The I of Secrets

Spies, family, and the need to know

Maggie Rogers

Published by Maggie Rogers

Copyright Maggie Rogers 2024

This is a work of fiction. Names, characters, places, and incidents are products of the author's imagination or are used fictitiously and should not be construed as real. Any resemblance to actual events, locales, organisations or persons, living or dead, is entirely coincidental.

All rights reserved. This book or any portion thereof may not be reproduced or used in any manner whatsoever without the express written permission of the publisher except for the use of brief quotations in a book review.

Thanks go to

Sue Horrocks for proofreading several draft copies. All my friends in the Nailsworth writers' group. My husband Terry for his support and encouragement. Matt Maguire from Candescent press for typesetting and the cover design.

Chapter One

Being a spy, if that was really what she was, meant everything in Katharine's working life had to be kept secret, even from her husband. Over recent years, particularly since having children, she had almost been inactive. She missed the stimulation of being in the field, but knew it wasn't compatible with family life. Her only involvement for a long time now was on the periphery of anything exciting, to say the least, and was mundane at best. She had considered herself to be a sleeper. So why did they wake her now, a few days into her family holiday?

Katharine paced around the villa's large sitting room, twitching at cushions and straightening magazines and books, none of which needed twitching or straightening. She made her way out to the balcony, welcoming the cool, early morning air on her warm skin. The sun was just rising above the horizon, casting a golden thread across the sea towards her and beckoning her into the day. This morning the beauty failed to work its magic, and she sighed as she settled onto a reclining chair, closed her eyes, and leant her head back, trying to switch her mind off. Sleep was far away, but at least she could attempt to relax. She wasn't sure what the time was and didn't bother turning to look at the clock on the wall behind her. What did it matter? It was too early, even for the early morning swimmers, with whom she often exchanged a cheery greeting as she enjoyed her first coffee of the morning, while soaking up the peace and anticipation of the day ahead. She promised herself, each year they holidayed here, that one day she would join them, but that day had not yet come.

This was one of the rare North Italian beaches that wasn't filled with rows of sunbeds and parasols, except for a few outside the beach bar, but often they remained empty. The area had changed very little over the years, and Katharine was pleasantly surprised that their paradise remained undiscovered by tour companies. Unable to settle, she turned to look at the clock, still only six a.m. For now, she was alone, and she tried once again to glean some pleasure from the quiet and peaceful scene, but with little success. The sun was already gaining in warmth; it would be another day of searing heat, like any other, except for Katharine today wasn't going to be like any other.

As time moved on, the sun rose higher in the sky and the swimmers appeared, but Katharine did not stir to acknowledge them today. She continued with her musing. Then something alerted her. She stiffened, but relaxed again when she recognised the familiar noises coming from the rooms behind her, indicating that her solitude was about to be broken. At least she would have something else to focus on for the next few hours. The sound of a flush followed by a tap running, then a door opening and the soft patter of bare feet across the cool tiled floor. The fridge door opened, then there was a pause.

'Hi mum, you up? D'you want some juice?'

Katharine could hear juice being poured into a glass and could envisage Dan, her eldest son, standing juice in hand and the fridge door wide-open, waiting for her reply.

'Please.'

Dan closed the fridge and wandered out on to the balcony holding an overfull glass of fresh orange for his mother. He took a gulp from it, grinned, and then handed it to her. Dan sat, or rather leapt, onto a lounger by her side, not speaking; he wasn't much of a morning talker, and for once Katharine was grateful. With a contented sigh, he rested his feet and long brown muscular legs on the rail around the balcony and drank his own juice.

Katharine looked at her son with pride, he was growing into a strong young man, he looked so like his father, Jake, at the same age, judging by photos she'd seen. She thanked her luck that, so far, he'd managed to steer away from trouble, and was still content to holiday with his family. She wondered how long it would last. He was now almost seventeen and would soon want to spread his wings. Already there were secret phone conversations with 'a friend' whom Katharine assumed must be a girl, or a boy she supposed, but thought that unlikely. She was itching to ask but knew better and would bide her time. He would tell her when he was ready. They sat together in companionable silence, both gazing out to sea, lost in their own thoughts, neither enquiring why the other was up so early. They were on holiday and in Dan's mind that meant anything goes, particularly related to getting up and going to bed. Sadly, their peaceful interlude didn't last very long.

As the sun rose, so did the rest of the household. Katharine's younger son, Oliver, full of vitality and noise, was next to burst into the room, demanding to know what was for breakfast, opening the fridge and cupboards, looking for edible morsels to satisfy his insatiable, growing appetite. His activity forced Katharine to her feet to carry out her maternal duties. Pancakes, fruit and yogurt were piled onto the table along with ham and cheese followed by jugs of coffee and juice. Jilly, Katharine's fourteen-year-old daughter, sashayed into the room once all the preparation was complete. She was already showered and carefully dressed in a bikini and matching sarong, wearing more makeup than was necessary for a day on the beach, or necessary at all for a fourteen-year-old, but, for once, it was left uncommented on. Today wasn't the day for a battle, but today, even more than usual, Katharine felt acutely aware of her daughter's vulnerability. Jilly looked much older than her years, but Katharine knew despite all her grown-up ways and attempts to be independent, she was still immature and could be easily led. Social media was a particular concern. Young girls these days were often influenced by stars and peers. At least, for now, Jilly still confided in her mother, and they sometimes laughed together over silly things people posted online, but some of the activities of her school friends caused Katharine to be anxious and feel out of her depth as a parent. It had not gone unnoticed that the boys at the beach bar already seemed to be paying her too much attention. Katharine also noticed Jilly's delight at being noticed, and her surprisingly confident way of responding. She always brushed away her mother's concerns with a shrug and a comment that she wasn't interested in the 'beach bums', but who else were her curling eyelashes and pouting lips meant to impress? Katharine bent forward and kissed the top of her daughter's head, provoking a startled reaction from her.

Breakfast passed in the usual chatter and laughter of her children making plans for the enjoyment of the hours ahead; kayaking, swimming, sailing and lounging around seemed to be the order for the day, as it had been for the days before, and most likely would be for the days that followed. Everything was as it should be–almost.

'What are you planning to do today?' she asked Dan.

'I might take the dinghy out later and do some fishing,' Dan said, filling his plate yet again with pancakes and fruit. 'See if I can catch anything bigger than a sprat.'

'Don't go beyond the bay,' Katharine felt obliged to say, and was rewarded with raised eyebrows and a slow shake of the head.

'Can I come with you?' Oliver, although just a few weeks away from his twelfth birthday, was always keen to emulate the actions of his older brother.

'Go on please, you can show me how to make it capsize, and right it again like we did before. Mum, can you tell Dan to take me?'

Katharine smiled, relishing the normality of family conversation, and turned to put something back in the fridge. She knew Oliver was desperate to be involved with his older brother, but it was up to Dan, not her. So, she said nothing.

'Oh, all right, if you must, but we're fishing, not messing around, OK?'

'OK, thanks. I won't mess around, promise.'

Dan was rewarded with a beaming smile from Oliver and a smile and mouthed thanks from Katharine.

'What are you doing today, mum?'

Katharine looked up, surprised, her stomach knotted; the children rarely consulted her on her plans, unless they wanted something. She didn't think that unkindly. They were good, considerate kids, but like most teenagers, she was more often thought of as the provider of food, money, lifts etc. rather than a person who might have plans of her own.

'Oh, a swim, then probably I'll just relax and read my book, maybe some sketching. Why?'

'No reason, you just seem a bit quiet.'

Katharine looked at her eldest son and smiled at his uncharacteristic perceptiveness. Her introspective mood of the morning must be even more evident than she thought if Dan had noticed. She suddenly wanted to hug him close, but instead just patted his shoulder as she leant across to remove the empty dishes. The other two stopped eating momentarily and looked at their mother, just to make sure they weren't missing anything.

'I'm fine, just didn't sleep too well. Now then, I'll make a salad for lunch, about one o'clock?'

The three faces looked at her, nodded, satisfied that she was all right, and normal service was resumed. After all, they thought, what could possibly be a problem here? As she cleared away the breakfast things, all the unanswerable questions that had been churning around Katharine's mind during the night came crowding back. It was impossible to push them away again. Her mind was in overdrive–Why now? Why me? Why during the holiday? Unanswerable, at least, until her father arrived. This was the first time for many years that her father, a senior operative in the Secret Service, had called on her to help with a seemingly important mission.

Also jostling for space in her brain were Jake's last words– 'Just tell your father no'. Words that continued to ring in her ears long after she had put the phone down. Easy for him to say, because he did not fully understand the significance of her father's position, or her own role, and she couldn't tell him.

She knew saying no was not an option. In theory it was possible, she had turned down his requests before, but only when she'd either been pregnant or unwell. She was neither now, and being on holiday didn't count. Part of the deal meant being available at any time, even though that aspect of her role had faded well into the recesses of her mind. But why did it have to be today?

Katharine picked up her phone. She would ring Jake to explain, yet again, why she must go, but she presumed he would already be at work, so put her phone back in her pocket. Yesterday she could not wait for Jake to join her and the children, so their holiday could really begin, but now her anticipation had faded. His late joining of the family was due to something important with *his* work, a deal that could not be delegated to anyone else to finalise. Katharine understood, and agreed without a second thought, to bring the children away on her own for the first few days. That she would now miss a couple of days of holiday because of *her* work was treated differently. Jake didn't understand. The feeling of injustice welled up inside her. What was the difference?

The difference was that this had come out of the blue. And, whereas she was aware of the details of Jake's work; they often discussed his projects and the intricacies of his office dynamics, there were very few aspects of her work she could share with him. He didn't usually ask too many questions. He just accepted when she said it was research work for her father. Was he even interested in what she did, she wondered? She shook her head to get rid of the thought, not wanting her mind to go there. Many of her tasks in recent years were routine and quite dull, usually paper or computer searches, but occasionally a breakthrough had her on the edge of her seat, feeling envious of the agents who would be following up the lead. It was years since she had felt the adrenaline rush of active service, and didn't really think she would feel it again, having assumed those days were behind her.

Was she up to the job? Doubt nibbled at the edge of her confidence. She was older now. Was she wiser? Probably not, but something about her father's tone conjured up that special tingle. She was still in the dark about what the task was, clearly not something to be discussed over the phone. Her father hadn't really *asked* for her involvement, more he quietly insisted that this task must be carried out by her. That intrigued her and brought up more questions. Her initial protests about being on holiday were swept away, and if she was honest, she wanted to be involved. It was just the timing. If only she could persuade him to wait.

Chapter Two

The day passed slowly, too slowly, for Katharine. She felt as if everything was happening in half time. She swam and read and to all intents and purposes was enjoying a lazy day in the sun, but her stomach was knotted, and she could not concentrate on anything for long. She couldn't resist looking frequently at her watch, willing, but not really wanting, the time to move on. She felt in limbo.

Lunch was the normal lively affair and Katharine tried hard to engage in her children's banter but was distracted. She knew she needed to mention something to the children and was just working out in her mind what to tell them, when Jilly asked what time their father was arriving.

'I'm not sure, it depends on work and flights. He's got a busy day of meetings today, so it might be late. Even after you've gone to bed.'

Jilly sighed and pouted.

'And I have to go away for a couple of days to help Grandad with something,' Katharine said, picking up an orange and peeling it with a studied air.

'Doing what? Where? How long for?' Oliver demanded.

'I'm not really sure, something to do with property I expect, and he asked if I could spare a couple of days to help him.' Katharine focused as casually as she could on her orange.

'But that's not fair, it's our holiday…'

'It'll be fine. I'll be back before you know it and dad's going to enjoy having you all to himself. It'll be a treat for him, but I'll have to warn him not to spoil you all.' Katharine was struck by the different reaction her absence was receiving to the one Jake's delay had provoked.

'Where are you going, mum?' Dan asked.

'I don't know, but I should know more later when grandad arrives.'

They mulled her words over for a few minutes in silence. Jilly said nothing, which worried Katharine more than Oliver's protestations. They finished their lunch and for once Katharine rejected their offer to clear up. As they scattered, she felt reassured that they seemed to have accepted the situation, hopefully heeding her warning not to swim straight away. Something she advised after every lunch but seemed to wash over them like water off a duck's back. It must be a mother's lot, she thought, to offer advice and warnings, usually to be ignored. She remembered herself at their age, and her Aunt Clare giving her the same warning. She never knew if it was a real risk, or just something adults said to children. Perhaps she'd look it up sometime.

Katharine cleared the lunch away, taking extra care to leave everything tidy, before returning to the beach. She lay on a sun lounger, not even pretending to read her book. Jilly had spread out on the sand beside her, flicking idly through a magazine.

'Mum…'

'Hmm?'

'Is everything OK with you and dad?'

Katharine sat up and swung her feet over the sun lounger so she could see Jilly more clearly.

'Of course. What makes you think otherwise?'

'Well, you're going away, just as dad arrives. You've never done that before. It seems a bit sort of not right.'

'Darling, it's just inconvenient that I must go now, but not significant. Dad understands.' Katharine mentally crossed her fingers at that last statement.

'Unfortunately, Grandad says it's urgent and can't wait, otherwise I wouldn't go.'

'You know Dalia, at school? Well, her mum and dad split up out of the blue. She said it was after they'd been on a great holiday. At least she thought they'd had a great time. Then when they got home, her dad just left. She only sees him at weekends now, she hates it. I'd hate it as well.'

Katharine looked at her daughter and wanted to hug her close. She sank down onto the sand beside her and stroked her hair.

'Nothing like that is going to happen to us.'

'Promise.'

'Promise,' once again Katharine's fingers crossed tightly. 'Would you like me to plait your hair?'

'Yes, please.' Jilly rummaged in her bag for her hairbrush and handed it to her mother. The gentle sweeping strokes of the brush soothed them both.

Late afternoon came, with no let-up in the heat and today no welcome cooling breeze either. Katharine must have dozed because a shout from her daughter startled her.

'Look, it's Grandad.' Jilly was waving madly and shouted 'Hello!'

Katharine sat up on the sun lounger and followed her daughter's gaze towards the balcony of their villa. Even from this distance she could tell her father was frowning. It was something to do with the tilt of his head and his hands holding the rail. A shudder of fear mixed with anticipation ran through her.

'At last,' she thought, not sure whether she was pleased or disappointed that her father had arrived before Jake. At least now there wouldn't be a row.

Dan and Oliver, who had just pulled the dinghy up onto the beach, alerted by Jilly's shout, were now racing up the beach. Katharine gathered her bits and pieces together and followed the children, at a slower pace, towards the villa. They greeted their grandfather excitedly, and she exchanged a peck on the cheek with him. He took her to one side and looked, not unkindly, at her.

'Are you prepared? Will Jacob be here tonight? I don't want to wait until tomorrow.'

Katharine nodded, surprised at the haste. She wasn't sure what he meant by being prepared, but she'd thrown a few clothes in an overnight bag.

'Good. Now, I'm looking forward to a few hours with my grandchildren.' He said, smiling at the three eager faces and settled himself into a chair ready to listen to their excited chatter. They loved his company. He was unlike other relatives, as he treated them with respect and always listened attentively, commenting but never judging.

Early in the evening, after a flurry of activity, washing out swimming costumes, showering and dressing for the evening, they all made their way on foot to their favourite nearby restaurant for supper. The meal was delicious, of course, and paid for by her father, but to Katharine, each mouthful tasted insipid and was hard to swallow. She willed Jake to arrive with every bite. His last text said he would try to get an earlier flight, if there was a seat available, and Katharine had heard nothing since. She sat at the far end of the table next to her daughter, who was surprised by the lack of admonishment from her mother for flirting with the young waiter. Usually, a look or quiet word stopped any attempts at what Katharine considered to be inappropriate behaviour, but tonight she seemed oblivious, and Jilly made the most of her inattention. Every time the door opened Katharine turned, hoping it would be Jake, but it wasn't. She knew the later it became, the less chance there would be to have a proper conversation before she left.

She had not told the children that she was in fact going away that night and knew she would have to broach the subject soon. This detail she had only discovered herself when her father arrived. She wondered why. Surely tomorrow morning would be soon enough. As she mused, she overheard her father telling Dan he was whisking her away that evening, for a day or two.

'Yeah, mum said, sounds cool,' was Dan's reply, and for the second time that day Katharine was impressed by her son's maturity. Oliver and Jilly just nodded when they were told. After the meal, they strolled back to the villa, amidst chatter and laughter, the children delighted by the unexpected appearance of their favourite grandparent. They regaled him with stories of their antics, many of which were also news to Katharine.

Tired after a day in the sun, and disappointed that their father had not arrived, the children went off to bed, and Katharine spent a few minutes with each one, explaining why, even though she wasn't sure herself, she was going to be leaving almost as soon as their father arrived. She was reassured by how calmly they took the news, even Oliver, and she promised that his father would look in when he arrived to talk to him, if he was still awake.

She returned to the sitting room, expecting her father to start filling her in about the details of the task ahead. But instead, after finishing his drink, he walked across and picked up his newspaper again, settling down to complete the crossword. Katharine shifted uncomfortably and wasn't sure whether she was relieved or not when the crunch of car tyres indicated Jake's arrival. She wanted to rush out of the room and down the stairs from the balcony to meet him, but instead of following her instinct, she waited beside her father.

'Does he...?' her father looked across the room as Jacob entered.

'Know?'

He nodded.

'Yes. Well, not really. At least not the details,' she said, but then neither did she, and it was partly the lack of detail that was causing Katharine anxiety.

Her father nodded again.

Jake's hair was dishevelled, and she recognised the familiar sign that he had been running his fingers through it, something he always did when stressed. He looked tired.

Presumably, work had not been straightforward. Following her instinct this time, she rushed across the room into her husband's arms. She hugged him and whispered apologies into his ear, promising to be back soon; earlier irritation forgotten. Her father walked out onto the balcony for a moment, not wanting to intrude on their private conversation, before returning and striding across the room to shake Jake's hand. Jake expressed his surprise and genuine pleasure at seeing his father-in-law already there. He felt certain Katharine had told him her father was not due until tomorrow, and he looked questioningly in her direction, but Katharine just shrugged. There had been no time to explain why she was leaving almost immediately.

Jake went to see the children and looked more relaxed when he returned. He poured himself a drink and sank into a chair. They sat and chatted about nothing in particular for a few minutes, then her father rose and said it was time to be off. Jake stood up as well. He looked surprised, and was about to say something to Katharine, but she spoke first,

'I didn't have time… but there's loads of food in, and the children are all right about it. I'll be back soon.' She hugged Jake. 'I'll be back soon,' she repeated.

'Wait in the car,' her father said, handing her the keys. He placed an arm on Jake's shoulder and steered him to the side of the room and began talking quietly and earnestly to him.

All Katharine made out were the words 'change of plan' as she made her way out onto the balcony. It was beautiful, no lights anywhere, only the moonlight sending silver shimmers across the calm sea. She listened to the gentle hypnotic swish of the waves lapping on the sand and did not want to leave. It was a beautiful evening; she enjoyed evenings like this most when it was just her and Jake, after the children retreated to their bedrooms. She leant on the rail to steady herself, her knuckles, white as the moon, as her hands closed around the cool metal. I'll be back soon, she told herself.

Katharine could hear the occasional sound coming from

the bedrooms but felt isolated from the children. She listened, and slowly and carefully pictured each individual child, relaxed and carefree, reading, on their phones, or possibly fast asleep in bed. A lump rose in her throat, and she felt the urge to run away as fast as she could and hide, but she did not move and suppressed the feeling of foreboding. She just stood and waited, consciously absorbing the beautiful scene, just in case she never saw it again, while admonishing herself for being melodramatic and irrational.

Her father's arrival onto the balcony made her jump. He didn't speak. Just inclined his head towards the steps, and without a backward glance, she followed him down, picking up the small bag that she had earlier left by the door, and climbed into the waiting car. Jake followed his father-in-law out onto the balcony and watched as they left.

'See you in a day or two,' Katharine said and blew a kiss, which was not returned.

'Be careful,' he called, but the car door was already shut.

Chapter Three

Katharine's return - over a week later

Sweat dampened Katharine's hands, as the taxi turned off from the main road towards the bay, and it had nothing to do with heat. She felt as though she was returning a different person from the one who had left. So much had happened, and she wasn't sure she would be able to just slot back into holiday mode. She had been away for over a week, which was far longer than the couple of days she expected to be away. Jake was entitled to be angry; if that was what he was. There had been no contact between them in all the time she was away, except for Katharine's brief call the previous night, to say she was returning. She was certain she told him, or if she hadn't, then her father would have reminded him, that she would not be able to ring him until it was over. Over a couple of days that might have seemed acceptable, but she knew having no contact for this long would take some explaining.

The taxi slowed round the bend, and she caught the first glimpse of the villa. Usually, at the end of the journey and start of the holiday, she would feel all her worries drift away, but this evening she felt almost sick as she looked across the bay. The evening was already dark, and for once there was no moonlight dappling the sea to welcome her. There was a light on in the villa and she could just make out Jake's silhouette leaning against the rail of the balcony. She could almost imagine that he had not moved since the night she had left, when he'd assumed the same position.

She always thought that the villa looked like a sugar cube sitting at the edge of the beach, even in the dark she could see, or did she imagine, a white glow from its painted exterior. It was not the most architecturally attractive of buildings, being little more than a plain white concrete block when seen from the road. The large balcony, or was it a raised veranda, she wasn't sure, was cut into the sea-facing aspect of the cube, with steps running down both sides, one set only a few feet away from the beach and the other twisting back to the parking area. It was the perfect holiday villa, in a stunning location. She presumed it was owned by an acquaintance of her father's, as he always secured the booking for the family. It never occurred to her to ask him who it belonged to, which she now realised was odd, and she wondered if they would come again. Katharine wound down the window and took in some deep gulps of sea air. The taxi driver asked which villa it was and after directing him she took another deep breath and closed the windows as they drove the last hundred metres to the villa.

Jake must have seen the car headlights as they swung around the road behind the bay, but he did not appear to stir, to be ready to greet her. A lump rose in her throat, and she sat without moving in the back seat, delaying the moment of her arrival. She anticipated a difficult time lay ahead. Throughout the journey she had worried about what, and how, she could tell him about her time away, not least about what had happened to her father. The driver cleared his throat, and Katharine knew it was time to face whatever was to come. Leaning over, she paid him, before gathering her bags and climbing out.

So often, during the preceding few days, Katharine had thought of this moment with anticipation and longing, but now, the reality of Jake not being as forgiving as she had hoped, took shape in her consciousness. Every fibre of her being wanted to delay the encounter. At the bottom of the steps Katharine stopped and hesitated, but still Jake did not appear. Any other time he would have been down the steps before the car door was open, even after a quick trip to the local town, but tonight all was still. She waited a few more seconds, hoping he would appear, and tried to imagine what must be going through his mind. He must now know that she was back. Of course, he did. Even if he was inside the villa, he would have been aware of her arrival, but standing on the balcony there was no way he could have missed the sound of the taxi pulling in.

Katharine fished around in her handbag for her comb and lipstick, a delaying tactic only, as she knew that what she looked like would not make the slightest difference to her reception once she climbed the steps. She dithered, not hurrying to move. Still there was no sign of Jake. The sudden thought Jake might not want her to stay flashed across her mind and filled her with dread. She swallowed hard and tried to chase the thought away. She would explain; make him understand and be able to win him round –wouldn't she?

The crunch of her shoes on the sandy gravel seemed abnormally loud, and with another deep breath she mounted the steps. Was it really only just over a week since she had followed her father down these same steps? She knew she had a mountain to climb once she reached the top. At the top of the steps, she paused. Jake was leaning on the rail looking out into the darkness; he didn't turn to look at her. A light, probably from a small fishing boat, appeared to hold him in thrall, but Katharine could tell from the rigidity of his posture that he knew she was there. He remained perfectly still.

'Hello,' Katharine said, and took a couple of steps towards the rail and stood closer to him.

Jake turned, an unreadable expression on his face.

'You're here then?' He turned towards her, but barely met her eyes. There was no smile or kiss hello. Not the faintest glimmer of relief that she was back. Katharine moved, her limbs felt heavy and despite the warm evening air, she shivered.

'Yes. I'm here. How are you?' she asked, and then straight away wished she hadn't.

'How am I?' he looked at her properly for the first time. 'I'm confused, I'm angry, but most of all, I'm disappointed. Disappointed that my wife could not bring herself to tell me she was still playing at being a secret agent. Angry that you lied about how long you would be away, and angry that I've had to manage our children's anxious questions without having a clue what the answers are. That's how I am.'

Put like that, the enormity of the task before her to regain his trust swept towards her like a wave and almost knocked her off her feet.

'I'm so sorry, really I am, but I'm not really a secret agent, I ...' her voice trailed off.

'I don't know who, or what, you are any more, Katharine. How do I know if that's even your real name?'

He walked back to the rail grasped it again, as if to control his hands, and stared out to sea. 'I thought we shared everything, trusted each other. Now I don't know what to think.'

She was about to tell him not to be so ridiculous but bit her tongue. His pain was real, and she felt almost relieved by his outburst and agitation. At least it was out in the open and they could now talk, or she hoped they could. She moved towards him but didn't stand next to him.

'Jacob, Jake, let me explain.' She stepped closer and touched his arm. He half turned towards her.

'Please, so much happened that I didn't expect. It was only supposed to be a couple of days, honestly. I didn't mean to hurt any of you. It was just...'

Her heart contracted at the hard look on his face, but melted when she recognised the etched lines of worry around his eyes. How could she have put him through so much? In truth, over the last week or so, there was almost no time to give him or the children a proper thought. Not once while away did she think about how the children might view her longer disappearance. She had not explained it properly to them before she left, but she couldn't have known what was to happen, so how could she prepare any of them? A hot flush rushed through her body, and she put her hand out to steady herself. What sort of mother, or wife, come to that, did she think she was? Selfish was the only word that came to mind, but she knew there was much more to it, and she had to try to make Jake understand.

'How long has this been going on? I guess I'm right in assuming this isn't the first assignment you've been involved in since you said it was all over. How many years ago was that?' Jake spoke into the night, not looking at Katharine.

She did not reply for a long time. For some reason, this wasn't a question she'd expected and wasn't sure how to answer. The truth was, that despite telling Jake not long after they married, twenty or so years ago, that she was no longer working for the security services, she had carried on, and because she'd only be involved with small jobs, it seemed OK to not enlighten him.

Sometimes her jobs were as simple as a discreet translation or passing on papers when needed. Her fluent languages and excellent memory made her useful to the service, and her father's senior position, of course, helped. She was not an employee in the same way most people were when they worked for a large organisation. There was never any formal interview or appointment, or resignation come to that. These minor jobs, she decided at the time, weren't necessary to worry Jake about. In fact, the service discouraged her from speaking about them to anyone outside the organisation, and they never took her away from home. This recent major job was the first for many years and now she decided, rightly or wrongly, not to mention the others. So, she kept quiet, because she could not face being accused of lying and didn't want to admit that fact, even to herself.

'Well? Or can't you tell me because you've signed the Official Secrets Act and after all, I'm only your husband?'

Katharine didn't immediately reply. She needed a moment to compose herself.

'Please, let me explain,' she said, and looked out to sea, trying to order in her mind exactly what she was going to tell him. What was she able to tell him? Officially, not a lot.

'Everything. I want to know everything. I want the truth about where you've been for nearly two weeks, without even contacting your children, otherwise…'

Katharine nodded, she didn't want to ask or think about what the otherwise was, and neither did she correct his exaggeration of two weeks.

'I'm sorry, you have a right to be angry, but yes,' she paused. 'I will tell you everything.'

Jake took her arm in a firm grip and looked into her face.

'I mean everything. No skipping bits, no glossing over. I want the lot. Not just the official hogwash,' he said.

'No, I promise, I'll tell you it all, but it's a very long story.'

'I'm not going anywhere,' he said, and turned away from her. 'I'll get some drinks and cheese, or something, to keep us going. I don't care if it takes all night.'

She stepped aside to let him pass, feeling like an unwanted guest. Looking at his retreating back, she fingered her wedding ring. What could she tell him? What should she tell him? She was finding it almost impossible to sort the details out in her mind. After thinking about it for a few minutes Katharine decided, whatever the consequences, she would keep her promise and tell him absolutely everything. After being kept in the dark for so long she felt she owed it to him. They had been married for over twenty years and more than ever Katharine felt she needed his love and support, wanted his strong arms around her, but she knew she would have to win his trust again before that could happen. She listened to him rustling around in the kitchen and wondered if he had been shopping to buy more provisions since she left. He must have been, or perhaps Maria, who came in to clean, had filled the cupboards again. She placed a small table between two lounger chairs. If they were in for a long night they might as well be comfortable.

After a short time, Jake reappeared and placed a bottle of red wine, a jug of water, glasses, and a platter of bread, cheese and olives on the table between them, before sitting on one of the loungers. How many times had they sat here with a similar supper between them, but in very different circumstances? She nearly commented about it, but this was far from the relaxed and happy evenings they usually shared on this balcony. They were like strangers, struggling to be polite. The familiar sound of the waves lapping the beach was the only discernible noise, until Jake's voice broke the silence.

'Right, I'm all ears. Everything mind,' he said, pouring wine into both glasses and handing one to Katharine.

'I'm not sure where to start,' she said, pouring herself a glass of water that she drank straight down, then lifting a wine glass and taking a long swig of wine.

'Try starting the evening you walked down those steps with your father, leaving me to manage our children's questions and anxieties for the last however many weeks.'

Katharine winced as he emphasized, yet again, her misdemeanours.

'How are the children? Where are they?' She suddenly realised that the unusual quietness was because the children were missing. Normally even after they'd gone to bed, their presence was still palpable, the sound of music from Dan's room, or the click, click, click as Jilly messaged friends at home. A lump rose in her throat, wondering what the implication of them not being there meant. How could that not have been her first question!?

'Worried, but they will be fine. They've gone to my sister's apartment for a couple of nights. I made up something to pacify them. Right, I need to hear what was so important that you left them, us, without a word, only some cock and bull story from your father.'

'He's dead.' Katharine's lip trembled. She took a deep breath to keep her feelings under control. There would be time for grieving later.

'What?'

'My father, he's dead. Sorry, I …' She took another drink of wine and looked at Jake's gaping reaction. Jake was fond of her father, and it wasn't her intention to just spring that piece of information on him. Perhaps it was to the good, as he was now staring at her, a mixture of emotion and disbelief playing across his face as he waited to hear what she was going to say next.

'Look, let me just talk without interruption from start to finish. Once I have told you everything, you can ask me anything. Anything you want, I promise I'll tell you the truth.'

Jake nodded, took a large gulp of wine himself, and refilled his glass.

'No interruptions, promise?'

He nodded again.

Katharine sat thinking, not speaking for what felt like many minutes, and then she started,

'When father came out onto the balcony, after speaking to you, I wanted to run back in to say goodbye properly and make sure you understood, but I knew it would cause more problems, there would be too many questions I couldn't answer. Not because of any official secrets, but because at that time I knew very little myself. I honestly didn't know what my task was.'

Jake was about to say something, but Katharine held up her hand, and he muttered sorry and settled back to the difficult task of just listening, as promised.

'I didn't go back I knew you would be angry and probably confused by my lack of openness, but as I said there was hardly anything I could reveal, because at that stage I only knew that I was needed to carry out an important task in Naples. I didn't want to leave after a row, so I thought it was best to just go. I really hoped you would try to understand and wait for a fuller explanation when I returned. My biggest frustration was that your delay, totally unavoidable I know, in joining us at the villa, meant we were unable to spend any time together before I left. Believe me, I'm not blaming you in any way for being late, and maybe it was just a twist of fate that meant there was no time for explanations and doubts, more doubts on my part at least.

At first, Katharine was consciously aware of Jake's eyes on her, listening intently for a credible explanation. She began by talking directly to him, but very quickly seemed to forget he was there, and soon was recounting the events as though telling a story to a stranger. In a way, losing herself in the telling was cathartic. It felt unreal and faintly unbelievable even to her, so she dreaded to think what Jake would make of it all.

Chapter Four

Katharine's story

I climbed into the car next to my father. The engine was already running, and I could tell by his tapping on the steering wheel that he was eager to be away. We travelled the first few miles in silence. We followed the track that swept round the bay, passed the restaurant where we had eaten earlier, and up the hill towards the main road. I looked back just as we turned away from the sea and could see the villa, now almost in darkness, apart from one light still on inside, which illuminated the balcony enough for me to see you leaning against the rail. I couldn't tell whether you were staring out to sea or following the progress of the car. I felt sick as we lost sight of you.

My father was concentrating on driving carefully around the potholes and looked surprised at the sudden break in silence when I spoke,

'What did you say to him?'

'Jake? I told him it was an essential job, that it would be safe and that you should be back in a couple of days. There wasn't anything more I could tell him.'

'Did he say anything or ask anything?'

My father paused before he replied, which made me believe that a lot more was probably said than he wanted to discuss.

'He wanted to know why we were leaving at such a late hour, and why there was so much secrecy, and he wanted to know precisely when you would return. He knew something like this was possible, didn't he? I got the impression he was unaware that you might be called upon at any time.'

'Yes, of course,' I lied. 'But it's been quite a long time, years even, since I did anything major, and I suppose he thought it was over.'

My father nodded, 'Sometimes it's never over.'

The tone of his voice concerned me, and I turned to study his face, fixed on the road ahead. He suddenly looked tired or was it tense? I couldn't tell, but once again an uneasy feeling settled in my stomach. I wondered whether this really was such a straightforward task, after all. He turned to look at me, aware of my eyes on him, and mistook my expression as a look of concern about my husband, rather than him.

'He'll be all right when he thinks it through properly, and it will only be a couple of days. You'll be back before he has time to get worried. It's just a simple courier type mission.'

I settled back in my seat and hoped he was right, although if it was just a simple courier mission as he said, and I'd carried out plenty of those in the past, when I was younger, why were we leaving at night and why did it all feel so uncertain? I tried to pull myself together; it was probably just that I was out of practice. I knew from experience not to ask him any more about the task for the time being, so just sat quietly looking out of the window and wondering where we were going. I knew I would hear all I needed to know when my father was ready. For now, we both sat in silence, thinking our own thoughts.

We drove for about an hour, only passing through small, Northern Italian, sleepy villages and hamlets, none of which I recognised. I might have dozed, I wasn't sure, but later, along what appeared to be another small rural road, I realised father was slowing the car. He was scanning the road, looking for something. A small light on a post seemed to be the sign he needed, and just beyond, we pulled off the road and followed a narrow dusty track for about a quarter to half a mile. As we bounced along, I saw faint lights in the near distance. The lights belonged to a small, whitewashed villa that even in the light of the headlamps I could see needed a coat of paint. It appeared to be an unused agricultural worker's cottage, or an old holiday let. A car was parked outside, and the front door was open, but at first sight, there was no one visible.

A few seconds after we stopped, and the engine was turned off, a tall, elegant woman appeared in the doorway. She looked about my age, possibly younger. Her naturally, curly, dark hair looked like it had been relaxed and fell into a bob on her shoulders. She wore large framed, blue glasses and a blue sleeveless dress. Stepping out from behind her was an older man, shorter than her and stick thin, with greying hair and a close-trimmed beard. He stepped forward as my father got out of the car, with me close behind. The man's initial anxious expression changed, and he smiled warmly and extended his hand towards my father.

'Duncan, good to see you again.' The men shook hands, and then gave each other a quick hug and pat on the back, which surprised me, as my father wasn't prone to demonstrative gestures. 'And you must be Katharine?' he held his hand out to me, and I placed mine in his firm, friendly grasp. 'I'm Geoffrey. I can't believe our paths haven't crossed before,' he said. 'This is Julia,' he said, turning to my father. 'I don't believe you've met each other either,' he said.

My father shook his head. 'No, it's a pleasure Julia, I've heard about you, of course.' he extended his hand.

Julia smiled at father, took his hand and nodded in my direction.

'Right, come on in, I presume you've eaten. We can only rustle up some bread and cheese' Julia turned towards the door. Small talk didn't appear to be her forte. I got the impression she was the one in charge and wanted to get down to business.

'We're fine, thanks,' said father, speaking for us both, but I was by now feeling quite hungry. It was many hours since we had eaten supper. We followed them through the front door into a small, but clean and comfortable room, and sat down where Julia indicated. Geoffrey filled a jug with water and put it with four large glasses on the table.

'Sorry, nothing stronger,' Geoffrey said in a tone that implied he wished there was. 'Would you like some cheese? I think I could manage some.'

Before father could intervene, I said 'Yes', and Geoffrey produced a meagre block of cheese and barely enough bread for a slice each.

'How much have you told Katharine?' Julia asked, getting straight down to business. She smiled. 'You must be wondering why you've made this detour?'

I nodded, but said nothing, just listened. Geoffrey moved to close the door, but not before stepping outside and scanning the immediate vicinity. Satisfied, he nodded to Julia.

'Right, let me get straight to the point. We think there's been a leak in the organisation,' she said, looking straight at me.

Father obviously already knew, as he showed no surprise. Again, I said nothing, just nodded and gave her my complete attention. Julia didn't elaborate too much about the supposed leak, but she went on to talk about the importance of this mission. She outlined the operational detail and what I was to do, which seemed primarily collecting and delivering a memory stick. The mystery that seemed to surround such a simple task surprised me. I knew it was well within my capabilities. She then carried on explaining what she called essential technical information, that quite honestly went over my head, or at least I was too tired to properly take in. I stored the details in my mind so that I could mull over them when I felt more alert. I wasn't clear why I needed to know so much technical detail or what it was essential for but didn't question her at the time. It was clearly something I should have been aware of, and my lack of knowledge made me feel uneasy.

After half an hour or so, Geoffrey stood up and picked up

a packet of cigarettes from a side table. He'd been shuffling uncomfortably for the last few minutes, and I suspected he needed his nicotine fix.

'Sorry,' he said with a slight smile. 'Filthy habit I know, but I just can't get to grips with giving up.' He headed towards the door.

'OK if I join you, Geoffrey?' Father stood up and walked with Geoffrey out into the still, warm darkness. 'I could do with stretching my legs. So, are you all right? I mean really, all right?' he asked as he closed the door behind them.

Julia and I smiled at each other across the table, then she stood up.

'Go and sit somewhere more comfortable, I'll make some coffee,' she pointed to an area off the room with a sofa and couple of armchairs and made her way to the small kitchen. I sank into a chair and struggled to stop my eyes drooping.

'So, what makes you so sure there's a leak?' I asked, when she returned with the coffee jug, and poured us both a cup of exceptionally good, strong coffee, which had the effect of reviving my brain cells.

'We've suspected for quite some time, but the person is being very clever, nothing too obvious, and not all the time.'

'Do you have any idea who it might be?'

'There are a couple of possibilities, but not yet enough evidence to confront anyone. That's partly why we're using a memory stick for this job.'

'I did wonder. It seems a bit outdated. Couldn't they secure the information and send it over the Internet?'

'They could, but we thought this was a safer way, because it's not what would be expected. Of course, we encrypted the stick and coded the information on it, so anyone finding it would not be able to read it. Unless they had access to a team of decoders.'

I nodded, understanding who might just have such a team of decoders. I couldn't help wondering, but didn't ask why they didn't just post the stick, if the information on it was so secure. I didn't because I thought it would sound facile. I looked at Julia. She was being very cautious, whilst at the same time trying to be open, but I wanted to know more. I felt as though a vital piece of the story was being withheld.

'Where has it originated? The data I mean?' I hoped this wasn't something she'd already told me in amongst all the technical stuff.

She paused, took a sip of coffee, and smiled at me.

'The less detail you know, the better. Just to say it's come from a non-European, non-Christian country. I can't stress enough how important this mission is.'

I nodded, presuming she meant the Middle East, somewhere like Syria or Iran, but I knew not to press her. However, she did nothing to allay my concerns. I knew how ruthless people could be when they discovered their organisations were being infiltrated and secrets being exposed. Previous assignments I'd been involved in had felt exciting, and never for one moment did I think I was in danger, but times had changed. Was I in danger this time, or was I just letting my imagination run away with me? I knew acutely that the risk from terrorism was greater now than when I was last engaged in anything similar. The rules of the game were changing, and I wasn't up to speed with them.

'Different people have couriered the stick, so its journey has been quite tortuous, so anyone trying to follow will hopefully have lost track by now. Also, there are only a very few of us who know its exact route.'

I nodded again. I assumed they were also hoping if the route was divulged, it might unmask their mole.

'So, is my drop off in Florence the last leg?'

Julia didn't reply one way or the other, 'Are you ok driving that distance?' was all she asked.

'Of course, I'm used to driving in Italy. Can I ask why me? I mean, I'm operationally quite rusty.'

'That's why. You might be rusty, but you are also unknown, at least amongst the sort of foreign agents we're dealing with these days. Most of the couriers are new or a sleeper, like you.'

'Ah coffee, good idea.' Geoffrey, followed by my father, returned and sat down with us. Julia looked relieved at their return and made sure the conversation turned to more general topics and shared acquaintances. She was in control and didn't want to be pressed to reveal any more information about the content of the stick or the mission. After a while, I was unable to stifle a yawn. It was by now very late, and that was the cue for the evening to end. Julia showed me to a small sparsely furnished bedroom, and after using the bathroom I fell into bed, exhausted because of the previous sleepless night, and all the information my brain was trying to compute.

Chapter Five

I found it difficult to sleep, despite being overtired, and woke often, listening to the unfamiliar noises in the house. When I slept, I dreamt strange, unsettling dreams, where my mother, or a woman who called herself my mother, kept following me, calling to me from a distance, then disappearing as soon as I tried to speak to her. I blamed the late-night strong coffee and cheese. Waking for the last time around six thirty, I lay for a few minutes listening to the birds singing, before deciding to get up and make myself some coffee. I pulled on my clothes and put my contact lenses in before taking them straight out again. My eyes were too sore after several nights of poor sleep; I could manage without them. I drew the curtains back and surveyed the large overgrown garden surrounding the villa before heading downstairs. It was one of those summer days where the sun slipped in and out behind fluffy white clouds that drifted lazily across an otherwise clear blue sky. I longed to be back on holiday with Jake and the children and wondered what he would do with them today. Oh well, I thought, despite Julia and Geoffrey's warning last night, it should be an easy, straightforward task, and I would be back with them in a couple of days. All it involved was a very simple collection and delivery job. What could go wrong to delay my return?

I made my way into the kitchen, not expecting anyone else to be up, so I was surprised to find my father already leaning against the sink with a cup in his hand.

'Good morning, sleep well?'

He was shaved and dressed, ready to leave.

'No, not really, you?'

He shook his head, 'I'm getting fussier about my bed and pillows as I get older. Kettle's still hot if you want to make a drink.'

I made my coffee and soon felt better, even after the first gulp, then rummaged in the cupboards for the remains of last night's bread or something for breakfast. At last, I found less than half a loaf.

'This won't go far between four of us,' I said, as I opened drawers, looking for a knife.

'Julia and Geoffrey left last night, so it's only you and me and I don't want anything. Use as much as you want.'

It surprised me they'd left, and I was about to ask my father why, but as I turned, he was already making his way out of the kitchen. It struck me as odd that they should leave so late, and without saying they were going, but then it was all a bit on the odd side. After all, my father could easily have told me everything that Julia told me. None of it appeared to be new to him. Unless I was missing something, this detour had been almost irrelevant. I still couldn't work out why Julia needed to inform me about all the technical details. They seemed as irrelevant as the detour, but that made it even more disconcerting. I doubted the details were anything to do with information stored on the memory stick. That would be too dangerous. So, what was the point? I must be missing something. I sipped my coffee and made some toast, trying to push doubts away. Perhaps Julia and Geoffrey left because there weren't enough beds in the building. I had no idea how many rooms the villa contained. It was small, but I would have thought it was big enough to sleep four people. It just struck me as odd that they didn't say goodbye before I went to bed. As I mulled things over, I opened the fridge looking for butter and, with luck, something sweet to put on my toast. I found two of the little packs of butter you get on airplanes and one small jar of marmalade. They weren't expecting us to linger for long, or to eat much.

I took my two pieces of toast and coffee outside into the

sunshine and sat on a bench, surveying the surroundings. The villa, built in a hollow and surrounded by trees on higher ground, did not offer much of a view, but made it very secluded and shaded. There was a small, neglected swimming pool and patio, which, if tidied up, would provide a pleasant sitting area, but the place had an air of abandonment about it. I wondered idly who owned it and what I would do to it, if it were mine. It had plenty of potential. I was still munching my toast when my father appeared round the side of the building and came and sat next to me. We sat for a few minutes outwardly enjoying the morning sun, like any normal father and daughter might.

'Have you known Geoffrey for long?' I asked after a while.

'We've worked together on many things in the past, but I'm concerned about him…'

'Oh, why?'

'He seems distracted, not quite himself. I think it's something to do with a woman, but he didn't open up to me. I hoped he would when we were alone last night.'

Not sure what else to say, I just nodded.

'I asked Julia why the information wasn't just sent electronically, and I wondered, but didn't ask why the stick wasn't posted?'

He considered my question for a moment.

'What did she say?' he asked but carried on without waiting for me to answer, 'Well, I suppose there are a couple of reasons. The post would be far too risky, too haphazard, and too slow. An electronic link, well, that would be instant, but it could still be traced.'

'Really? I thought there were all sorts of untraceable ways for disguising the sender and receiver of information these days.'

'Yes, you're right, there are. The whizz kids at HQ seem to find their way around the internet more easily than I can read a train timetable. So, if they can do it, presumably the source country for the data has similar whizz kids on board.'

'Doesn't a memory stick seem a bit old hat?'

'True, a memory stick is the least likely way to transport the data, hence why it would be unexpected, and bearing in mind we suspect a leak, an old-fashioned courier system, when all considered, seemed the safest.'

I didn't reply, just absorbed his explanation. He was right of course. Even my own children were way in advance of me on just basic computer skills, and I considered myself to be fairly computer literate.

'It's one of the reasons I've decided to withdraw from service. It's time for younger people to take over. I'm starting to feel left behind. I'm one of the old brigade.'

'Really? I thought you were in it for life.' I was surprised by his revelation, but then he was already well beyond the age when most people retired. I just couldn't imagine him gardening or playing golf all day, but I suspected he would have something more interesting planned. 'Are you all right, I mean your health?'

'Like I say, this game's not for people my age. I'm getting tired. Besides, it'll give me more time with my grandchildren, and you, of course.'

I nodded, not convinced.

'Do you think there is a leak?'

'Yes, I do. We already think the downloading of the information has been detected. That might not be a leak of course, just detection on their part. They might know it's gone, but not where it's going, or the format it's in.'

'Hence the circuitous route,' I said.

'Indeed. Only a very few people know who all the handlers are, and each handler only knows their immediate contacts.'

'What's really on it?' I asked, knowing he would not or could not tell me.

He shook his head, 'Information that will make huge strides into the war against terrorism.'

A shiver passed through me. This was turning out to be bigger than anything I'd been involved in before, at least to my knowledge it was. In truth, when I'd carried out tasks in the past I was only ever told as much as I needed to know, which sometimes was very little. Perhaps I should have asked more, but in those days the world seemed less complicated, and I always felt there was a clear distinction between what was right and wrong. Now everything felt blurred. Right and wrong seemed to have been thrown out of the window, and with terrorism, no one knew or played by the rules. If there were any rules.

'When you're ready, I'll drive you to the town. From there you can get a taxi to the airport. There's a flight to Naples later this morning. Your ticket is booked.'

I nodded and drained my cup. He didn't elaborate, but he didn't need to. I knew from Julia what was expected, and my meeting with the person I was to contact to collect the stick wasn't until the next day.

'There's no desperate hurry. You've got plenty of time,' he said, but got to his feet and appeared more eager to leave than his comment implied. I washed up my cup and plate and put the few things I'd taken out of my bag back in and was ready for what was to come.

Chapter Six

Half an hour later we were driving away. Father left the key in the front door of the villa; presumably someone was tasked with looking after the place and would come along later that morning to tidy up. We travelled in silence, father concentrating on the road, and me lost in thought. Eventually, we pulled up in an anonymous looking side street, away from the main square, in a scruffy-looking village. I had no idea where we were, and I didn't recall even seeing a sign for the airport, but I trusted my father when he assured me it was not too far away.

Before I got out of the car, father gave me the plane ticket and a new phone. He stressed a couple of times it was to be used only to contact him, no one else, and then only in case of emergency or if anything untoward happened. Under no circumstances was I to use my own phone or contact Jake. I agreed, relieved that he didn't insist on me leaving my phone with him. It was reassuring to have it, just in case. He also gave me a zipped holdall, which, when I looked questioningly at him, he informed me contained bits and pieces that might come in useful. I found his statement intriguing, but I resisted the temptation to look inside and just managed to squeeze it into the bag I was already carrying. We hugged, and he wished me good luck and pointed towards the square where he said there was a taxi rank.

I set off and turned back to wave just as I reached the square, but his car was already almost out of sight down the road. I felt irrationally disappointed and abandoned. Father had seemed distracted, more so than normal. I'd hoped that as an adult he would feel able to talk to me more, confide in me, maybe even rely on me, but except in a work context, it didn't appear that was going to happen. I turned my attention to finding a taxi, which wasn't quite as easy as father implied it would be. Tatty little shops and cafes lined the square on three sides, most of which appeared to be closed. A large church completely overshadowed the fourth side of the square. That wasn't unusual, but the architecture was bland, and the stonework was tarnished with years of traffic exhaust. It wasn't the charming Italian piazza with the beautiful church shown in tourist literature. This clearly was not a town on any tour guide's route.

Walking briskly around the square, I came across a taxi office just down a side street. The man leaning on the desk, absorbed in his newspaper, looked up with a just audible tut of annoyance at being disturbed. After some shouting to a man outside, I was settled in the back of a rather decrepit Fiat, to be driven by an apparently kamikaze driver, to Bergamo airport. My flight was on time, and I relaxed a little, and passed the short waiting time trying to complete the crossword in the paper. My Italian was good, but crossword puzzles were always a challenge, one that I usually relished, but today just frustrated me.

As well as my flight to Naples, there was an earlier one to Rome listed on the board, and soon the departure lounge filled with over-excited school children, who were off to see the antiquities of that amazing city. The two adults accompanying them, who I guessed were their teachers, gave off an air of elegant indifference. The children were not running riot but were noisy and irritating and my meaningful glares at the two in charge went unnoticed. They seemed more interested in each other and the tender way he placed his hand on her back as he guided her towards the gate spoke volumes. I wondered how I would have felt as a parent of one of the pupils being supervised by this romantic pair, but then the parents would have been in blissful ignorance.

The airport felt even more quiet once all the children had left for their trip to Rome. My flight was next to be called, and I discreetly viewed the remaining passengers, who were also waiting for the flight to Naples. Most of them were suited businessmen, looking expensive and important; a trio of young adults who I guessed were students; and an ordinary-looking middle-aged woman. I was about to return to my crossword when I noticed that the woman kept looking in my direction but looked away whenever our eyes were about to meet. She unnerved me. Was she watching me, or was I being paranoid?

I rolled up the paper and wandered over to the small book stall. When I looked around, there she was, close behind me. She gave a nervous nod and smile but said nothing and began flicking through a book without appearing to take any interest in its contents. While she was pretending to be absorbed, I studied her in detail. She was petite, dressed in trousers and a cheap blazer. Her dark hair was twisted into a tortoiseshell clip, and she wore little makeup. She did not look sinister or suspicious at all, but you never can tell. After all, who would suspect me? However, I kept my eye on her to make sure she couldn't follow me later when we arrived in Naples. I had been too absorbed watching the school party to notice when she'd arrived in the departure lounge. As we boarded the plane, I let her go ahead of me so I could choose a seat behind her. From now on, I would keep her in my sight and my wits about me, just in case.

It was midday when the plane arrived in Naples. Most of my fellow passengers rushed off to taxis or buses to take them into the city. I hung back, fishing in my bag, but always keeping my eyes firmly on the woman from the flight. She stopped, didn't rush for the exit like most other passengers, and looked around. I felt certain she was looking for me, and ducked behind a magazine rack, always keeping her in sight. Then, she waved and hurried towards an elderly couple who were standing by the doors. My shoulders dropped in relief. I moved closer to where they were embracing and overheard that the couple were her parents. She was explaining to them that she had managed to overcome her fear of flying and had identified a fellow passenger she might call on if she felt overwhelmed. I felt mean for being suspicious and a little foolish. I turned and smiled at the woman as I passed her on my way out to the taxi rank, and she rewarded me with a smile and a mouthed thank you from her and also her parents. I felt ashamed, but I knew I had to be on full alert.

Chapter Seven

My journey from the airport to the hotel was another heart-in-mouth experience. The drivers in Naples seemed to follow a different highway code, if there was such a thing here, from anywhere else I had been in Italy or beyond. The taxi driver drove most of the way with one hand on the horn and the other intermittently gesticulating out of the window. I held my breath as we dodged into small gaps and gasped at the numerous near misses. I pitied any tourist who made the mistake of hiring a car and trying to drive around the city. I often drove in Italy but would never drive in Naples. The driver pulled up outside the hotel, looking unruffled, as though he had just had a leisurely drive down a country lane. He grinned as I paid him, and I felt relieved to be back on firm ground. I guessed Julia had booked the hotel for me, it was in an excellent position overlooking the waterfront and although it was not luxurious, was pleasant enough. My room was on the small side but had a balcony and lovely view over the bay and the two peaks of Vesuvius, which were clear over towards the left, against the bright blue sky.

After a quick splash of water on my face, I wandered across the road, where there were several restaurants overlooking the marina. I chose a small, lively place with an open terrace and enjoyed a delicious lunch of seafood while looking out across the bay. I could easily have forgotten the reason I was there, as I sat relaxing in the shade of a large canopy watching the boating activity. Not many of the boats looked like they were going anywhere soon. Most sat moored, looking sleek and expensive, shining in the Italian sunshine, waiting for equally sleek and expensive owners, and their entourage, to step on board. After eating, I still had the afternoon at my disposal, and I walked along the waterfront wondering what to do. I made my way back to the hotel. It was hot and still, and I was wearing the wrong shoes for walking, but I knew I couldn't settle to read or sit by the hotel's rooftop pool. I needed to be doing something more stimulating to keep my mind occupied until my meeting the next day. I remembered from an old guidebook the sculpture of the Veiled Christ, which was something I always wanted to see. When I had last been in Naples, which must be several years ago, I didn't have the time to seek it out. So, I decided now gave me the opportunity to put that right. After changing into flat shoes, I set off with a sense of anticipation. I thought I knew whereabouts it was but wasn't sure. So, with a tourist map picked up in the hotel, and the directions from the man at the reception desk I felt confident I could find the right street, and the small chapel where the sculpture was displayed.

The heat seemed to bounce off the buildings and I felt sluggish as I walked along, even though I clung to the shady side of the street. Nothing seemed to slow down the bustle and chaos of the city. Cars jostled for position along the crowded roads, with total disregard for lane discipline or pedestrian crossings. Anyone attempting to cross the road was taking their life in their hands and often rewarded with a blast from a horn. Naples felt mad, but I loved the sense of history with a tinge of danger, which made it feel exhilarating. It could not have been more different from the quiet bay where I had left the family.

I walked in the right direction and soon found myself in another small square, off which, according to the hotel receptionist, the chapel was located. It should have been on the right-hand side. It wasn't. Feeling hot and frustrated by the lack of detail on the inadequate map, and not being able to match the names of the alleyways or buildings that surrounded me, with the tiny, out-of-line print on the map, I was about to give up and return to the hotel. A young woman, seeing my confusion and sensing my inability to orientate the map, asked if she could help. I explained my predicament in Italian, which surprised and pleased her. The woman looked at the map and, after a couple of seconds; grinned and turned it around. She showed me on the map where the chapel was and pointed me in the right direction. Feeling a fool, I thanked her and pushed the map in my bag. The smell of coffee and fresh pastries wafted across the square and I was tempted to follow my nose and give up the search for the sculpture. I resisted and instead followed her directions and found the right place easily.

I bought my ticket from the ticket office and joined the long queue, which comprised mostly Chinese or Japanese tourists, and another group of over-excited school children. The queue moved at a snail's pace, as only a certain number of people could be admitted at a time. At least we were in the shade, and once my turn came to enter the chapel, I was thankful I had not returned to the hotel. It was worth the wait. The sculpture, by Sanmartino, when at last I set eyes on it, took my breath away. Pictures of it did not do it justice. I found it difficult to comprehend how something so fine and delicate could have been created from a single block of marble. I walked around the figure in total awe, entranced by its beauty. The body of Christ was laid on a marble couch. I don't consider myself to be religious, but the suffering of Christ below the veil was palpable and moving to behold. The technique of the sculptor made the figure appear so lifelike, I could see each feature, even the veins in his forehead looked real, under the translucent veil. So realistic was it, that I felt an almost overwhelming temptation to reach out and try to lift the delicate fabric, despite knowing it was marble. I resisted, due to the eagle-eyed staff, poised to pounce on anyone who looked like they might lean over the guarding rope to have a crafty touch, or who might raise their camera or phone to take a picture.

It was peaceful and calm inside the chapel and I lingered, admiring the other impressive sculptures around the Veiled Christ. I don't know how long I stayed and wasn't aware that most of the other tourists, having been deprived of taking their selfies in front of the sculpture, had left the chapel. I was also preparing to leave the coolness of the interior and re-enter the sauna of the afternoon city, when a young woman, who I thought must be Italian, moved too close to me, considering the chapel was now almost empty. She looked to be in her late teens or early twenties, with dark hair and an intense stare. She whispered something that I couldn't quite catch and passed me a piece of folded paper. I took it but was so surprised that by the time I had gathered my thoughts, and looked up to speak to her, probably only a few seconds, she had gone. I hurried out of the chapel, hoping to catch up with her, but she was nowhere to be seen, having disappeared into the thronged, narrow street. My heart was thumping, and I had an overwhelming sense of fear. Who was she? What did she want? I'd taken Julia's talk of a leak as something disconnected from me, but now I felt vulnerable and exposed. How would the girl know where I was, unless I was being followed?

I paused for a few seconds, leant against a wall and took some deep breaths to compose myself; my mind was racing, but my body felt rooted to the spot. Where was she now? What did she say, and what did she want? Without looking at it, I pushed the piece of paper into my bag. Before I did, I needed to sit down somewhere quiet. I looked around to see if anyone was looking in my direction, or, more likely pretending not to look in my direction. I used to be good at spotting people who were pretending not to look. No one in the vicinity was acting strangely–except me. No one glanced twice at me in my agitated state. Everything and everyone appeared normal.

The street was less crowded now, and I wanted to be amongst people, so walking as fast as I could, I made my way back to the small square where the other girl had earlier helped with directions. Could it have been her? Did she tip someone off? After all, she approached me. I didn't ask for her help, but I willingly told her where I was going. I had let my guard down. Feeling weak and as though I could not breathe, I made my way to a small café. I sat down at a table with my back to the wall to ensure no one could pass behind me. It was not until an extra strong coffee was in front of me that I calmed down and began to pull myself together. From my vantage point on one side of the square, I scrutinised the crowd again. No one was looking at me, no one appeared furtive. The majority were all young people, chatting and laughing in the sunshine, some Italian and others, clearly tourists, poring over guidebooks and maps. I was probably over-tired and just overreacting.

As I sipped my coffee my heart rate slowly returned to normal, and I relaxed. A young man, dark-skinned and possibly Arabic, pulled out a chair and asked if he could join me. A reasonable request as most of the other tables were occupied, but my heart rate sped up once again. I nodded and waited tensely for him to say something to me. I watched his every move, but after ordering his coffee, apart from thanking the waitress, not another word passed his lips. In fact, his eyes never left the screen of his phone. Intermittently, his fingers tapped away on his mobile in response to the messages that frequently pinged through, or maybe he was playing a game, the sort of game Dan and Oliver spent far too much time playing. His total lack of interest in me helped me to relax again. As I was drinking my second cup of coffee, and biting into a delicious pastry, I pulled the piece of paper out of my bag, remembering that I hadn't read the message, or whatever was on it.

I checked that my table companion was still absorbed in his phone, before I slid the sheet of paper out. He looked up, probably aware of my eyes on him; I waited and managed a weak smile before he returned to his phone.

I unfolded the paper. It was written in Italian, but translated as:

"Beware, time is running out. You are in danger."

I gasped as I read the words and stared at them until they danced across the page. I felt sick and for a moment felt as if I was going to faint. The man once again lifted his eyes from his phone and looked across the table, concerned. He laughed and tapped the piece of paper lying on the table in front of me. What could he want? I needed to leave but couldn't move.

'Ah, you have one too,' he said, and reached into his back pocket. He pulled out a similar piece of paper. It said something different, but equally disturbing.

'It is some sort of crazy group.'

A wave of relief swept over me, so strong I almost leapt up and kissed him.

'Oh, thank goodness, I thought it was personal.'

The waitress came to clear my cup and saw the pieces of paper on the table.

'Idiots, ignore them.' She nodded towards the table.

'Who are they?'

'I don't know, activists or something, kids mainly, they seem harmless. They chose people standing on their own to give this rubbish to. The police chase them away, but they still come back. They're just trying to be clever.'

The waitress moved away, and the young man explained that they were supposed to be environmental activists. He said he passed their demonstration earlier that morning in Garibaldi Square. Apparently, it was getting a bit out of hand and the police were trying to break them up.

'Environmental!' the waitress tutted, overhearing as she passed by again. 'They leave these pieces of paper everywhere, and all of them carry plastic bottles of water. They are idiots.'

'Pity,' said the young man. 'A good cause can get lost if it's not put across well.'

I nodded in agreement.

'I'm not sure this is the best way to get the message across.' I picked up the piece of paper. 'It seems quite threatening to me and doesn't even say what their cause is.'

'You are right, they are young, idealistic,' he smiled. 'At least they don't have guns,' he screwed up his face, shook his head, but he didn't say anymore. He stood up and picked up his bill, ready to pay.

'Please let me,' I took the bill from him. It was the least I could do.

He thanked me profusely, shook my hand and then hitching his rucksack over his shoulder set off across the square. I wondered what his story was, the way he mentioned guns so vehemently made me feel he might have seen much worse than a bunch of unruly environmentalists. I paid for his coffee, then sat and slowly drank another one, just people watching for a while. Three coffees in a row were not good and I hoped I wouldn't pay the price later. When I'd finished, I decided to return to the relative tranquillity of my hotel room, where I could sit on the balcony and enjoy the view overlooking the bay. I had had enough excitement for one day.

Chapter Eight

I made my way back through the crowded streets, then stopped. It was ridiculous to go back now. After all, when was the last time I had the luxury of being in such a fascinating city on my own? The strong coffee was now giving me energy and I dismissed my plan of returning to the hotel, just to sit down and waste the rest of the day. I turned round, and slowly at first, made my way back the way I'd come. I mulled over what I should do next and decided to seek out the museum. Having made my decision, I walked as briskly as the heat would allow in the direction of the archaeological museum.

It was quite a long way from where I was, and I needed to stop often to refer to my map, this time making sure it was the right way up. At last, I came to the end of a street and the grand pink façade of the museum was in front of me. I remembered it from the time when we brought the children into Naples after a trip to Pompeii, but much as they'd loved Pompeii, the children were too young at the time to want to linger over the artifacts in a museum, so we didn't do it justice. I crossed the road and climbed the steps to the main entrance and went, once again, into the delightful coolness of the interior. Now I relished the opportunity to linger for as long as I liked. I made my way up to the floor containing the exhibitions from Pompeii and Herculaneum. They were the most popular, of course, but surprisingly, it was not too crowded. I was absorbed in reading the details about the Carpe diem mosaic showing a skeleton, in black and white, holding two wine pitchers, when I became conscious of someone on the other side of the room staring at me.

I glanced up and just caught the eye of a man, who, as soon as he saw me looking at him, looked away and left the room. My pulse quickened. Not again! Or was it once more my overactive imagination? I hurried to the entrance, hoping to spot him. Not seeing him, I stepped into another larger hall, full of glass display cases and several large groups of people. I could not see him anywhere; he was either mingling with the crowd or had already left the room. I told myself to stop being paranoid. Not everyone in Naples could be following me. I was allowing my imagination to take hold and blow simple situations out of all proportion. Once again, just to be sure, I scanned the people in the hall. All seemed to be either looking intently at the displays or having earnest discussions about individual items. No matter how hard I tried, my previous mood of anticipation had faded, and I decided to join onto the tail end of a tour group, rather than continue looking around on my own–just in case.

It turned out to be a good decision. The young guide, a university student who was studying archaeology, was full of knowledge and enthusiasm, and soon had the small tour group hanging on his every word. I was once again relaxed and was enjoying the experience, when the man I'd seen earlier appeared from behind a sculpture and stared around the room. He was clearly looking for someone. I ducked behind an exhibit before he saw me, and watched as within seconds he decided whoever he was looking for, presumably me, wasn't there. The tour guide was indicating for us to move on. Luckily, in the opposite direction from the man, and I went with the group, keeping close to the guide. I made a great effort to concentrate on the guide's explanation as to how the huge mosaics had been transported from the Pompeii site to the museum. I still found it hard to believe that they had survived in such an intact condition.

As we moved into yet another room, there he was, staring

straight at me. He dodged out of sight as soon as he saw the group, but I moved to a position where I could watch him as he circled the room. He was trying, unsuccessfully, to look as though he was just another tourist, but his darting eyes and air of agitation gave him away. Who on earth could he be? And what could he want? My stomach was knotted, but I felt I had the advantage. He didn't know that I knew he was following me. I would have to be cool and clever to lose him. Something I used to always be good at, and years ago would have been high on the thrill of the chase, but now I seemed to be losing my nerve. Where was the woman who years ago had been involved in an exhilarating cat-and-mouse chase with a foreign agent in Bulgaria? Gone I feared, but that was then, and I could do without it now.

Keeping with the tour group, but now very much on the periphery, we moved to look at the pottery displays. I moved around the cabinets, keeping my eyes on the man. He was not good at surveillance; he stood out like a sore thumb, now he seemed to have given up any pretence of being a visitor. He just stood with his hands on his hips, staring at everyone entering the room. His incompetence reassured me. I felt certain I could shake him off, if necessary. He wasn't tall, about five foot nine or ten and looked quite young, mid to late twenties. He was dressed as many young Italian men are, in a tight pair of jeans and white T-shirt, a brown leather bag slung over his shoulder and typically beautiful Italian brown leather shoes. From that point of view, he blended in well with everyone else, but his actions were, to me at least, a giveaway. He didn't appear to be very well trained. I committed to memory his face, quite good looking with dark hair, dark eyes and a straight long nose and an earring in one ear. There was nothing really outstanding about him, but I knew I would be able to recognise him again and would make a note of the details later.

We continued playing a bizarre game of hide and seek as we went from room to room. By now, my enjoyment of the museum had faded, and I only managed to flick cursory glances at the beautiful items on display, so as not to lose sight of my follower. The tour group moved into a small room where the walls were lined with mosaic tiles of people in sexual poses. The guide described it as a menu for the brothel in Pompeii. I remembered this room from the visit with the children when Dan sniggered excitedly at each depiction. The group moved on through an opening at one end of the small room, which was annexed to a larger room, and then out through another exit, back into the larger area. The man had been close behind when we entered, but when we emerged on the other side, he was nowhere to be seen. I left the tour and retraced my steps, back to the room with the pottery and then round and once more through the 'menu' room. He was not visible anywhere. When I knew where he was, I felt in control, but now… I sat on a bench at the side of the room where I could see all the entrances and waited. Surely, he would show himself soon.

Many individuals and another tour group passed through the room, but the man I was looking for did not appear. At last, I stood up and decided to go back to my hotel. I walked out through the main entrance and was about to walk down the steps when I spotted him again. He was standing about halfway down the steps and staring straight at me. In the instant I hesitated, trying to determine my next move, he shouted and leapt up the stairs towards me, or rather passed me. In fact, he was oblivious to my presence. I turned to see where he had gone and overheard him admonishing another young man, saying he'd spent ages looking for him in the museum. The other man began gesticulating and swearing blind that they'd agreed to meet at a different time.

I slumped onto the steps and rested my head in my hands. What on earth was wrong with me? I was usually so cool headed and unflappable, but here I was behaving like a complete novice. Suspecting that everyone was out to get me was exhausting. I decided I must just be over tired after two restless nights, a flight and the stifling city heat. The two young guys, presumably now having made up, sauntered passed me down the steps and disappeared arm in arm across the street.

I could not face the walk back to the hotel in the heat, so bought a ticket for the open-top bus, which I knew stopped right outside the museum and I felt certain it stopped near my hotel. I didn't have long to wait and boarded the half empty bus, then settled myself into a seat on the top deck. My ticket came with a complimentary set of earphones, so I settled back to enjoy the commentary and ride around the city. The bus stopped on Garibaldi Square, where the noisy group of environmental protesters, mostly young people, were shouting and waving placards. They were being observed by several bored-looking policemen leaning against motorbikes. A young man jumped on the bus and started handing out the notorious slips of paper before being shooed off by the conductor.

A young family climbed on the bus at the stop near the Catacombs, just before it turned round and made its way back into the throng of the city. I felt empathy with the mother, who looked weary with the effort of keeping two small children entertained in the heat of a big city. I moved over to allow the boy, who looked about seven, to sit next to the window. He chattered almost non-stop about going into the Catacombs, telling me it was full of dead people, although he didn't see any. I smiled at his obvious disappointment. His younger sister sat on her father's lap with her thumb in her mouth, clearly being so close to dead people didn't excite her in the same way as they did her brother. They dismounted outside the museum, where the mother and I exchanged knowing looks. I heard her promising her daughter they would be having an ice cream soon, and I hoped that was enough to sustain her through the museum. My stop was the terminus, and I strolled the short distance back to the hotel, feeling quite upbeat and looking forward to relaxing on my balcony with a cup of tea and putting my feet up and having a nap, before thinking about finding somewhere for dinner.

Chapter Nine

The hotel reception was quiet, just another family with hot, tetchy, children booking in and struggling with their paperwork and bags. I waited for them to finish, then asked for my key. Just as I turned towards the lift, the receptionist who had been dealing with the family called my name.

'A lady left this for you, and a gentleman was asking for you.'

She pushed an envelope across the desk and was about to turn away. I must have looked alarmed because she stopped and reassured me, she had not revealed my room number to the man, and that he left without leaving a message. Apparently, the woman didn't ask if I was in, just left the letter. I thanked her, and with a shaking hand, picked up the envelope.

'Did either of them give their name? What did they look like?'

The receptionist shrugged, 'Nothing outstanding. I think they were middle-aged. I didn't take much notice. Sorry. I expect they'll be back if it's important,' she said, turning away to speak to another couple who'd just arrived.

In a matter of seconds, I had moved from being quite calm to yet again being a complete bundle of edgy nerves, and my hand still shook as I pressed the button to call the lift. This time, it was real. These people knew where I was, but who were they?

Today had been a roller coaster of emotion. I had caused myself unnecessary stress over imagined followers, but now it seemed someone, no, two people, really were looking for me.

No one apart from Julia, and possibly my father and maybe Geoffrey, knew where I was staying and even then, I wasn't certain father or Geoffrey knew all the minute details. It was Julia who oversaw making all the arrangements. Perhaps the man was my father, maybe there was a change to our plans, but then he would have left a message, even if it was cryptic, so I would know it was him. Anyway, there was the phone he had given me, and I was certain he would have just rung. I wondered if the woman might be Julia, but why would she come here, and in any case, I felt certain that if it were Julia, the receptionist would have mentioned her skin colour. My mind was whirling with all the possibilities and not coming up with any explanations.

The lift stopped at my floor but before stepping out I scanned the corridor to make sure I was alone, then satisfied it was empty and no one was lurking, I hurried to my room and fumbling with the key card, eventually opened the door and slipped inside, locking it behind me. The room was how I left it; my bag dumped on the rack where I'd put it. I sat on the bed and opened the envelope. Inside was one small sheet of high-quality cream note paper, dated today, but with no address. It was a brief note handwritten in bold, round, script. My eyes travelled over the words, but it took me a couple of reads to work out what it said.

> *Katryn,*
> Forgive my intrusion; I am your aunt, your mother's sister. Your father told me you were in Naples. Please ring the number below if you would like to meet. I have so much to tell you.
> Raisa

Was this genuine? I didn't know my mother had a sister, but then in reality I knew very little about my mother at all. Everything in my body was screaming at me to ignore the letter. It could be a trap. I looked at the letter again. She said my father had told her where I was; that seemed genuine, didn't it? Maybe the man the receptionist mentioned was my father coming to let me know. I puzzled why Raisa called me Katryn, but somewhere in the depths of my mind, that name rang a bell, and I wondered if it was an option for my name before my parents settled on Katharine. I wanted so much to speak to someone who knew my mother well. I had so many unanswered questions, and I knew deep down I was going to ignore my sensible inner voice and contact her. What harm could it do?

Neither my father nor Aunt Clare were forthcoming, when, as a child, I asked them about my mother. Father said the memory of her loss was too painful to talk about, and Clare said she didn't have the opportunity to get to know my mother very well. That may be true, but now I wondered if they were hiding something from me. I remembered father saying that my mother had no living relatives, no one else in the world were his exact words. Why, if it wasn't true would he say that? Maybe my mother had fallen out with her family, or they had disowned her for some reason. As I grew up, I learned not to ask too many questions, and gradually, my curiosity faded or was at least overshadowed by the demands of growing up and establishing my own life.

Once again, I wondered whether I should call my father about Raisa or even call Clare. But I didn't. I could imagine my father's reaction if he found out I had called his sister on the emergency phone for family business.

My desire now, to find out more about my mother, was so strong it blocked out any common sense or questioning. Why, after so many years, mother's sister would want to find me, and while I was working virtually under cover, went unquestioned. I also failed to question the method of her contact. I should have contacted my father just for confirmation that Raisa was who she said she was, but again, I didn't. Neither did I question how she knew where to contact my father, if, as he said, he was unaware of her existence. I wanted to believe she was my mother's sister, and I needed to know more about my mother. In fact, it was not until days later I allowed these thoughts to surface and chastise me with my own stupidity. I did nothing about it straight away and folded the letter back into my bag. I needed to think first, and I was, for now, more concerned about an unknown man asking for me by name, so there was no mistake it was me he wanted.

    I poured myself a drink and paced around the room, avoiding the balcony, just in case anyone was watching the hotel. So much for a quiet sit down! Two unknown people, even if one was my aunt, knew where I was staying, and it made me feel uneasy. I felt certain the man was not my father; he would contact me on the phone he'd given me that morning. I checked the phone just to make sure I had not missed a call, but there was nothing. After several minutes of pacing backwards and forwards, I reached a decision. I would move. I focused on my new plan. I changed my clothes and tucked my hair carefully into the light brown wig that was in the bag my father had given me on the way to the airport that morning. Was it really still the same day?

    I looked in the mirror, making sure that no strands of my own dark hair were showing. I'd thought the wig was unnecessary when I first looked into the bag but was now thankful it was there. I left enough of my belongings in the room to make it look as though I was still occupying it. I pulled the sheets back and rolled around on the bed, so that when the housekeeping staff arrived the next morning, it would look as though it had been slept in. I splashed water on the towels and ruffled them up. Then I was ready to go.

    I stood in the doorway for a moment before leaving the room, checking both ways along the corridor to make sure I was alone; I walked up two flights of stairs and along to the other lift, the one that descended into the far corner of the reception. Not being sure why, but I just felt I needed to cover my tracks as much as possible, even though I was certain no one was watching me inside the hotel. A man and woman were waiting for the lift, so I walked past them, going further along the corridor, until I heard the lift doors glide shut behind them. All was silent, so I made my way back and waited for what felt like many minutes before the lift arrived on the floor again. The doors slid open to reveal an empty cubicle. Once inside, I positioned a floppy hat on my head to conceal my face and put on a pair of large sunglasses. Looking in the mirror that lined the side wall, I hardly recognised myself, so felt certain anyone looking out for me would not realise it was me.

To my relief, the lift didn't stop at any other floors, and when the doors opened onto the reception, I was met with a cacophony of sound and activity. A party of American tourists must just have been deposited at the hotel. They were all milling around, talking loudly, and stretching the patience of the frazzled receptionist. She appeared to be on her own and was struggling to understand the American accent. None of them seemed to speak Italian and thought their demands for certain requirements in the rooms would be understood if they raised their voices. Under normal circumstances, I would have offered to help, but that moment was not classed as normal circumstances.

Unnoticed, I strode out of the hotel, walked around the block heading away from the waterfront, then back round towards the bay, coming out further along the same road. I chose an unassuming hotel a couple of blocks away from the original, and again, with an air of confidence, walked through the revolving door and up to the reception desk. Luckily, the reception was empty, and a room was available. I hadn't thought through the scenario of them being full, which was stupid of me considering it was the height of the holiday season. It was with a welcome, distinct lack of interest that the young male receptionist booked me in. My Italian was good enough for him to assume I was a native, or at least not a tourist, as he did not promote any of the excursions being advertised boldly on the reception desk. If I had been a tourist, I would have been less than impressed with his welcome, but for once I didn't care about manners.

My new room was small and without a balcony or sea view, but I felt, in the circumstances, that it was a small sacrifice to pay. I ordered room service, then lay on the bed and watched TV. It was halfway through the evening when I remembered the letter from Raisa. I reread it, and without giving myself too much time to think it over, decided to ring her. As I was about to dial her number on the mobile phone, my father had given me for 'official' use only, I remembered what he'd said. I knew it would also be a mistake to use my personal phone, so made my way down to reception. While waiting for the lift, I remembered the wig and rushed back to my room to put it on. A rookie mistake, I thought, and silently admonished myself for being slack, although I doubted the bored young receptionist would even have noticed my appearance.

It was the same man, leaning on the reception desk, staring into space. I asked if I could use one of the hotel's phones, giving him the excuse that my mobile had no signal. He shrugged his shoulders and muttered something about the signal being perfectly all right for most mobiles, and that there were phones in the rooms. I thought he was going to refuse, but then he smiled and indicated a phone on a desk at the back of the reception. He took the piece of paper I had scribbled the number on and obligingly dialled Raisa's mobile. The phone at the back of the reception gave a modicum of privacy. I did not want to use the phone in my room, just in case someone could trace it, but I couldn't explain any of that to the receptionist.

My hand shook as I held the receiver. Raisa answered almost immediately, as though she was holding her phone waiting for me to call. She sounded delighted when I said who I was, and she implied, although did not say, that she had very recently spoken to my father, which was when he had told her I was in Naples. She clearly knew a lot about me, things that only a family member would know. Her friendly, familiar tone swept away any of my previous doubts. I felt excited and was eager to know anything she could tell me about my mother and her family. Raisa wasn't in Naples anymore. She asked whether I wanted to talk over the phone or if I would prefer to meet. This again helped to give me confidence in her. I said I would love to meet her. She offered to come into the city again but thought it would be nicer if we met somewhere less chaotic. I told her I was spending some time looking around and would be in the city for one more day, but after that I would be happy to travel to meet her as I would be driving north.

We arranged to meet at a little place she knew in the hills further up the country, north of Naples. A little luxury break for us to get to know each other, she'd said, and I was excited by the prospect. Although I stressed I could only spare one night. It was on the way to Florence so would hardly be inconvenient and I was sure a minor delay in my task would not be a problem. I put the phone down and felt a glow of anticipation. At last, I might find out details about my mother's family. I thanked the receptionist and made my way back to my room. I needed to put thoughts of my family to the back of my mind for now. I had work to do.

Chapter Ten

The next morning, on my way to meet my contact, I walked along the waterfront to the port in plenty of time to catch the commuter ferry, rather than the tourist one, to the island of Procida. Part of the route was along the main road and although there was a reasonable pavement, the madness and fumes of the traffic made it quite unpleasant, and at times unsafe, making me question my judgment in walking rather than taking a taxi. The ferry terminal was heaving with people; it seemed many tourists used this route as well as locals commuting to and from the city for work. By the time I'd worked out the chaotic ticket system, as well as trying to help a rather confused English couple, who couldn't speak Italian, I only had a couple of minutes to wait, before being swept, in a tide of people, onto the large ferry. I had never been to Procida before and was looking forward to seeing it at last. It was the lesser known, but possibly prettiest of the islands in the bay, less glamorous and commercialised than Capri, the usual destination of choice for day-trippers.

The breeze out on the open water, even if slightly tainted by the fumes from the engine, was delightfully cool. I leant on the rail and admired the view of Vesuvius as we crossed the bay and wondered at the wisdom of the huge number of dwellings that had been built on and around the volcano. It had not erupted for many years but was by no means dormant. Although the sky was a clear, cloudless blue, there were a couple of white wispy clouds that hung just above the summit of the volcano. I assumed it was steam from the crater, rather than cloud, and tried to imagine what the famous eruption of 79AD must have been like. I promised myself another trip to Pompeii, although not this time. This visit was not for sightseeing, and besides, I wanted to bring Oliver, who was yet to marvel at the city frozen in time by volcanic ash. I remembered Dan and Jilly when they visited being fascinated by the history and stories of people who lived there at the time. The irony of not wanting to visit Pompeii yet being happy to visit an unknown aunt was lost on me.

The crossing didn't take long and Procida was the first stop. I watched, impressed, as the ferry was expertly manoeuvred into the tiny port, before I disembarked with probably less than half of the other passengers, the rest carrying on to the larger island of Ischia. Once on the quayside, and without the breeze, the mid-morning heat hit me, along with the enticing smells coming from a small bakery, unfortunately interspersed with the less enticing but ever-present fumes from scooters, that buzzed like a swarm of demented bees just about everywhere in Naples.

I was in plenty of time for my rendezvous, so rather than heading straight off to find my meeting place, I wandered along the pretty, bustling quay and found a café with large sunshades protecting the tables. I sat down, ordered myself a long, cool drink and a pastry, and enjoyed them while I watched the boats bobbing in the marina, and people passing by. For a small place, there was certainly plenty of activity to keep me entertained for a short time. I checked my watch and studied the small map Julia had given me. It looked straight forward. My destination was on the other side of the island, and after a conversation with the waiter, I worked out that it would take about twenty minutes to walk across.

After paying for my drink, I reluctantly left the shade of the café and made my way up a narrow, mostly residential, street. There were one or two shops selling local food delicacies, but it was very quiet. Most of the tourists clustered around the harbour or took the small, frequent buses to other parts of the island. The street led steeply away from the harbour, and I needed to stop a couple of times to catch my breath and cool down and part of me wished I'd had the sense to catch a bus. Although the heat persisted, I noticed clouds were gathering way out at sea, only a few at first, but enough occasionally to flit across the face of the sun.

As I reached the top of the hill, the road opened out into a small, shady square. I crossed the square and a previously hidden small harbour came into view below me. To catch my breath, I sat for a few moments on a low wall beside an ancient yellow painted church, which stood out in contrast to the deep blue sea beyond. I checked my watch to see if I had time to peep inside, but decided it would have to wait, perhaps later, on the way back.

A winding cobbled street led down towards the sea; flowerpots clustered on steps and beside doorways spilling brightly coloured flowers onto the grey cobbles. It was delightful. Rounding the last corner, I found myself at the far end of the small harbour beside the profusion of fishing and day trip boats. There were boards next to some of the boats, and people shouting to any passing tourist, enticing them to take trips around the island. In other circumstances, I could imagine how much the family would enjoy one of the trips and vowed to come back with them one day.

The multi coloured houses glowed in the sunshine as they clung to the hill and tumbled down onto the quayside, which seemed to be almost completely filled with tables and chairs; they were grouped by different coloured tablecloths and umbrellas, which I presumed indicated each individual establishment. I checked my map for the name of the café where I was to meet my contact, Giuseppe, and hoped it would be easily identifiable when I reached the melee of tables. Julia had provided very little information about how I would find Giuseppe, I just hoped he would be looking out for me. I was carrying my map, but the majority of other people milling around were also carrying maps.

I walked along past the boats; there was still had a few minutes to spare, and I hesitated when I noticed a young woman coming towards me with an apologetic smile on her face. I wondered if Giuseppe had sent her to meet me but thought that highly unlikely. Julia had emphasised that I should see him and no one else, and I assumed he would have been told the same. No middleman. The woman did not look like a tour operator, although that seemed possible, touting for business, or perhaps, she was a lost tourist, not that you could really get lost here. The harbour side settlement was very small. Apart from the quay, where restaurants and cafes struggled for space, there did not appear anywhere to get lost. There was the street I had walked down and a couple of alleyways between buildings, and I could see another small street leading away from the harbour on the other side. I smiled at the woman and was about to walk purposefully on, hoping she wouldn't stop me.

'Sorry, excuse me,' she said.

She looked older than I'd first thought once she was close. An attractive, well-dressed woman.

'Is this the way to the port?' she said and pointed back up the narrow street I had just come down.

'The ferry port?'

'Yes, I asked someone along the road. Their English wasn't very good and I'm afraid my Italian is even worse. They directed me here. I think they thought I wanted a boat ride, but I need a ferry, not a pleasure boat,' she scrabbled in the bottom of her bag and pulled out a crumpled ticket. 'This is the port I need,' she handed me the ticket.

I gave her directions and pointed to the street on her map and said I thought it would take her twenty to thirty minutes to reach the ferry. She looked at her watch and headed off,

'Thank you. I should just make it if I hurry. They'll be getting anxious if I'm late.'

She seemed unduly agitated, so I pointed out that her ticket wasn't for a specific time and that there were plenty of ferries. I was just beginning to feel a twitch of suspicion, but she smiled, thanked me, and turned away.

'Bye,' I said, and watched her as she headed off up the cobbled street, clearly in a hurry. I didn't envy her having to rush in the heat. As soon as I turned away and walked on, I forgot about her. I looked at my own watch. Right now, it really was time to find Giuseppe.

Chapter Eleven

Walking towards the multitude of tables and chairs, a man suddenly stepped in front of me and took my arm. I thought for a split second it must be Giuseppe, but soon realised it wasn't.

'You come for boat trip?'

'No, thank you, not now,' I tried to shake off his hand, but he was holding it impertinently tight, and I knew I couldn't get away. Something felt wrong.

'No, you *are* coming for a boat trip,' he emphasised and started to walk towards a jetty, his arm now around my waist, making it impossible for me to get away. I had no option but to walk with him.

'Struggle or scream and you'll regret it,' he hissed in my ear in English, and I was at once both incensed and afraid.

Then, as though a switch had been triggered in my brain along with a rush of adrenaline, I was at once on full alert and could think with total clarity. This situation demanded calm control. I was not sure what was going on, but instinct and experience told me I needed to play the role of the innocent tourist while I worked it out. For the time being, I said nothing. I now felt certain this person wasn't anything to do with Giuseppe, but although his identity and motive were a complete mystery to me, he must know about my mission in some way. No doubt I would soon find out. I scanned the jetty as I was roughly steered along but could see no one who might help. In fact, we had already walked quite a way from the cafes and groups on the quayside. As we passed a rubbish bin, I pretended to stumble and slipped my map, which had Giuseppe's name and the café where we were to meet written on it, to the side of the bin by the wall.

'How dare you! I do not want a boat ride. Let go of my arm,' I said, deciding that a tourist would protest, not just keep quiet.

'Just walk and shut up.'

We reached the end of the small jetty; we had passed all the small, brightly painted pleasure boats, and he pushed me towards a medium-sized launch. Another man was standing alongside, holding a rope, and the engine was already ticking over. I weighed up the pros and cons of making a scene and attracting attention to myself. The only other people on the jetty were a few tourists, waiting excitedly for their trip, at the far end, and they were talking loudly in a language that was neither English nor Italian. To shout out enough to attract anyone's attention on the quayside seemed pointless.

'This is ridiculous. What's going on?' I tried to sound indignant and forced myself not to overreact, as the man manoeuvred us on to the boat and unceremoniously shoved me down into a cabin. Within seconds of boarding, the man on the jetty untied the rope, jumped onboard and we were moving, slowly at first, so as not to collide with one of the many other boats. Then as the boat passed through the opening of the small harbour it increased its speed, and the momentum flung me against the table. Trying to regain my balance, someone roughly pushed me back on to the long bench seat behind the table and told me to stay put.

I knew anything I did or said now was critical to my safety. A strange surge of excitement mixed with indignation and a touch of fear now replaced my initial feeling of anger. This was what my training was for, although that training was very rusty, and I was determined to rise to the occasion.

'Now look, what do you think you're doing? This is totally out of order. Take me back at once. This just isn't on,' I said, warming to my role.

A momentary look of confusion crossed one of the men's faces, and I decided that playing the naïve upper-class tourist was going to be my best cover. I just needed to keep it up. The men were speaking in Italian and despite being fluent, I played ignorant. If they thought I couldn't understand them, I reckoned I stood a better chance of working out what was happening, so long as they stayed within earshot.

'Please, can you speak English? This is ludicrous. Tell me what's going on. You've made a terrible mistake!'

'Stop talking! You talk too much.' The man who first grabbed me on the quay glared, then turned back to the other man and carried on his conversation in Italian. From what I could glean from their conversation, it seemed they were heading out towards another boat, but I couldn't make out what they planned to do with me once we got there, or why. Nothing from their language shed any light on who they were or, more importantly, who they were working for. It seemed certain whoever it was knew about my mission, and this was not just a random kidnapping.

'Listen, I don't have any money, if that's what you're after. I'm not anyone rich or famous.'

'Quiet,' the first man barked, and turned away.

I could see through the cabin window we were leaving Procida behind, and we weren't going to another harbour on the island. Neither were we heading back to Naples on the mainland. Apart from a long-ago holiday on Capri, I was unfamiliar with this area of coast, so it was difficult to get my bearings and form a mental picture of where we were. I really was on my own.

I thought it was just the two men and myself on the boat, so was surprised when a woman appeared from a forward cabin I had not noticed. She looked to be in her mid-thirties; I found it difficult to tell. She spoke to the men before turning her attention to me. Her lips were thin, made to look fuller with inexpertly applied lipstick, and bent into a humourless smile. Her dark hair was scraped back from her face and her equally dark eyes had a hard, cold look about them; I instinctively knew to be wary of her. She appeared to be the one calling the tune, and I knew she was the one I needed to watch and try to fool into believing that they had picked up the wrong person.

'Give it to me,' she said. Both her English and Italian seemed fluent, but she spoke with an accent that I couldn't place, possibly Eastern European.

I stared at her, and she repeated herself, then leant forward over the table so that her face was too close to mine. Her pale green shirt was an expensive designer brand, but now appeared grubby and frayed around the collar. She smelt of cigarettes and cheap cologne, which made me think that like the two men she was not the boss, although, by her manner, I knew she was the one in control on this boat.

'Give you what? I don't know what you're talking about. Is it money you want? You can have all I've got, which isn't much, but I demand to be taken back to shore, immediately.'

The woman laughed, but it was obvious she didn't find the situation funny.

'We saw you; we saw the exchange with the woman.'

'What woman, what exchange? This is getting ridiculous. You aren't making sense? I insist on being taken back. *Now!*'

A fleeting look of doubt crossed her face, and she turned to the men and barked at them in Italian, asking if they were sure. I realised from their exchange that they must have seen me talking to the woman on the quay and assumed we were liaising, not just meeting by chance. They also assumed that she had given me something. That something must be the memory stick. I felt deeply grateful that it wasn't yet in my possession. I felt quite shocked that they knew about it, if in fact they did. It put me in a more vulnerable position, but I was determined to deny all knowledge of everything.

'Don't pretend. We saw you; she gave you something and we want it, now. Why else were you meeting another woman on the quayside?'

'No, honestly, I don't know what you mean. The only person I've spoken to before I was grabbed by that thug,' I nodded towards the man who'd accosted me on the quay, 'was a lady looking for the ferry port. It certainly wasn't any sort of clandestine meeting; I have no idea who she was and have never seen her before in my life. Now, I don't know who you are, or who you think I am, or what charade you are involved in, but I demand to be taken back at once.' I hoped the slight quiver in my voice didn't give my fake righteous indignation away. If they were after the memory stick, anything could happen. They didn't seem to be the most effective or professional team, and people like them were often more dangerous. They could become unpredictable under pressure.

'Empty your bag,' the woman said, and banged on the table with such force she made me jump and judging by her expression, hurt her hand. She threw a comment over her shoulder to the men along the lines of they would be in big trouble if she found nothing. They in turn threw angry glances in my direction and stared stony faced as I picked up my bag. I almost felt sorry for them; they were going to be in big trouble. I tipped the contents onto the table in a heap. The woman spread them out, then picked up each individual item. The tourist map of Procida, that for some reason I'd picked up on the ferry, despite already having a map, used tickets from the museum and the chapel in Naples where the veiled Christ was displayed. All this gave credence to my tourist image.

'What is this?' she thrust a short, multi coloured chunky pen, that I'd bought at the airport, under my nose.

'A pen, let me show you.' I reached to take it from her hand, but she passed it to one of the men.

'Undo it,' she barked in Italian.

The taller man, with a scar along his forearm, seemed to be all fingers and thumbs as he clumsily unscrewed it. He pulled out the ink holder and scattered the spring and push mechanism onto the table.

'Hey, you can't do that! That's my favourite pen.'

They ignored me, but I could tell that the woman was starting to boil inside. They stared at the dismantled pen as if willing it to be what they were looking for. Next, she picked up my lipstick, opened it and twisted it up and down, before putting it back on the table. I was pleased that she didn't snap it, as this really was my favourite. She then emptied the contents of my purse, which amounted to a couple of hundred euros and a few coins. Luckily, my credit card, which would have confirmed my name, if they knew it, was in the safe in the hotel, along with my passport and other information that might have given me away.

'Take it all if you want, but just take me back. I won't report you to anyone. Please. I've done nothing, just please take me back,' I said, thinking a bit of anxious pleading might sound genuine at this stage.

She stared at me but said nothing, then picked up my phone. My pulse quickened.

'Unlock,' she thrust the phone at me.

I would have to think up an explanation, and fast. She looked at the screen; apart from the standard icons, it was blank. She then tapped the phone icon. No calls were listed, then she tapped contacts and frowned when she saw it was also empty. I knew my father's number by heart, so didn't need to save it in contacts. She tapped on emails, nothing. Then placing the phone on the table drummed her fingers on the screen. She looked puzzled, frowned even deeper, then looked at me.

'Why nothing? Check it,' she passed the phone to one of the men.

'It's new. I had my phone stolen yesterday outside the museum.' Even to me, the explanation sounded plausible, and I felt pleased with myself.

There was a pause while she digested this information. The man handed the phone back to her with a shrug. I breathed a sigh of relief. My father's method of hiding apps and contents had worked.

She dropped the phone back on the table.

'It's Naples. What do you expect?'

'I'm a tourist. I expect to be treated with respect, not have my phone stolen or to be kidnapped when I'm sightseeing,' I said, although I knew her question was rhetorical. She stared at me with a scathing look on her face, picked up my bag and shook it, felt inside the pockets and patted the lining. I didn't care about the pen being in pieces, but I really didn't want her to rip the lining of my bag.

'Cretino.' She spat the word in Italian at the two men as she flung my bag back on the table.

I gathered my things together and shoved them anyhow back in my bag. She looked but didn't stop me. I was feeling certain she now believed I was just a tourist, but that didn't mean I was safe, far from it. I was no longer of any use to them, so could be regarded as disposable, and this far out at sea, no one would ever know where I was if I was pushed overboard.

'Look, please just take me back. I don't know what you want or what's going on, but if you just take me back that will be the end of it.'

She whirled round. 'Shut your mouth,' she said. She almost whispered the words, but there was an undertone of threat, so I did as she said. I sat still, just watching, and waiting, and wondering what else I could do.

Chapter Twelve

The three of them moved away to the far end of the cabin and were having a heated debate, which, with the drone of the engine, was just out of my earshot. I studied them, trying to imprint their faces in my memory. The man with the scar, which I presumed was where a broken arm had been pinned and plated, looked about thirty. He was a tall, powerful man with no other identifying features. When he spoke, he sounded well educated, although he said little, and wore very dark sunglasses, even inside the cabin, so I couldn't see his eyes. The other man who was older, stockier and swarthier, seemed more volatile. A tattoo of a snake curled up his right arm, and on the back of his left hand there was a crude anchor tattoo, which looked as though it was an amateur, homemade attempt. I wondered if he was an ex-merchant navy sailor, and whether this was his boat. Maybe not, as it occurred to me, there must be someone else on board skippering the boat. His face was weather beaten and deeply lined. I felt sure I would recognise him again, if I needed to at any time.

The woman's face and bone structure were quite distinctive. She was thin and angular and very tense. On her cheek, I noticed, was a mark that was either a small birthmark or an irregular shaped mole, maybe even a melanoma. After a few moments, they stopped speaking and looked in my direction, then looked away and carried on with their heated, muffled conversation. I could make out a few words from the woman's low, agitated voice, but not enough to make any proper sense of it. I guessed she was trying to work out their next move, which I imagined included what to do with me. They glanced in my direction a couple more times and I wished they would move closer, or speak more loudly, so I could hear what was being said.

I looked out of the cabin window; we were now quite a long way out to sea. I could still just about see the coast, but there were very few boats out this far. In fact, I could only see one and we were heading full speed towards it. Within a couple of minutes, we were alongside the bigger boat and the engine idled. Now we were no longer speeding along the swell became more noticeable and keeping close to the other boat without banging into it was quite tricky.

'I need some air, I feel sick,' I said, putting my hand to my mouth.

They weren't to know that I'm a very good sailor, but I wanted to get out on deck to inspect the other boat. Again, they went into debate about what to do with this new situation. The woman was inclined to leave me to get on with feeling ill, but the older man confirmed my hunch that, if it wasn't his boat, he was responsible for it and categorically expressed that he didn't want me to vomit in his cabin. They debated interminably whether going outside would be all right; after all, there was nowhere I could go and no one I could shout to for help. To speed up their decision, I made gulping noises and put my other hand over my mouth.

'Ok quick, get out here,' the woman said, and pulled on my arm. Once I was on my feet, she gave me a shove in the back and pushed me through the open door.

I lurched to the side of the boat nearest to the other boat and did a pretty good imitation of being seasick. My only concern was that I had increased the risk of being pushed overboard. I would not stand a chance of survival, unless I was very lucky, and another boat found me. I was a good swimmer, but you would need to be superhuman to swim the distance back to the island.

What they didn't know, of course, was that there was no

friend or family on shore waiting for me, and who would raise the alarm as soon as they knew I was missing.

As I hoped, no one came to check what I was up to, assuming that the row I was making was proof enough of my previous meal ending up in the water.

The boat we were now bobbing beside was a much bigger launch. It was a sleek cabin cruiser, which in its heyday probably hosted a glamorous set for luxurious holidays, but now was looking a bit tired. In between my bouts of supposed vomiting, I looked up and scanned the side of the boat. It was called "Boreas" and was registered in Antalya. From my position hanging over the edge, I could just see the raised pilothouse and the outline of a figure at the wheel. It was difficult to pick out any other identifying features.

I sat back up and could hear the crackle of voices. The woman on the boat I was on was talking to someone on the VHF radio. I guessed to someone on the boat beside us, although it was clear they knew we were alongside. I sat breathing in the fresh air. It was welcome after the stuffy interior, and I hoped I would be left to enjoy it for as long as possible. A minute later the radio went quiet and a shout from someone on the other boat startled me. Something was happening, and I was once again on full alert. The woman, now red in the face and agitated, banged open the cabin door and almost fell onto the deck. She told me to move with a shove on my shoulder. She actually said,

'Go below', but I slid across the seat to the other side of the small deck area and keeping silent, kept my eyes and ears wide open.

The woman went to the side of the boat, nearest to the Boreas, and shouted to a person who was now leaning over the rail of the bigger boat. They were even more in danger of bashing together now on the heavy swell. I moved back along the seat towards her, making sure I was out of her eyeline, and observed everything that was taking place. It was hard to determine whether the person on the other boat was male or female. They wore a baggy all in one boiler suit type of outfit, with a hat pulled down low over their eyes. The only give away were the hands, which were holding a small package. They were quite large, but smooth with short well-manicured nails and a rather large emerald signet ring. My guess was that it was another woman. However, I changed my view when the person spoke, or rather shouted across the bow to the woman in front of me. The deep tone made me think it was more likely to be a man.

He spoke to the woman in a language I recognised as Turkish. I knew a few words but my understanding of their conversation, despite it being shouted clearly, was very limited. For some reason, he pulled off his hat, and I was able to get a clear look at his face. Despite speaking in Turkish, he did not look like a Turk. His hair was fair, almost red, and his eyes looked pale blue or green. If I'd been asked to guess, I would have thought he was a Scot, but there was no trace of a Scottish accent. The boats continued to be pushed away, then back towards each other on the swell. When the boats were almost level, the fair-haired man tossed the package that he was holding across to the woman, who only just caught it.

He shouted something else, and the woman just shrugged. He turned away and disappeared into the boat's cabin. The woman turned to go below but seeing me still sitting on deck swore under her breath and grabbed my shoulder. With a sharp irritated jerk of her head, she indicated for me to go back inside. Reluctantly, I got to my feet, protesting that I still felt sick, but she was insistent, and I went back to my seat at the table in the stuffy cabin. I was trying hard to piece together the few words I'd managed to decipher from the shouted instructions. There was something about a drink and sleep, but nothing that really made much sense to me. Once back inside, the woman explained in Italian to the two men what was happening. I put my head on my arms on the table, still pretending to feel sick, while my ears were straining to hear what she said. It seemed the plan, now they were convinced I was the wrong woman, was to make me drink something with a drug in it to make me sleep. They would then return me to shore and when I woke up, the effect of the drug would be such that I wouldn't be able to remember anything in any detail.

I knew the sort of drug it was, having learnt about something similar many years ago. It would leave whoever took it feeling woozy and unable to decipher the truth from a muddle of images. I needed to make sure that somehow, I didn't take the drug, but at the same time make them think I had. It would be tricky, but I knew it was essential not to let myself lose the information I had gathered. It could be key to identifying them and the mole in the Service. The boat was now heading back in the other direction, and as expected, I heard them pouring water into a glass.

'Here, drink this. It will stop you feeling sick.' The man with the scar pushed on my shoulder to make me sit up and held out a small glass of what appeared to be ordinary water.

'Thank you, what is it?' I took the glass. 'Are you going to take me back now?'

'Just drink, don't keep asking,' he said, not taking his eyes off me.

I raised the glass, desperately trying to think of a way not to swallow its contents. As luck would have it the radio crackled into life, and all three of them turned away from me for just long enough for me to tip the glass onto the upholstery of the seat. It soaked into the worn fabric very quickly and I shuffled along to sit on it, ignoring the unpleasant dampness soaking through my dress. By the time they looked round, I was apparently, draining the glass and putting it on the table.

'Thank you,' I said, and pushed the glass across the table. 'Could I have some more, please?'

He picked up the glass, peering in to make sure it was empty, but ignored my request for more water. I genuinely would have liked a drink of water. It felt like hours since my last drink but decided not to push my luck.

'How long does it take?' the older man asked the woman.

Just the question I was asking myself, and listened for the answer, so that I could feign my sleep at the right time.

'Five or ten minutes, might be quicker as she's quite small.'

So, five minutes later, I yawned, folded my arms on the table and rested my head. I still wasn't confident they were taking me back to Procida, but all I could do was wait. My fear was that once, apparently asleep, they might decide to throw me overboard. It would be easier if I couldn't struggle.

The boat was now speeding along, bouncing across the waves as the sea was getting very choppy. I listened to them talking even more freely now they thought I was in a drug induced sleep. It seemed they were being paid to carry out a job and were now blaming each other for failing to do that. As I thought, the older man was the boat owner, and only became involved to get a bit of extra cash ferrying the other two backwards and forwards. It still wasn't clear who was driving the boat, but I decided that wasn't too important. The boat owner was demanding to be paid, even though the other two were unlikely to be receiving any cash. He argued that his side of the bargain had been fulfilled. It wasn't his fault if I was the wrong woman.

He was now saying he would refuse to take them back to the bigger boat unless they paid in advance. I wondered what sort of man would willingly take part in what was, to all intents, a kidnapping without asking any questions, but remembered this was Camorra country and I suspected a trip like this was nothing for someone like him to get alarmed about. As long as he was paid, no questions would be asked. They must have agreed a very good price because the holiday market was quite lucrative for a small boat owner.

Apart from listening to them arguing over money, I didn't pick up any useful information about who they were or which organisation they were working for, although I racked my brain for organisations with Turkish links. I knew a couple but could not be certain. The journey back seemed to take a long time and my neck was getting stiff, but I dared not move or open my eyes to see if I could get a glimpse of where we were. I just hoped we were heading to Procida.

Eventually the boat started to slow, and I could hear the throb of other engines nearby, and people talking to each other on the jetty.

'Don't tie up, just hold it while we get her off. Then you will take us back.'

The woman was giving the orders, and the boat rocked as the man with the scar jumped off and pulled the boat alongside. The boat hit the jetty with a gentle thud, and I felt a wave of relief sweep over me.

'Wake up.' The woman was shaking my shoulder vigorously. 'Wake up. Time to get off.'

I stood up, remembering to wobble and look a bit dazed.

'Where am I? I feel sick.'

'Not again. Quick help me get her off.' She reached under my arm and the other man pushed me towards the door. I slipped my hand through my bag that was still on the table and clutched it to my chest.

They manhandled me off the boat and pushed me onto a bench seat at the side of the jetty.

'What's going on? Where am I?'

'You've been on a nice boat ride, and now you're back. Goodbye.'

'Bye, thank you,' I said, slurring my words.

The woman snorted. 'She won't remember a thing,' she said to the men as they climbed back on board. Almost as soon as their feet were back on the deck, the boat moved away from the jetty and was soon speeding back out across the bay. I presumed they were going back to re-join the bigger boat. I could not help wondering what sort of reception would be waiting for them, when they boarded the Boreas, after their miserable failure. They would have a lot of explaining to do, picking up an innocent tourist by mistake. I laughed to myself, feeling quite proud of my amateur dramatic skills. Now I had my proper job to complete.

Chapter Thirteen

I waited for a minute or two, just getting my mind back onto the task in hand, then stood up; I could still see the boat bouncing over the waves as it headed back across the bay. I watched until it was almost out of sight, and then, after looking up and down the jetty to make sure there was no one else about to pounce on me, made my way back towards the still bustling quay and busy cafes. The people touting for customers for their boat rides seemed to be having a break, leaning against the wall smoking and chatting. As I reached the end of the jetty, I noticed the distant, gathering clouds of earlier were now filling the sky, and large raindrops began to fall. I walked with a purposeful stride towards the cafes and restaurants, where people were suddenly jumping up and rushing inside or under the rapidly wound out awnings to avoid a sudden drenching.

Walking along the quay I examined every café, trying to work out the one in which I was supposed to be meeting Giuseppe, my contact. Blue and yellow cloths and parasols, I remembered, was scribbled on my map. I passed one with blue cloths and another with yellow parasols, but none seemed to quite fit the description. I hoped I would find it soon as the rain was beginning to soak through my thin summer dress, which, along with the wet patch on the skirt, was starting to make me feel uncomfortable. I doubted that Giuseppe would still be waiting, as by now I was well over an hour late. He'd probably messaged in a 'no-show'. I wondered what that would trigger but didn't dwell on the thought.

Anyway, I needed a drink; I was desperately thirsty, and a brandy wouldn't go amiss either, to help me decide on my next move.

'Katharine, quickly come with me.'

A man appeared at my side and put his hand on my elbow, and I instinctively pulled it away. I wasn't going to be caught twice. I whirled round, ready to fight or run.

'Sorry. I didn't mean to startle you. I'm Giuseppe; I saw what happened earlier. Come with me.' He held out his hand, which I took. 'Let's go. I don't want you to get wet or caught up in the stampede of diners trying to get out of the rain.'

He steered me between two buildings and up a narrow staircase into a small, unoccupied room looking out over the sea. It was an attractive intimate room with large open windows which provided views across the tops of the parasols below and beyond to the blue horizon. As I glanced out, there was no sign of either of 'my' boats.

He smiled and his eyes sparkled in his deeply tanned face. It was difficult to estimate his age. He could have been anywhere between thirty-five and forty-five. His dark hair curled behind his ears and overall, he was very good looking. Years ago, I would have been delighted to spend time with such a handsome man, and would have switched into full flirt mode, but now I was just relieved to have found him, or rather, be found by him. He could have looked like a gorilla for all I cared, and my pleasure would have been the same. His clothes were casual, long beige shorts and a plain green t-shirt, and, I observed, he was wearing well-crafted leather sandals.

I sat down on the chair he pulled out for me at a table beside the window.

'This is my sister's trattoria; we can talk up here without being disturbed. This area is closed to the public until later,' he said, before I'd said a word.

'I need some paper and a pen, and a glass of water, please.'

'Of course, just a moment.' He stood up without questioning

this strange request and went to an area at the back of the room. Moments later he was back with a large glass of water, which I gulped gratefully, and another glass of pale amber liquid. 'I thought this might help, after your ordeal,' he said, and smiled.

I picked up the glass and downed it in one. He must have read my mind; it was just what I needed.

'And this,' he said as he placed a sheaf of paper, a pen and a couple of coloured pencils on the table.

I wondered whether he thought I wanted to sketch the view from the window, but charming as it was, at this moment, it was of no interest to me. I picked up the pen and jotted down all the key points I could remember; the name of the larger boat and where it was registered, and underneath made a sketch of what it looked like; then the smaller launch, "*Luce del Sole*" it was called and was registered in Naples. I then drew the snake and anchor tattoos that were on the stockier man's arms, and a quick sketch of his face.

Giuseppe watched without moving or speaking.

'You're very good at this,' he said, when I paused for a moment, nodding towards the paper.

'I've got a very good memory for details; I think it's why my father thought I would be a good asset,' I said, without looking up.

Chewing the end of the pen to help me concentrate, I recalled other details and then carried on sketching. First the scar on the taller man's arm. Then I drew what I could of his face, but to be honest, because he wore sunglasses, it had been difficult to pick out any distinguishing features. The portrait of the woman was more detailed and when I stopped to think for a few moments, Giuseppe pulled it towards him and pointed to the mark on her face.

'Do you recognise her?'

'Possibly, I'm not sure, but this on her face looks familiar. You said there were two boats. Did any of them make connection with anyone on board the Boreas?' he tapped the paper where I'd written the names of both boats.

'Yes, hang on a minute, let me get everything down while it's still fresh, then I'll tell you what happened.' I knew he was desperate to ask questions, but I needed to work in silence for a few more minutes.

He smiled and nodded. I picked up the pen again and thought about the man on Boreas, I made an outline sketch of his face, showing through shading that his hair and eyes were a light colour, and then made a more detailed drawing of the signet ring, which I thought was probably unique to the wearer.

'OK, I think that's everything.' I took another gulp of water and pushed all the pieces of paper across the table to Giuseppe. He scrutinized each one closely for several minutes without asking anything, and I didn't interrupt his train of thought. Then he looked up and smiled.

'Good work, excellent, but before we start discussing the details, would you like something to eat?'

I realised that I was starving hungry, having not eaten anything since my pastry when I arrived on Procida, which felt like a very long time ago. I nodded. Giuseppe pushed his chair back and went to a door at the back of the room. He called to someone down the stairs. I heard a woman shout back. He requested two pizzas and a bottle of wine, and my mouth began to water.

He returned and sat back down at the table and turned the papers over. We sat in silence for a few minutes, both mulling over the morning's events.

'The rain will stop soon.' Giuseppe nodded towards the church on the hill, behind which blue sky could already be seen pushing the clouds out to sea.

He was right; by the time our pizzas and wine arrived, the afternoon sun was once again shining, dazzling on the wet street and people were again filling the tables in the quayside cafes. Their chatter and laughter floated up and through the open windows of the quiet dining room where we sat.

The pizza was the most delicious I could remember tasting. Not that I should be surprised considering it is a specialty of the Naples area. Although I felt better with each mouthful, my mind was too preoccupied to savour it as it deserved.

'OK,' he said, pouring another glass of wine. 'I saw you, or who I thought must be you, come down the street, then stop and speak to a woman for a couple of minutes. I presumed it was just a random meeting. Then a man grabbed you by the arm and walked you along the jetty. At first, I thought maybe it wasn't you, but I could tell by the way he was holding you it wasn't a friendly encounter. I contemplated whether to run after you, but I thought you would be safer if I left you alone, and in any case, the boat would have moved away before I could reach it. I walked along the jetty and found your map with my name on it, so I knew it was you. Smart move leaving it. So, apologies for leaving you to your fate, but tell me everything that happened from when they took you on the boat.'

It took almost an hour for me to cover all the details. From my decision to play the dumb tourist, to the woman searching my bag, the smell of her perfume, my feigning seasickness, and then pretending to drink the drugged water. Giuseppe listened, leaning towards me so as not to miss any detail, only interrupting once or twice to clarify something.

'So that's about it. Does it mean anything to you? Any idea who they are or who they might be working for?'

He looked out to sea, absorbing all the details of my description. 'I think you had a very lucky escape. I'm not certain who they were but your description and this.' He tapped the papers again. 'Will go a long way to finding out. With your acting and drawing skills, you're wasted in this game.'

'I was amazed they fell for it! How did they know about me, do you think?'

'I don't know. I doubt they knew who you were, or who you were meeting, which is good for you, good for us both, but it seems they knew that there was to be an exchange, here, today, which is enough to ring alarm bells.' He sat, eyes closed, once again deep in thought, then shook his head. 'I have no idea how they knew, but hopefully they will think they've missed the handover and move on. Can I keep these drawings?'

'Of course. I wonder if they know the next handover point.' I was about to tell him that there was a suspected mole but stopped myself. Not that I suspected him, it just felt better to keep some things quiet.

'I'll pass them on. They're a good start.' He folded my sketches and rested his hand on them. Almost, it seemed, to stop me taking them back should I change my mind.

'Do you think the memory stick is some sort of decoy?'

'Decoy?' he said, frowning. 'What makes you say that?'

'Well, it just seems a strange way to move sensitive data. I just wondered if there was something else, I don't know, something that we're unaware of going on in parallel.'

'Could be, I hadn't thought of that, but it seems a bit over elaborate. I think using the stick is quite clever. It's not an expected method.'

'No, but someone is on to it, or on to something.' I paused, wondering if I should tell Giuseppe what else had been confusing me, and decided I would.

'When the details of my task were explained, I was also told a lot of technical data, which seemed at the time, and still does come to that, completely irrelevant. I don't suppose you've any idea?'

He shook his head. 'I haven't been given any other details. Can you remember it?'

I nodded, and he slid the paper and pen across the table. My mind turned back to the evening with Julia. If I could picture the scene, I would remember it more clearly. It came back in surprising detail, considering how tired I'd been at the time. Giuseppe watched as I wrote out the details, then passed the paper back to him.

'Any idea what it could mean?' I asked after he'd studied it for a few minutes.

'No, not really, but if there is a decoy, I think this is it.' He looked up and smiled when he saw the look of surprise on my face.

'How can it be? I wasn't told what it was or what to do with it.'

'No, I think it was something that if you were pressurised, under duress, it would be information that would come to mind, and you would give it up. It would seem very genuine that it was something you considered to be secret.'

His words sank into my brain, and I felt rather foolish, but I knew what he meant. Of course, information planted almost subliminally would come to mind, as Giuseppe said, 'under duress', and would sound more authentic than a cock and bull story about a memory stick. Although the woman on the boat was looking for the stick, not technical data. Somehow, the details were known. There was a mole, and whoever it was knew everything.

I then remembered and told Giuseppe about the man making enquiries about me in the hotel, and how feeling unnerved I'd changed hotels. He nodded in approval of my actions but couldn't throw any light on that man's identity or motive, either. An admirer, perhaps, he'd said with a twinkle and to my annoyance, I blushed. He smiled and became more serious and advised me, particularly after what happened today, that I should be extra vigilant from now on and to make certain, as far as I could, I wasn't being followed. Not easy in the chaos of the city I thought. I didn't want to become paranoid, well no more paranoid than I already was, although strangely after the morning's events I felt calmer, more in control, and the old familiar buzz was tingling through my body, but Giuseppe was right I must be more cautious. He didn't offer advice on what to do if I thought I was being followed, but I would cross that bridge if it happened. Besides, I'd handled this last situation well, so didn't think I needed advice, after all this was what I was supposed to be good at.

I didn't mention the contact with Raisa. It wasn't a deliberate omission; it was more because I felt it was personal and nothing to do with the mission, and because, at the time, I genuinely forgot. He picked up my sketches and put them inside a small leather man bag. That seemed to mark the formal side of our contact and for the rest of the meal, we laughed and chatted as though we were old friends. I relaxed and almost forgot I wasn't just having a convivial meal with a friend.

Chapter Fourteen

'Right then, are you ready?' He emptied his second glass of wine and folded his napkin on the table. 'I don't have it with me,' he said, in response to my raised eyebrow.

'Of course. Very wise,' I said, feeling foolish that the memory stick had slipped to the back of my mind. Perhaps I wasn't as good as I thought I was! I stood up, wondering where we were about to go.

Giuseppe led the way back down the stairs, through the main indoor dining area, and out onto the quay. The buzz of relaxed chatter filled the air as we wove our way through the once again fully occupied tables, most diners either indulging in long leisurely late lunches, or by now early dinner sittings. He strode out along the quay, and I followed close behind, not sure where we were going but hoping it wasn't too far. At the far end of the quay he stopped, glanced around, then nodded to me before turning into a narrow alleyway. He stopped again, scanned the empty alley, then entered a door halfway along. The door led into a small courtyard with several rooms leading off. It looked like someone's home, but we didn't linger. We went up an external staircase into a small, but surprisingly light and airy room.

'Take a seat, I won't be a minute,' he said and nodded towards a small sofa in the corner. It was hard to work out what the room would normally be used for. There wasn't a lot of furniture apart from the sofa I was sitting on, a couple of hard chairs against the wall, and a huge dark wood bookcase that was empty of books. Perhaps someone was in the throes of either moving in or out, but it didn't look lived in as it was.

Giuseppe, who had not said a word since we left the restaurant, now walked out of the room. I could hear him open a cupboard, and then a familiar sound I was sure was a safe being opened. He returned and sat beside me. He took the memory stick out of an envelope and pushed it into a tight mesh cover for added protection, then passed it to me. I closed my fingers around it.

'Right, that's it, over to you now. Just keep it, and yourself, safe at all times. You know what to do now?'

I nodded and was about to speak, to tell him my next steps, but he held up his hand to stop me. I knew, of course, the fewer people who knew what was happening, the better. Each person was only briefed on their own piece of the jigsaw; it was always considered safer that way. I was just out of practice, so I shut my mouth and smiled, but could not resist asking one more question.

'What's on it? I've been told nothing.'

'That's probably for the best,' he said, in a tone that dissuaded me from pursuing the topic but made me think he knew.

For some reason, his reply unnerved me, more than if he had said he wasn't able to tell me anything. I would have felt happier if he'd told me he had no idea either. I looked at him and his casual composure dropped for a second, and he looked grave. Why had he been told, and I hadn't? I sat quietly, mulling it all over. It was strange but the smaller risks seemed bigger these days, and now the initial buzz had subsided, I felt unable to take it all in my stride like I used to; perhaps it was a symptom of getting older, or tiredness, or wine. Probably all three. I tried to pull myself together. I was being ridiculous. I was overthinking everything. I took the memory stick and unzipped a small pocket on the back of my belt and pushed it inside. Whatever was on it, it could only be information that someone wanted to keep out of what they considered to be the wrong hands, and it was my job to make sure it reached those hands.

'Good.' Giuseppe stood up and held out his hand to pull me to my feet. He smiled. 'It'll be fine now, yes?'

'Yes, of course.' All right for him now, I thought. His part was over. 'Providing I don't get kidnapped again.' I laughed, making out I was joking, but my stomach didn't quite get the joke.

'I'll take you back to the ferry,' he said, and patted my arm.

As I followed him back out the way we'd come, I noticed for the first time the children's toys scattered in a corner of the courtyard. He stopped and called through one of the open doorways, a woman's voice who I presumed by the tone used between them was a relative or close friend or even his wife, called out something I couldn't quite hear. I was surprised that he used his own home to store the memory stick, if it was his home, but then this part of it was none of my business, so I kept quiet and followed him out. We continued into the alleyway, where again he checked to make sure no one was loitering, before he pulled a small scooter out from behind some bins, pushed it on to the road and started the engine.

'Jump on and hold round my waist,' he said.

Despite spending extended periods of time in Italy, I had never been on a scooter before and didn't relish the idea now. I did as I was told. I hitched up my dress and climbed on behind him. Neither of us wore helmets, so I held on tighter than was absolutely necessary for the very short ride back to the ferry. Giuseppe was a careful rider, and he had little option but to drive slowly with all the people wandering around. The ferry was already in, and people were starting to board as we pulled up on the side of the dock. I climbed off the scooter and laughed, surprised how much I had enjoyed the short trip. I pulled my fingers through my hair and thanked Giuseppe for the ride. He grinned at me. Clearly amused by carrying such a novice passenger. He parked the scooter and walked with me to the gangplank.

'Take care, lovely to meet you, and be careful,' he said, and bent to kiss me once on each cheek.

'Thanks, I will,' I said. 'Hope to meet you again one day.'

He nodded. 'I hope so,' he said, but we both knew that was very unlikely to ever happen.

I made my way up the ramp onto the boat, turning to wave before disappearing into the almost empty interior of the boat. Most people had headed straight out to the open deck. I was tired and consciously aware that it was now up to me to deliver the stick to the next rendezvous. Not such an easy task as I imagined before, judging by recent events. I touched the slight bulge at my waist before finding a seat, intending not to move again until we reached Naples. Most of my fellow passengers were tourists, mainly couples except for one large group of very loud middle-aged British women who appeared to have overindulged in the local wine. I spent the journey dozing and daydreaming, wondering about who Giuseppe was and how he came to be involved in all this. He had given very little away about his personal life, which was how it should be, but I enjoyed a few moments thinking about him. I dare say he was also wondering, how a middle-aged English woman could be involved in work like this, but I supposed that was it. The more diverse we were, the less likely to be spotted. So far, I wasn't doing a very good job on that front.

It was almost dark by the time the ferry docked in Naples, so, rather than walk, I took a taxi back to my original hotel. No messages were waiting for me at reception, and I asked the receptionist if I could settle my bill. I told her I would be leaving early the next morning, and it would be easier to pay now. She was dubious; probably worried I might drink the mini bar dry and then leave without paying. After conferring for many minutes with a colleague, they agreed, and I paid in cash. I scanned the reception area, before getting in the lift. No suspicious looking characters were concealed in the shadows, and so I made my way up to my room. All was in order. The bed was made, and fresh towels hung in the bathroom, but nothing else had changed. I packed my bag, then as I'd done the day before, I rolled around on the bed to make it looked slept in, splashed the clean towels with water and tossed them on the bathroom floor. I changed my clothes, the wig, I realised was in the other hotel, so I pulled my hair back and tied a scarf around my head. Not a good look, but at least it made me look different. After a quick check to make sure I had left nothing in the room, I set off. No one was in the corridor, but to be certain, I made my way back up the stairs to a higher floor before getting into the lift at the far end as before.

When I emerged from the lift, I could see that the reception area was empty, which struck me as unusual. The two girls on desk duty had taken the rare opportunity of a few minutes quiet to relax and were gossiping in the room at the back. I paused to see if the sound of the lift alerted them. It hadn't. I hooked the strap of my bag over my shoulder and slipped out of the front door. No one in the street, except probably me, looked in the slightest suspicious. Most were couples strolling along after a leisurely dinner. I followed my previous circuitous route to the other hotel again just in case anyone was watching.

Once back in my room in the other hotel, I stored the memory stick in the safe and raided the mini bar before taking a shower and ordering room service. I ran over in my mind the events of the day. It seemed Julia was right about the leak. How else would the location of the handover be known? It was just pure luck that they bungled it, and as Giuseppe had said, I had had a lucky escape. What worried me was how they knew what I looked like. Or did they? Was it purely the act of the other woman asking for directions that made them think it was a handover? It must have been, they would be looking for a woman on her own, and in amongst families and holiday makers, it was easy to see how they deduced it was me.

I sat for a while writing everything down in the secret code I shared with my father before falling into bed. I was more tired than I could ever remember, but I slept fitfully, disturbed by strange and illogical dreams. Needless to say, I awoke early. So, I got up and packed up my few bits and pieces and returned the memory stick to the inner zipped pocket on my belt. Forgoing breakfast, I could eat on the way, I checked out of the hotel. I asked if there were any messages for me and was relieved when there weren't.

The car hire firm I had booked a car through was on the edge of the city. I had the address but wasn't sure where it was. Rather than battle public transport, I took another taxi, into the game of Dodgems which is the Naples rush hour. This time I felt more exhilarated than terrified. The taxi driver dropped me at the door of the car hire office, and I was thankful that I could see the sign for the motorway junction, just down the road at a large roundabout. As I had hoped, I was saved from the trauma of trying to navigate my way through the crazy streets of Naples. I remembered the saying 'see Naples and die' and thought the outcome would be quite likely for anyone attempting to drive there.

Chapter Fifteen

The Sat-nav told me my journey to the hotel where I was meeting Raisa would be about one and a half hours. The hotel was not just outside Naples as she had said, but at least it was in the right direction. I took it slowly and aimed to arrive around mid-afternoon. I enjoyed driving, except in cities, and the Italian penchant for undertaking or driving too close didn't faze me. In fact, in the car, I felt safe and relaxed and was almost certain that no one could follow me. I stopped at a small town en route for lunch and to stretch my legs. What had passed for my breakfast only comprised a small chocolate bar, and so I tucked into a large bowl of delicious pasta. I resisted the temptation to visit an amphitheatre that the town advertised on the road sign; I was already doing enough that didn't count as essential to my task. A wave of guilt swept over me regarding my detour to see Raisa. I justified it by convincing myself that one more night would not make that much difference and it might make a big difference to the family if I could bring it together. At the very least, it would help to answer my questions. If I left after breakfast tomorrow, I should be able to meet my contact, pass over the stick and get a flight back in the evening and the job would be done. The heat was rising by the time I climbed back into my car, and I was relieved to turn on the air conditioning and let the coolness permeate my skin before setting off again, feeling refreshed.

The route to the hotel soon took me off the main road and along smaller roads, passing through small villages and countryside. Before too long, I was winding along a small bumpy road up into the hills near to Rome. I was starting to doubt Raisa's directions, and the Sat-nav, when a small sign strategically placed by the side of the road announced my arrival at the hotel. The sign pointed to a long winding driveway, which seemed to go on to the horizon and my anticipation rose as I turned a bend and saw the jumble of low-rise, stone buildings ahead. It was not what I was expecting for a luxury hotel, but it looked charming. Pleased that I had at last arrived, I steered the car into a space at the edge of the driveway, the small parking area being already full, and climbed out, instinctively touching my belt to feel the small bulge of the memory stick.

The beauty of the surrounding countryside forced me to pause and take it all in. An open view that seemed to go on for miles across a valley and up the other side to rolling, wooded hills. The sweet scent of a plant or tree that was familiar, possibly Oleander, though I couldn't be sure, was delicious and I took a deep breath, filling my lungs. Standing next to the car, I stretched my arms in the delightful temperature, which was several degrees cooler than in the city. I felt excited about meeting Raisa, but if I was honest, I was also looking further forward, and with more anticipation, to going home the next day, now my mission was almost complete. There was only another day to go, two at most.

I looked around at the cluster of small, ancient buildings, but I could see even before I reached them, they were well-maintained. Large, open wooden doors indicated the main entrance, which was framed by enormous stone pots overflowing with flowers. To the side stood an old delivery bike with the front basket also full of flowers. It looked delightful. I reached into the back of the car for my bag, but before I could pick it up, two men I hadn't noticed previously, approached. One of them lifted the bag from the boot and walked off with it, before I could grasp what was happening. The other man said something to him before turning to me. Feeling confused and on the back foot, I was about to protest. At least the memory stick was in my belt, not in my bag. My mind was going into overdrive as to how I was going to get out of this situation, when he smiled and spoke.

'Buongiorno,' he said, and reached out his hand and took mine in a warm clasp. He had the easy good looks and charm that many Italian men have as they gracefully age. He looked to be in his mid-fifties, but could have been older, and his warm smile made me relax and forget my suspicions.

'Welcome, I am Francesco, and you must be Katryn?'

'It's really Katharine, but Katryn is fine.' I corrected him but didn't know why. I rather liked being called Katryn.

'You must be tired after your journey. Your aunt is on the terrace, but maybe you prefer to go to your room first?'

I nodded. 'Yes, a tidy up would be good before meeting her. Thank you.'

He smiled and gestured towards the entrance,

'Follow me. It is very hot, even here in the hills. Would you like a cup of tea or cold drink brought over to your room?'

'Tea would be lovely, thank you,' I said, following him towards the low stone buildings at the side of the main reception. They looked like tiny cottages straggled along a cobbled street. Francesco called to the man who had relieved me of my bag, asking him to bring a pot of tea. I followed him across the cobbles and round to another building with a beautifully carved wooden side door, which he opened and then stood back to let me pass in front of him. My bag was already on the stand next to the wardrobe. The room was furnished in an understated country style, and the large bed was beckoning to me, asking me to just curl up and sink into its soft downy feathers.

'This is lovely, thank you.'

'Should I tell your aunt you have arrived, or would you prefer to...' he waved his arms towards the bed, as if reading my mind.

I hesitated. 'Perhaps don't say anything. I'll be along in about half an hour.'

He nodded and stepped aside to let a young woman enter with a tray of tea and some dainty cakes.

'The terrace where your aunt is sitting, is just past the reception area when you are ready. Just pick up the phone if you need anything,' he nodded towards the phone on the bedside table, smiled and left me to my tea.

I thanked him again and watched as he followed the young woman back to the main building. I poured my tea and took it out into the little garden attached to my room. I sank into one of the lounge chairs in the shade of a small tree, my room looked out over views of the verdant countryside, it was delightful and there wasn't a sound to be heard, apart from the buzz of bees and the hum of cicadas. Feeling relaxed after a few minutes sipping my tea and nibbling the cakes, I got to my feet and unpacked a few essentials. If I sat there much longer, I would fall asleep.

The heat was making the elasticated belt around my waist uncomfortable, so I searched the room to find a secure place to leave the memory stick. As I thought when I first opened the wardrobe, there wasn't a safe anywhere, which was unusual for a hotel of this calibre. They were usually inside the wardrobe, but after looking again, I was certain there wasn't one. I hesitated, unsure about leaving the memory stick unsecured, so I resigned myself to keeping the belt on, but then remembered a trick I had used before. I unwrapped a tampon and inserted the memory stick into the cardboard tube, pushed it back into the box, and then locked it in my bag. This was a remote location and clearly considered to be safe. At least that was what I assumed the lack of security meant. I told myself I was being over cautious, but I felt happier with it hidden away.

After a quick splash of cold water over my face, and a touch up of make-up, I felt ready to meet my aunt. I turned the large old-fashioned key in the equally big keyhole in the wooden door and dropped it into my small handbag. I dithered again about leaving the stick but could not imagine anyone could break in through such a solid door. Pulling on the handle I made sure it was locked and then walked back to the reception, passing by and continuing on to the large terrace beyond, where Francesco said Raisa waited.

Comfortable chairs were arranged in groups around small tables with large parasols offering shade. Once again, there was a plethora of old pots and urns with flowers tumbling over the sides. It was a delightful place to sit and enjoy the peace. A middle-aged couple sitting at the near end of the terrace, deep in conversation, barely glanced in my direction as I approached. I stood still and scanned the entire length of the terrace, and just as I was about to move towards the far end, a woman dressed in a loose kimono style dress jumped to her feet. She looked mid to late fifties, or older, and was very glamorous in a casual way, with expertly styled dark hair and immaculate make up. At once I felt under groomed, in my light cotton dress and hair pulled back into a loose ponytail, and wished I'd made more of an effort. I knew even before she spoke that this must be Raisa.

'Katryn, darling; I would know you anywhere,' she said, and rushed towards me, arms outstretched and grasping my shoulders, kissed me on both cheeks.

I wondered how she could know me, as we'd never met before, but I assumed Francesco told her I was here, or it was just a figure of speech, after all, she was waiting for me.

A young waitress who must have been hovering close by appeared, and Raisa, without asking what I wanted, ordered a bottle of Prosecco, which materialised almost before I'd sat down, and was being poured into two glasses. I studied her as she reached for her glass. She was loud and bubbly and excited to see me. She also gave the impression of being used to being in control. I thought of my mother's photograph and tried to remember if there was any likeness, but that photograph was taken many years ago and there was no knowing what my mother would have looked like had she lived into her sixties and beyond.

'Salute,' Raisa raised her glass. 'You have grown into a beautiful woman.'

I must have looked perplexed; in fact, I was feeling a little uncomfortable and at a disadvantage. Raisa was supremely confident and gushing and the way she spoke implied she knew me but, how could she? We had never set eyes on each other before. Was it so strange to be familiar? I asked myself. After all, I was her niece, and she was just demonstrating Italian flamboyance. I was being oversensitive, more used to the British reserve.

'You look surprised,' she smiled at my confusion. 'Of course, you won't remember me. You were just a baby when I last saw you and not even two years old. You were such a pretty baby and look at you now. A beautiful woman.'

'Well, yes, I am surprised. I knew nothing about you until a couple of days ago when I read your letter. I had no idea my mother even had a sister or any living relatives. How, or when, did you see me?'

She didn't answer my question straight away, just continued talking.

'Well, here I am. I was six years younger than Mariana. She was my idol. I was devastated when… but no, this isn't the time to be sad,' she smiled, and reached over and squeezed my hand. 'There is so much to catch up on, but I suggest we leave the details until later, so first tell me all about your trip to Naples. Did you enjoy it? Such a crazy city.'

For a second time I felt wrong-footed, but of course, she already knew I was in Naples. I had no intention of telling her the real reason for my trip and assumed my father would have told her it was just a pleasure trip. So, I told her my main reason for visiting was to see the Veiled Christ and the museum. I spoke at some length about the beauty of the sculpture, which to my surprise, she didn't know. I then told her about the museum and the fascinating objects rescued from Pompeii. She listened quietly, smiling and nodding.

'Personally, I'm not a fan of that city, too noisy and dirty for me, but worth one visit, I suppose. I'm not so cultured. I prefer visiting dress shops rather than museums, although the sculpture sounds fascinating.'

I smiled at her honesty, and I knew what she meant about the noise and dirt. It certainly wasn't everyone's cup of tea, but I loved the Naples' madness.

'Where have you travelled from?' I asked.

'Oh darling, these roads are so awful I prefer to forget my journey. I hate driving these days, don't you?'

'I don't really mind; I suppose I drive quite a lot, so it's not too much of a problem, but it can be quite tiring.'

Our conversation took a detour onto cars, travelling in general, and Raisa's preference to always travel first class given the choice. I agreed, although didn't say that travelling first class was a rare treat rather than the norm for me. We chatted easily, sipping Prosecco, but our conversation didn't touch on anything significant. I was eager to hear about my mother's family, but there was no real hurry. I knew Raisa would tell me when she was ready.

Once I had adjusted to her manner and relaxed, (or was it the prosecco?), I found she was delightful company. It wasn't long before I felt as though I'd known her for years, but then she was family, so there was probably already a genetic bond. She was not the sort of person I could imagine my father enjoying spending time with, so maybe that was why he'd never mentioned her. I was determined to ask him, as things were not quite adding up in my mind, but I buried my concerns–for now.

'Well, I think it's time for me to freshen up before our dinner,' Raisa said after we'd been chatting for quite a while. She looked at her watch, got to her feet and held out a hand to me. 'I always like a few minutes rest before dinner, don't you?'

I stood up and walked with her along the path, wondering

what I could wear for dinner. I knew for certain my bags didn't contain an appropriate outfit.

'This is me,' she said, stopping outside a small walled garden in front of her room.

'You're further up the path, aren't you,' she stated rather than asked.

'Come and tap on my door in about an hour. We can talk some more.' She leant forward and kissed both my cheeks again. 'It really is so lovely to see you again, dear Katryn.'

The hotel was quite charming, the way each room was an individual little unit. With either a garden or a flower strewn balcony, and all the rooms appeared different. I walked along the scent filled path to my room in a warm glow, feeling for the first time that I belonged to a family with a history. Raisa was charming in an eccentric way, but I liked her and wondered whether my mother's personality was anything like hers. I realised apart from being told that my mother was lovely; I knew nothing about her as a real person. I suppressed my irritation, or was it anger, that my father had kept the details of my relatives to himself all these years? What reason could there be? I was determined to ask him when we next met. I couldn't believe he didn't know or had forgotten about Raisa.

Once back in my room, I turned all my clothes out on to the bed and sighed. There weren't many as this trip was only scheduled to be a couple of days, and nothing was suitable for dinner in a good hotel. In the end I chose a light-coloured linen skirt that wasn't too grubby and a sleeveless top. I showered and washed my hair and renewed my make up. I draped a soft silk scarf around my neck and studied my reflection in the mirror. The scarf looked wrong, so I took it off and refastened my necklace. For some reason, I decided to put in my contact lenses. I only wore them occasionally and could see quite well without them, but Jilly always said they enhanced my eyes, particularly the tinted ones, which I wore for fun, so in they went. I would have to do. At least I could look well-groomed even if I couldn't manage glamorous.

Chapter Sixteen

When I was ready, and after I'd packed everything away and checked that the stick remained secure in my bag, I sat outside my room, closed my eyes and tried to think of the most important questions to ask Raisa. It was difficult, as everything was important. In the end, I decided just to let her tell me what she could. It would nearly all be new, as I was ignorant of most information relating to my mother and her family, so it would all be significant to me. Just under an hour later, I picked up a pashmina that would do if it got chilly and strolled back along the path in the soft evening light to Raisa's room. The low sun, and stored heat from the day, made the honey-coloured stone buildings glow in the evening light.

Raisa was sitting outside her room flicking through a magazine but got to her feet when I approached. She looked elegant and expensively dressed in loose navy trousers and silk shirt; her hair was tied up in a casual arrangement that left tendrils curling onto her neck and shoulders. I guessed from what she'd said earlier that she must be fifty-six or seven, but she didn't look it.

'Come and sit down. I'm having iced tea, or would you prefer wine? There's some in the mini bar.'

'Iced tea would be lovely,' I said, and sat in the chair she nodded towards. Then I noticed a few grainy photos on the table that I presumed were of my mother's family. My pulse quickened, but I resisted the urge to pick them up straight away. With difficulty, I kept my hands still until Raisa returned with my drink.

'So, Katryn darling, tell me what you actually know about your mother, and I can try to fill in some of the gaps.'

'Well, I know very little. I know she was Italian and died soon after I was born. I've seen a couple of pictures of her, and she looked very attractive, but I was hoping you would tell me all about her.'

She smiled but said nothing, so I continued,

'My aunt Clare, my father's sister, mainly brought me up, and she didn't know my mother very well either, so we never really talked about her, except on a superficial level. I don't really know why.'

'Yes, of course, it must have been difficult for your father. I think he was heartbroken when Mariana died. We all were.'

'He was always so busy, working away a lot. I don't know what he did, something in finance, I think.' I decided to keep my father's real role secret. It wasn't relevant. 'I went to boarding school when I was older, just Monday to Friday. Father always tried to see me in the holidays, but he seemed detached, preoccupied. I don't think he knew what to do with me.'

Raisa leant across and touched my arm, and I felt tears prickle my eyes.

'Poor you, it must have been difficult. I expect it was all too painful for your father to talk about, don't you think?'

'Maybe, but it wasn't so difficult for me. It was all I knew, so I didn't feel too hard done by. I loved school and for some reason, my friends thought it was romantic in a tragic sort of way that I never knew my mother.'

'Well, let me tell you, you were wrong about one thing, your mother wasn't pretty…'

I gasped, not expecting her to say such a thing.

'She was beautiful. Very beautiful. You have inherited that beauty. Mariana looked like our mother, who was also beautiful. Sadly, I resemble my father, not so beautiful, you see.'

We both laughed. I suspected Raisa was being falsely

modest as she was herself a very good-looking woman. She reached across again and touched my hand.

'Our mother was such a kind woman, always there for us. I just can't imagine how sad it was for you never having that sort of relationship with Mariana.'

I looked at Raisa and her gentle manner and genuine concern touched me. My childhood had been happy, and Clare was a kind and thoughtful aunt, always doing the best for me. The tears I could feel stinging the back of my eyes threatened to spill over for the memory of the mother I never knew. I thought of my father, such a private man, not given to personal or delicate conversations with his growing daughter, and I felt less angry. His grief wasn't anything I'd considered before, and I felt ashamed and mean. It was apparent there was a lot I didn't know, but I hoped I would soon know more.

'Please tell me more about my mother. I want to get to know her, to fill in the missing links.'

'Yes, of course. Now let me think. OK, let me start at the beginning and I'll do my best not to miss anything out.'

She talked for a long time, telling me about her and my mother's childhood, how they grew up in a small town near Verona. She described their home, a large villa set in a magical, at least to children, rambling garden, with trees to climb and places to hide. Raisa made it sound like an idyllic childhood, and I felt quite envious. The family spent holidays either with relatives on Lake Garda or at the seaside north of Venice. The picture she painted could have come straight from the pages of an Enid Blyton book, except it was in Italy. I made a mental note to seek out these places another time.

At last Raisa handed me the photographs that for all the time she'd been speaking were sitting tantalizingly on the table in front of me.

'This is Mariana and me when, let me think, I was about six, so she must have been about twelve.'

I looked at the willowy young girl who beamed at the camera, one arm draped around her little sister's shoulders.

Raisa passed another, the same two girls, but this time in a group of adults.

'That's our mother and father, your grandparents,' she touched the photograph gently. 'And this was our aunt Sofia, father's sister, and the others are just friends, I think. There were always so many friends. Here, this one is Mariana just before she left school.'

The small black and white photo was old and quite blurred, so it was hard to distinguish her features, and I felt a bit disappointed that there weren't more. I tried hard to remember how she looked in the one photograph my father carried around in his wallet. The only other photograph I'd seen of my mother was on her wedding day, when she looked quite different with her hair covered by a veil.

'It's not very clear I'm afraid,' she said, sensing my disappointment. 'I didn't have time to pick up many.'

I looked again at the group photograph. Both my grandparents looked tall and slim with an air of elegance about them. My grandfather was dressed in a suit and my grandmother wore a well-cut skirt and jacket in some sort of lightweight fabric. They both wore hats, my grandmother's set at a jaunty angle, and both stared directly at the camera, laughing.

I handed them back.

'Keep them if you'd like. I'm sorry I haven't got more,' Raisa offered, and I snatched the photos up as if they were rare treasures.

'Are you sure? Thank you.'

She smiled and nodded. 'I wish I had better ones for you, but maybe when we meet again, I can try to find some more.'

'Oh yes, I'd love to see more recent ones, well of course there won't be more recent ones of my mother.'

'There should be more recent ones of some of the family, but there aren't many of us left now, and I don't really know where the photos would be kept.'

'Are your parents still alive?' I asked, although I felt certain from the way Raisa had been speaking that they wouldn't be.

'My mother died many years ago, before you were born. She had cancer, and father died about thirty years ago. He never recovered from losing mother, like your father, and then, when Mariana died, he was bereft.'

Raisa herself, in that moment, looked overcome with grief. I imagined that talking about such things must be difficult for her. Before we could resume our conversation, a gong rang out, summoning us for dinner.

'Oh dear, we've missed our aperitif and canapés. I've been talking too much and dwelling on so many memories. Shame, Francesco makes a perfect white Russian cocktail. Never mind, we'll have to make sure we don't miss it tomorrow.'

I put the precious photos in my bag, then Raisa took me by the arm and steered me away from her room. Maybe I could squeeze another night here. It couldn't do any harm, could it? My sensible brain was already forming the answer, but I said nothing to Raisa. I didn't want to break the spell.

'Raisa's a Russian name, isn't it?' I asked, as we walked towards the main building.

The dining area was outside on a terrace nestled up against the old wall of the building, away from any sudden gusts of wind, with a rush canopy smothered in vines to provide shade in the middle of the day. There were lights along the wall, and a centrepiece with a candle on each table. The tables themselves were set a discrete distance apart and each was covered with a pristine white cloth and sparkling glassware.

'Yes, it is. We had some Russian relatives on my father's side, but I think it was just because my mother liked the name. We thought Mariana had called you Katryn to reflect the family history and by the time we realised it was Katharine, Katryn was stuck in my mind. So, to me, you've always been Katryn.'

'I rather like Katryn,' I said, as Francesco held my chair out for me.

We paused our conversation while Francesco explained in detail each of the evening's dishes to us. I was surprised that there didn't appear to be a menu, but Raisa whispered across the table that the food was delicious, always fresh and planned daily by Francesco. I remembered that when I arrived, Francesco asked whether I had any specific dietary needs or requests. I'd thought it a strange question to ask as soon as I arrived, but now realised he would have adjusted a dish to meet my needs if I was unable to eat anything in particular. A waitress brought our wine, which Raisa must already have chosen, which was a soft red that she assured me would complement that evening's meal perfectly.

Throughout the meal, which was as good as promised, Raisa continued to tell me about my mother. I could visualise the sisters learning to cook and dance, and enjoying the idyllic childhood that Raisa portrayed. She said my mother was a very studious child and young woman, going on to study politics at the university in Milan. Raisa was hazy about my mother's actual working career. I understood why. She knew my parents met at work, but little else. She laughed, saying she used to tease her about being involved in something very hush-hush, because she was always so vague about her actual job. I smiled and felt a closer link with my mother through our shared secret lives. Raisa said she was too busy being a student and having fun to worry too much about her studious big sister's rather dull, as she saw it, lifestyle. She told me my parents married in London, which I already knew. She also talked about some of the other aspects of their early life together, most of it, but not all, were things I didn't know. I didn't mind hearing familiar stories; it just made me hang on to the new information she was telling me. Although my mother was a stranger to me, I felt her presence and my loss even more acutely that evening.

Not for the first time I wondered what my life would have been like if my mother had lived. I imagined long summers spent with a big family in Italy, rather than quietly in Dorset with just my kind, but rather staid, Aunt Clare and sometimes, my father when he could get away from work. Would she have steered me away from my line of work, into something safer, rather than encouraging me as my father had done? She would have I felt sure, and for the first time I wondered if by encouraging me, my father was trying to rebuild their working partnership. Even if it was subconscious.

'Of course, when Mariana died, we wondered whether you should come and live with us,' Raisa seemed to read my mind. 'But by then my mother was no longer with us, and I was single and busy with my life and father was just too broken-hearted. Besides, I think your father, wanted to cling on to you as a lasting reminder of Mariana. You have grown to look so like her.'

I smiled at the thought but cringed at being considered some sort of commodity. I couldn't quite imagine my father being so sentimental as to want me as a reminder of my mother; it was more likely that he thought it the proper thing to do, but I tried to imagine how different my life would have been being brought up by my grandfather.

We were almost at the end of our meal, just waiting for our coffee, when Raisa started rummaging through her bag.

'Yes, here it is, the one I was looking for. I knew I'd brought it with me.' She pulled another photo from her bag and passed it across the table to me.

I looked at the picture of a woman I could just recognise as a young Raisa, holding a child of about eighteen months, possibly younger.

'That was taken when I came to England. This was the last time I saw you,' she said, keeping her eyes on me the whole time.

'Where was it taken?' I studied the photo, not recognising the setting. It was a garden somewhere, but nowhere I knew. It didn't look like Aunt Clare's Garden.

'Oh, I can't remember. It was so long ago. I think it might have been your aunt's house or a friend of hers. I'm not certain we seemed to see so many people in those few days.'

I nodded, feeling surprised that Aunt Clare never mentioned Raisa's visit. What could have been the reason she didn't? Unless by the time I was old enough to understand she may have forgotten, or more likely she didn't want me asking lots of questions that she couldn't answer. As I stared at the photo, I felt frustrated that I couldn't work out where it was.

'Dear Clare, I enjoyed her company so much. How is she now?'

'She's very well, quite a lot older now, of course, but still living in the same house. I try to see her as often as I can. Did you keep in touch or visit again?' I was curious why Raisa failed to maintain the family ties, especially if she and Clare hit it off so well. She looked away and busied herself with her coffee, and I felt guilty for embarrassing her.

'There were reasons. I would like to see Clare again one day,' she stirred, then sipped her coffee. 'I don't think your father was keen to keep up links with our family.'

Unable to imagine why, I was about to quiz Raisa for more details, but I bit my tongue, now didn't seem the right time and I added it to the list of questions I would have no such compunction in asking father when we next were together. She composed herself and picked up the photograph of her with me and smiled at it, then looked up at me.

'You had, and still have, of course, got your mother's beautiful brown eyes.'

I took a sharp intake of breath but managed to conceal it as a cough. It felt as though a shard of ice had pierced my chest. I tried to nod and smile but kept my eyes averted from Raisa and it was my turn to be busy with my coffee. It could be a genuine mistake. I wanted it to be, but deep down I felt the first stirring that something was wrong. Who was Raisa, who was she really? I asked myself. I was grateful for the dimly lit dining area as I looked up and composed myself enough to smile at Raisa.

'You look tired darling, there's a lot to take in.' She put her coffee cup down, folded her napkin. 'Let's call it a day and carry on tomorrow. I'm sure once everything's sorted in your mind, you'll have lots more questions for me.' She reached across and squeezed my hand.

'Yes, good idea, I am exhausted,' I stood up and together we walked to her room and said our goodnights at her gate.

'Sleep well darling,' she kissed me on both cheeks.

'And you, goodnight, and thank you. See you in the morning.'

Chapter Seventeen

I hurried back to my room, my mind in total confusion. I went straight to the bathroom and removed my contact lenses, revealing my blue eyes, inherited from my father. I couldn't be certain, but I thought my mother's eyes were more of a greyish green not brown. Somewhere in the depths of my mind, I recalled Aunt Clare commenting on how unusual her eyes were, considering her dark hair.

How could Raisa make such a mistake? If she really knew me as a young child, she would know. Everyone always commented on my bright blue eyes when I was a younger. They were less bright now, more pale blue, but definitely not brown. Feeling a knot in my stomach, I paced around the room trying to convince myself that her comment was nothing more than a mistake, but the more I thought, the less convinced I became. I would wear the tinted lenses again tomorrow but would pay more attention to other details and listen out for obvious flaws in her story. But why? What was her purpose if she didn't know me? If she wasn't my mother's sister, who was she? One thing she was right about, I was tired and finding it difficult to make sense of anything. There must be a logical explanation; after all, as she said herself, I was about eighteen months old the last time she saw me and that was a long time ago. It would be easy to forget, particularly as there I was sitting in front of her with brown eyes. I relaxed a bit. That must be it. Seeing me with brown eyes made her assume they were natural, but then again, she said I had the same brown eyes as my mother. How could she make a mistake about her own sister, who she said she idolised?

I was about to get undressed when I remembered that I'd left my pashmina shawl on the back of my chair, and rather than leave it there overnight and risk forgetting about it, I decided to go and fetch it. The path to the dining terrace passed near to the entrance to Raisa's room, and as I walked towards it, I noticed a curl of cigarette smoke spiralling into the clear air from her garden. She must be sitting outside or someone else was with her. I was surprised that Raisa smoked. She had not lit up in my presence earlier. As I was about to turn away towards the terrace, I heard her speaking rapidly in Italian. It took me a second to realise she was speaking on the phone, not to someone there with her. The words I heard rooted me to the spot. Feeling sick, I stepped away from the terrace and back into the shadows closer to her room so I could hear more.

'Of course, she believes every word. Why wouldn't she? I'm very good at my job.' She chuckled.

There was a pause while she waited to hear the other person speak. I rubbed my hands down my skirt, which were now feeling hot and sweaty.

'Yes, quite naïve. I feel almost sorry for her.'

I bristled at the naïve description, but it was proving to be true. Not only naïve, but incredibly stupid.

'No, not yet. I'll gain her confidence more and then try to raise it.'

I crept closer; she must have moved away as her voice was fainter.

'Well, if she doesn't, then I'll have to find a way of searching her room. It won't be difficult. There's minimal security here, no safes, so it shouldn't be hard to find.'

She laughed then at something the other person must have said.

'Yes probably, it's a classic place to hide something like that. I'll ring again when I've got it. Don't worry, I don't anticipate any problems. Ciao.'

I dared not move. She must have ended her call, and after a moment I heard what I assumed was her stubbing out her cigarette and going into her room, closing the door behind her. All thought of my shawl went from my mind, and in a complete whirl I headed back to my room, shut the door and leant against it, my heart pounding as though it would burst.

At first, I couldn't gather any coherent thoughts together. All that was spinning around in my head was, 'Oh God. What a fool I've been!' and 'How could I be so taken in?' Slowly, after taking several deep breaths, my mind cleared. It was obvious that Raisa was no more my aunt than the woman that cleaned the room, but she seemed to know so much about my childhood, about Aunt Clare and my father, and more particularly about my mother. I also now doubted that she'd spoken to my father about my whereabouts. No, there was no doubt. Of course, her story about my father telling her I was in Naples was a complete lie. So how did she know so much? Shaking, I sank into a chair and put my head in my hands and traced back over everything we'd spoken about in our conversations. Slowly, at first, it dawned on me that I had, unwittingly, fed her the information she needed to build up a credible story. Her skill at subtly asking the right questions made me walk straight into her trap. She asked what I already knew before filling in the gaps as she said. I told her the little I knew about my mother already, so she could continue without contradicting the little details I clung onto as real. I told her about my school, about living with Aunt Clare, what else, I racked my brains.

We'd discussed so much; it was hard to remember how much of the information that came from me she had used to recycle my mother's life, and what was fabricated. Then there were the photographs. Where did she get those? Of course, when I thought back, every photograph was old, black and white and grainy. They could have been taken anywhere and be of anyone. No one in them was a person I knew, and I wanted, more than anything, to believe they were my mother's family. My stomach contracted when I thought about how close I'd come to being taken in. I dare not let myself think about what might have happened if I hadn't left my pashmina behind. Which was probably lost forever now. But now I knew the truth; I had the upper hand. I couldn't make any more mistakes.

The other thought that would not be suppressed was how desperately I wanted to know more about my mother. As a child I felt all my queries were brushed away, but then Aunt Clare always said she didn't know my mother very well. I now felt sure she wouldn't have known details about the rest of her family, and I wondered if my father really knew much about them, either. When this was over, I was determined to make my father sit down and tell me every detail, however insignificant, that he knew.

I pulled myself out of my reverie. Now was not the time for dwelling on my family, that was what got me into this mess. I needed to think, to be clear-headed, and decide about my next move. I quickly concluded that I must leave as soon as possible. It would have to be that night; if I risked waiting until the morning, I might leave myself open to… open to what, I had no idea, but nothing good came to mind. All I knew from the overheard conversation was that I could not trust Raisa; she was not who she said she was, and for certain was no relative of mine.

Splashing cold water on my face helped, as did drinking a big glass of water. How much alcohol had I consumed at dinner? I couldn't remember. We'd consumed one bottle of wine between us, followed by a digestif. Raisa, I felt sure, drank more of the wine than me. Regardless, I knew I had to leave.

I stood in the middle of the room for a few seconds trying to pull myself together, then changed my clothes and gathered all my belongings, which were very few, and packed them into my bag. I picked up the wig and left it on top of my now full bag; I would put it on just before I left. I concealed the memory stick, still in its tampon wrapper, in my belt. Then I threaded it through the tabs on my trousers and pulled a shirt over the top of it.

I opened the door of my room and stood just inside listening for sounds of activity. It was just gone midnight. There were a few lights on at the far end of the main building and I could hear the occasional voice. The kitchen staff, still clearing up and preparing for tomorrow, I presumed. I would wait until they finished. I walked along the side of my room, pressing myself into the shadows, and looked across the courtyard and down the path towards Raisa's and the other rooms. They were all in darkness and silent. My pulse started to settle, all I needed to do was wait for the staff to go, then I would leave.

I went back into my room and waited. Twice I stood by the door, but the lights were still on in the kitchen. I wondered if they were left on all night, but I went back inside when I heard a voice. The kitchen staff seemed in no hurry to leave. I paced backwards and forwards then forced myself to sit down and have a cup of tea. Every swallow almost choked me. At last, I heard the distant sound of people saying goodnight. Footsteps echoed up the path and disappeared towards another small building, which I had noticed earlier, and assumed it must be staff accommodation.

When I next looked out of the door, the kitchen area was in darkness. With difficulty, I made myself wait for another thirty minutes, just to be certain everyone was in bed. It was now well past three in the morning. I tucked my hair up under the wig, checked every corner of the room to make sure I left nothing behind, and put what I hoped was an appropriate amount of Euros on the table to cover my stay. After a final look around, I closed the door and walked as quietly as I could to my car. Every footstep seemed to reverberate around the stone walls, and I kept close to the buildings, expecting every moment for someone to appear.

At last, I reached the car, climbed into the driver's seat and let the handbrake off. I didn't close the door properly, and didn't start the engine, just let the car moved forward under its own momentum. I realised how lucky it was that there had been no spaces in the car park when I arrived, so my only option was to park on the slope above the long driveway. I congratulated myself for having turned the car round to face down the slope. The clouds drifted apart just as I set off and a full moon illuminated the dry dusty surface, showing it up as an almost white ribbon leading me to the main road. The car rolled down the hill and once or twice I thought it was going to stop, but it didn't. I kept an eye in the rear-view mirror. The hotel was quiet. Everyone was sleeping. No lights came on, and no one appeared to stir. Once the car reached the main road, I relaxed a little and started to breathe more normally. My hands had been clinging so hard to the steering wheel I'd almost lost the feeling in my fingers. I turned the engine and lights on and sped along the almost empty road; feeling better with each mile I put between Raisa and myself.

Chapter Eighteen

After driving for about half an hour, I pulled in and braced myself to ring my father. All the way along, I had been waging an inner battle with myself. One part of me had a strong urge to drop the memory stick down the nearest drain and return home and pretend nothing had happened, but I knew that was the least likely option I could take. My father's words were reverberating inside my head; use this phone to contact me in an emergency, only in an emergency, he had said. Did my current situation constitute an emergency? Yes, it did, but did it warrant calling at this time of night? I could not decide. Why was I hesitating? Was I afraid of my own father? I answered my question by admitting that even though I was now a grown, middle-aged woman, I was not afraid, but was anxious about displeasing my father. All my life, I realised, my aim was to please him. I had always wanted him to be proud of me and was always disappointed when he seemed indifferent to my achievements. This time I had failed. I had been stupid and fallen for an easy trick, which would annoy him. Perhaps, I would leave out the fact that it was pure luck I discovered the con.

    A sudden thought crossed my mind, maybe I could get away without mentioning anything, I could just carry on to Florence deliver the memory stick as planned and no one would be any the wiser. That option grew in my mind and was tempting. After all, no one knew I was here. As I was mulling everything over, a car pulled in behind me. I froze and rather than starting the engine and driving off, I just sat rigid with fear with my eyes fixed on the rear-view mirror, watching. It was difficult to make out who was in the car or what they were doing, but I presumed by the faint glow they were using a phone. Were they alerting someone to my presence, I wondered? If I drove off now, it could result in a chase, and I didn't feel up to that. I locked the doors and sank low in my seat. After what felt like an interminably long time, the car sped off into the darkness. I let out a sigh of relief and, shaking like the proverbial leaf, picked up my phone and, without another thought, rang my father.

I explained everything in detail to him. From the receptionist handing me the note in the Naples hotel, to the overheard phone conversation between Raisa and an unknown person this evening. His voice was steady and reassuring, not critical as I'd expected, and he even confirmed that my mother was, as I had always been told, an only child. There were no recriminations, and his gentle questioning, for some reason, made me feel even more guilty. Once he'd established where I was, or as near to where I was as we could work out, he told me to wait where I was, and he would ring me back very soon. After a short time, the phone rang, and he told me to make my way to Rome, not Florence. He said he would meet me the next day in a small café we both knew, set away from the tourist hubbub of the major attractions. I had driven blindly with no actual destination in mind and just hoped Rome wasn't too far away. No one else apart from the two of us knew my destination to be Rome. Anyone else would assume I'd gone to Florence for the handover.

'Katharine be very careful. I love you. See you tomorrow.'

When I put my phone back into my bag, I realised tears were pouring down my face. I couldn't remember the last time my father had told me he loved me, certainly not since I was a young child. Why, why now? I suddenly felt afraid. This was now far from an easy, straightforward mission, in part because of my actions, but also because the mission had been compromised from the start. I wound down the window, took some gulps of the fresh night air and told myself to pull myself together and complete this task like the professional I was supposed to be. I was very thirsty and rued the fact that I left a bottle of water in the fridge in my room.

After a couple of minutes, I came to my senses and did what I should have done when talking to my father and looked at the sat nav to work out exactly where I was. The map pinpointed my location. I programmed it for Rome and discovered I was still about forty minutes away. It did not matter, as I was in no hurry now. My meeting with my father wasn't until tomorrow. I drove towards the autostrada and stopped at the first service area, which, for that time of night, was surprisingly busy. I lingered over a strong cup of coffee and sandwich and bought a bottle of water to take on the journey with me. In the toilets, I took off the wig, which was starting to be uncomfortable, and returned to my car feeling better and more up to the task of driving on to Rome with no sleep.

The traffic built up even before I was in what I considered to be the outskirts of the city, and when I was still a long way from the area I needed to reach. As I pulled off the autostrada, I spotted a sign for the company I had hired the car from in Naples and decided to try to drop it off with them and use public transport or a taxi the rest of the way into the city. Even fully alert, the thought of driving in the centre of Rome was daunting. I followed the sign and soon found the car hire office. It was still early, and the office was closed, but due to open in about twenty minutes. So, I parked outside and dozed while I waited.

A man banging on the window woke me with a start. My first instinct was to drive off, but I soon made out from his shouting and gesticulating that the car was blocking the entrance to the car hire parking area. I told him I was returning the car, and he nodded and beckoned me into the tightly packed car park. I just managed to squeeze the car in between two other cars without scratching it, and then squeezed my bag and myself inelegantly out of the door. I followed the man into the office. Despite my bad parking, he was in quite good humour, and I explained my plans had changed since leaving Naples and I no longer needed the car. He agreed it wouldn't be easy driving into the city and I got the impression he bit his tongue before adding, for a woman. After filling out various pieces of paperwork, he pointed me in the direction of a taxi firm.

Out of habit, I scanned the almost empty street before setting off along the route he had indicated. Despite it now being rush hour, there were very few pedestrians in the street and the few people who were around, were busy preparing for the day. A man opening his shop said Buongiorno, an elderly lady walked past with a small dog, nodded, and we smiled at each other, otherwise no one took the slightest notice of me. The day was already warming up, and I began to feel weary, and my head was aching. I reached the taxi office but walked straight on, realising that I didn't know where I was going. I would need a specific destination before I got into a taxi. Rome was a big place, and I didn't want to spend time wandering aimlessly. I walked through the gates of a small park and sat in the shade of a large tree near to an empty fountain and racked my brain for the name of a hotel, not too far from where I was to meet my father the next day. Nothing came to mind, and I didn't want to use the Internet, to look up hotels, just in case. I could remember the name of a street, so I decided to take a taxi to that area, and I would look for a suitable hotel on foot.

The taxi driver was, for once, a slow, careful driver, and after only about ten minutes, he dropped me at my destination. After walking the length of the street, I settled on a small, tidy looking hotel set back from the road behind a pretty lawned garden. To my surprise and relief, not only did they have a room available but also it was nearly ready for me to occupy, if I didn't mind waiting a few minutes. I was more than happy to wait and sank into a chair in the lounge, feeling that my legs would not carry me another metre.

'Signora.' I came to with a start. I must have almost nodded off. 'Signora, your room is ready.' The girl from reception leant over and touched my arm gently; she smiled when I looked up confused. 'I will find someone to take up your bag.'

I followed a porter up a flight of stairs and into a small, but clean and well decorated, room. As soon as he left, I kicked off my shoes and fell onto the bed, asleep within seconds.

Chapter Nineteen

I awoke around midday feeling refreshed and hungry. The information pack in the room showed me that the hotel was only about a mile from the Pantheon, a place I always loved to visit when in Rome. So, after a quick wash, I decided to find somewhere for a bite to eat nearby, then walk over to marvel yet again at the Pantheon's amazing structure. Just around the corner from the hotel was a café selling tempting bruschetta and focaccia bread, so armed with the daily paper, I settled myself at a table on the pavement and enjoyed my food; relaxed knowing that no one apart from my father knew I was in the city.

The memory stick was now locked in the safe in my room and the sooner it was out of my possession altogether, the better. As I ate, my mind wandered over the events of the last couple of days, causing an involuntary shudder, but by tomorrow it would all be over, and I'd be on my way home. I still could not believe how easily Raisa took me in, and I felt ashamed of myself. I couldn't change that now, but I was determined not to be fooled again. After eating, I strolled along in the sunshine, crossing the Tiber by one of the many bridges, pausing every now and again to enjoy the sights and sounds of the city. The crowds increased with every step towards the centre and the key tourist sites. To all intents and purposes, I was just one of the many sightseers and relished once again, as in Naples, the opportunity of indulging myself, without having to bend to the whims and short concentration spans of the children. Although that thought caused a momentary flash of guilt, it was only momentary.

When I reached the Pantheon, the crowds were even denser, and I wondered how leisurely my visit was going to be. Once inside however, the atmosphere was one of cool and calm, with surprisingly few people milling around compared to the numbers outside. In no hurry, I lingered in the fascinating space, using one of the audio-guided tour headsets to remind me of the history and architecture, drinking in every aspect of the commentary. I was standing in the middle of the floor staring up at the oculus when a hand touched my shoulder. I turned and found myself staring straight into Raisa's eyes. Time stood still for a few seconds as my brain went into overdrive. What was Raisa doing here? How did she know where I was? I was sure, no, certain, that no one followed me from the hotel. Every stop I made, I checked to make sure I was alone. So how could she be here? It wasn't possible and yet here she was. My body went into fight-or-flight mode, despite the fact that I was standing rigidly still.

'Raisa.' Her name was the only word that managed to pass my lips, and I prayed my voice didn't sound too strangled. I hoped she would interpret the look of horrified disbelief as surprise.

'Darling, you left without saying goodbye,' she said, and smiled a mocking smile, or was that my imagination?

Every fibre of my being was on high alert, and I felt as though my brain was unscrambling a coded message and feeding the answers to my conscious mind in the form of a reasonable explanation. I smiled back at her, trying hard to keep the quiver on my lips out of sight, but now, clear in my mind, was how I was going to play the situation. I had pulled off my role as an aggrieved tourist in Procida. Now my acting skills were even more important.

'I didn't want to wake you,' I said, leaning to kiss her on both cheeks. 'But you obviously got my note, because here you are. I wasn't sure the night porter would give it to you. He seemed so dozy, but I impressed on him he must make sure you received it as soon as you went for breakfast.' I tried and, hopefully, added a note of relief in my voice. Raisa looked taken aback by my words but covered her confusion with a nod of her head. I slipped my arm through hers and steered her out of the Pantheon into the bright sunshine beyond. I needed to take control.

Outside in the piazza to the right of the fountain was a crowd of people, a protest or political gathering according to the placards that a few of them were holding. It crossed my mind to make a dash for them and hope I could get lost in the melee, but I quickly dismissed the thought as being unfeasible. Instead, I stretched a welcoming smile on my face, even though seeing Raisa was as welcome as a fox in a chicken coop.

'I didn't mean for you to come all this way, but I'm so glad you did. It's at times like these you want family beside you, thank you so much,' I said, and squeezed her arm and nodded my head manically. She was still unable to speak. I could almost hear the cogs of her brain grinding as she tried to make sense of what I was saying. She was now on the back foot, and I was determined to keep her there for as long as possible, at least until I could work out my next move.

'Come along, let's go and get a coffee. There's a table free over there.' I pointed to a café in the piazza, the last thing I wanted was to sit still with a coffee, my fight-or-flight reflex was urging me to do something active, but I suppressed it and tried to let my logical brain work out how on earth I was going to be able to get out of the situation.

'Darling, I was so worried, what happened? Tell me everything,' Raisa said, when we were sitting down sipping our coffee. Her tactic being to play along with my story. She was good, I had to give it to her. She was once again, outwardly at least, composed and doing an excellent job of pretending she knew what was going on, while asking the right questions to gather information. I needed to be careful and not let anything slip.

'Well, I was fast asleep when my phone rang, it must have been around three in the morning. It was the hospital; I was so worried I knew I must get to the hospital as quickly as possible. I thought about waking you, but to be honest I just needed to get on the road, so I scribbled the note instead. I'm so pleased you were given it.'

'How is he now?' she asked, and I recognised she was treading very carefully so as not to give herself away. I avoided saying who it was in hospital, assuming she should know if she'd read my note, if there had been one. She would have to be clever to find out who 'he' was without asking, but I had no intention of giving anything away.

'Comfortable,' I nodded gravely. 'Yes, comfortable is about as far as the doctors would say, but they are very positive.'

'That's good,' she said, reaching into her bag for a cigarette.

She was rattled, I could tell because now she was smoking and before she had tried not to smoke in front of me. I was enjoying having the upper hand and mentally reminded myself not to go over the top, but to just keep everything feasible.

'I was going to give you a call later to let you know what was happening. I was hopeful I would be able to return to the hotel tomorrow. I didn't want you to cut short your break.'

'Well, I'm here now darling, so I can support you, but you haven't told me the details yet. Your note was quite vague.'

I felt a tightening of my stomach. I needed to be careful. After all, she knew exactly where I was. In the whole of Rome, she came straight to where I was. That could not just be luck on her part. No matter what I thought, she still had the upper hand and probably knew full well I was bluffing.

'So how did you know where to find me? I mean, Rome is so big I could have been anywhere?' I asked, desperate to know, but feeling certain she wouldn't tell me.

'It was pure luck,' she said. 'I thought I would kill a couple of hours looking around, then go to the hospital for visiting time, assuming, of course, that you would be there. Imagine my surprise and delight when I saw you here. I haven't checked in to a hotel yet, so I can try to get a room where you are. I can't tell you how delighted I am that I found you.'

As she spoke, I felt as though I was losing ground and needed to buy some time. After a few more seconds, I stood up.

'Why don't you order us another coffee, and one of those yummy pastries while I just pop to the ladies? I haven't been since I left the hotel.' I laughed and picked up my bag but left my cardigan hanging over the back of the chair, as a signal that I would be back. It was the only way I could think to remove myself for a few minutes, to formulate a plan in the quiet of the loo. At that moment, I couldn't think of any way out of the situation. I needed to think, and fast.

As I walked into the café, I indicated to the waiter to go to our table, feeling Raisa's eyes burning into my back. No doubt she was wracking her brains about what to do next, as well. It was as though we were playing a game of chess and the one that slipped up first would lose. As I made my way towards the toilets at the back of the café, a man stepped out of the shadows and grabbed my arm. I froze and thought I was about to have a heart attack and just stifled a scream. Then I wrenched my arm away from his hand and was about to jam my elbow in his ribs when I recognised Giuseppe. I just gawped at him, opening and closing my mouth without emitting any sound at all. I didn't think I could cope with another shock appearance, and this time instead of my brain going into overdrive, I felt as though I was about to crumple.

Giuseppe recognised my wobble and took control.

'Go in there and change into this,' he said as he thrust a carrier bag into my hands and nodded towards the toilet cubicle. 'Give me your handbag,' he held out his hand. I was about to protest and hesitated. What could he want with my bag?

'Now, we haven't got much time. Be as quick as you can.'

I handed him my bag. Went into the toilet and closed the door. I leant against it for a few seconds, feeling confused, but realised Giuseppe was my saviour and sprang into action. The how and why he just happened to be in the right place at the right time I could sort out later. A sudden thought crossed my mind: Was he league with Raisa? No, I felt sure that wasn't the case. I pulled on the trousers and loose jacket; somehow Giuseppe seemed to know my size. I tied the scarf around my head, covering my hair so none of it was visible, and put on the sunglasses. Looking in the mirror, I felt sure Raisa wouldn't recognise me. I opened the door and Giuseppe nodded his approval.

'Look, it was in your bag,' he held out a small disc about the size of a watch battery.

I stared at it; certain it wasn't mine. 'What is it?'

'A tracking device. She must have dropped it in your bag yesterday when you were at the hotel.'

The waiter appeared and before I could say anything, Giuseppe took my arm, and we followed the waiter, who was carrying a tray of coffee and cakes, towards Raisa's table. We kept right behind the waiter, so he blocked her view of us as we strolled very close, too close I felt, to the table where Raisa was still sitting. Her cigarettes and matches were out on the table again and she was drumming her fingers on the packet, while appearing to be staring into space. She turned to acknowledge the waiter and for one moment I thought Giuseppe was going to speak to her when he leant over the waiter's shoulder, but to my relief he didn't and with a squeeze of my arm he steered us out onto the piazza. To any casual onlooker, we appeared to be just one of many couples enjoying time together. I gave a wistful glance at my cardigan hanging on the back of the chair, one of my favourites, and now gone forever, along with my pashmina left at the hotel last night.

Chapter Twenty

As soon as we were far enough away to be out of sight of the cafe, we increased our speed until we were almost running down a small side street that led away from the main piazza. At last, we slowed down, and it took me a few seconds to regain my breath and allow my heart rate to return to somewhere near normal. Normal enough for me to be able to speak for the first time since Giuseppe's miraculous appearance.

'Giuseppe, what on earth are you doing here? I mean, thank God you are, but how, why? Only my father and I knew of the change of plan.'

'Your father rang me early this morning. He suspected something like this might happen.'

'But how did you get from Procida to here in such a short space of time?' My mind was trying hard to make sense of the proceedings of the last few hours, and not making a very good job of it.

'I live in Rome,' he said, and took my arm before I could ask anymore. 'Come on; let's get back to your hotel. We need to move somewhere else, just as a precaution.'

'But why were you on Procida? I don't…'

'Questions later. Come on now.'

We started walking along the road, not fast, but fast enough to make me pant, and then Giuseppe stopped.

'I don't actually know which hotel you're in, so you lead the way.'

'Well, at least you don't know everything about me,' I laughed.

He grinned, and we set off again.

'Your father suggested the Pantheon. He said it was the place you always visited first when in Rome.'

'Yes, seems like I need to be less predictable in the future.'

'Good job in this case, that you are, or I might not have found you in time.'

I shivered, wondering what would have happened if I'd been left to my own devices. I hoped I would have worked out a way of losing Raisa, but it seemed Giuseppe didn't think that would be the case, and part of me thought he might be right.

We reached my hotel, and I explained to the receptionist that I wouldn't be staying as my nephew was taking me to stay at his home. I would, of course, pay for the night. She nodded and looked approvingly at Giuseppe and made a discount for breakfast. It took only a few minutes to clear my room.

'The memory stick?'

'In the safe,' I said, extracting it.

Thank goodness Giuseppe mentioned it; in the madness of recent events, I might have forgotten all about it. He smiled, as if once again he was able to read my mind.

'Do you want to take it?' I asked, then pushed it once again into my elastic belt and secured it round my waist. He shook his head.

'OK, let's go. I know a place just along the next road where we can stay.'

'We? Are you staying with me? I thought you lived in Rome?'

'Of course I'm staying,' he said.

I wondered why, if he lived in Rome, he didn't want to go back home, but I didn't ask. I presumed he wouldn't want to do anything to jeopardise his safety, and I welcomed his company.

'Wait, that tracker, where is it? Shouldn't we do something with it, to put them off our trail?'

I had only just remembered the tracker that Giuseppe retrieved from my bag in the café.

'I dropped it into Raisa's bag as we walked past. She'd left it open, hooked over the back of her chair. A stupid mistake for anyone in Rome; it's usually things being taken out not put in,' he grinned, pleased with his actions. 'It wasn't a very sophisticated device. No doubt she'll think you're following her for a while until she finds it.'

I laughed, amused by the thought of her looking over her shoulder trying to work out where I was, but at least it would be almost impossible for her to find me now.

'She must have put it in my bag the previous night when it was hanging over the chair at dinner.' I couldn't think of a time when I'd left it unattended. I wracked my brain, trying to remember if I'd left the zip undone. She must have used sleight of hand leaning across or passing me something. How could I have missed it? I was losing my touch. Perhaps it was when she kissed me goodnight.

'She was playing safe, just in case she couldn't get the stick from you at the hotel. She's a clever woman. A dangerous woman.'

I felt a little irked by the admiration in his voice, even though I'd thought the same myself.

'Not so clever, if you figured it out almost at once.'

'She must have been in shock when she realised you'd gone this morning. She made mistakes as well; talking on the phone outside, a rookie mistake, but thank goodness she did.'

I cringed at the 'as well' comment. I was making too many mistakes.

'I knew there must be something like a tracking device when she knew exactly where to find you, and that was without your father's instinct about the Pantheon. It was just a hunch on my part that there would be something in your bag.'

'When did you first see us?' I asked.

'I was in the Pantheon when you arrived. After your father's call, I went straight there.'

I must have looked surprised, because he grinned,

'I made sure I kept out of your line of vision. I just kept an eye on you, so saw when Raisa approached you, then followed you both to the café.'

'I had no idea and I've been so careful up to now, checking all the time that I wasn't being followed.'

'Once she arrived you were concentrating on what to do next.'

I nodded, grateful that he didn't think I was just being unobservant.

'Could there be other trackers?' it struck me that Raisa might have doubled up on her chances.

'Unlikely, but we could check.'

Before he could stop me, I lifted my bag onto the bed and emptied its contents. Giuseppe felt all around the inside of the bag, while I checked all my pockets and my wash bag, even though to my knowledge, Raisa never set foot inside my room. I checked the pockets of my trousers and when I was satisfied all was in order, I repacked, and we headed out onto the street.

Giuseppe leant over the counter and whispered something to the receptionist on the way out of the hotel. She nodded and giggled. I raised an eyebrow as he joined me, picked up my bag, and pulled my arm through his.

'What was that all about?'

'I told her if anyone came asking for you, to say nothing, only that she'd never heard of you.'

'Don't you think that would raise her suspicion even more?'

'She got my meaning; she said she didn't think I was your nephew. She winked and wished us good luck. Our secret is safe with her.'

I laughed at his cheek, but it was a good ploy and when I looked back over my shoulder, I could see the receptionist looking our way with a wide grin on her face. The tracker meant Raisa would already know where the hotel was and might come making enquiries.

We crossed the street, dodging a swarm of scooters and small cars and cut down a small alley onto another, busier street. There were no pavements and the shops and cafes opened straight onto the cobbled road. Cars were parked all along the street and one café had claimed a small area protected by low fencing and large pot plants, to put out tables and chairs. In other circumstances, I would have enjoyed sitting there to while away the time and people watch, but not now. Giuseppe guided me along the street and through an archway into a discreet, attractive hotel, set at the back of an enclosed courtyard. A rampant climber covered the front of the hotel. Struggling out from under it were small, cream canopies over the ground floor windows and main entrance. There were a few people sitting at the tables and chairs in the courtyard sipping drinks without a care in the world. The air was full of the scent of flowers mingled with food preparations, but it was a welcome relief from the fumes of Vespas and other scooters that buzzed around the streets like annoying gnats. It looked expensive.

I followed Giuseppe into the reception and to my surprise he booked us into one room, keeping up our cover I presumed. Before I could comment or protest, we were being shown to the lift and taken up to the second floor, and into a large room overlooking the courtyard. Momentarily, I wondered if he was going to try anything on. I didn't think I could cope with that as well.

'See! Two beds,' he indicated the small single in the corner behind the large double as soon as the door closed behind us. 'This is mine,' he said, sitting on the single bed.

I thought again about protesting, but decided not to, so just nodded my agreement and dumped my bag on the other. We sat in silence for a few minutes before I remembered and asked him something that had crossed my mind earlier.

'So, if you live in Rome, why did I have to travel to Procida to collect the stick?'

'It came in by sea, to Procida. Coffee?' he picked up the kettle and headed towards the bathroom for water.

'Please, but I could have liaised with whoever brought it in.'

'Ah yes,' he returned with the full kettle and switched it on. 'But the person who brought it in didn't know about it. It was stowed away before he set off; he was in the dark. It's safer that way, so I had to retrieve it first.'

It wasn't a satisfying answer, but I didn't pursue it. I didn't ask where he retrieved it but had an image of him sorting through piles of fish, gutting them until he found the right one to extract it from.

'It was inside a book. I waited for the owner to go ashore then boarded and found the right book. It was well hidden, but I knew which book and where to look. I go to Procida often to see my sister, so it wasn't unusual for me to be there.'

'Yes, that makes sense. At least the book sounds more civilized than I was imagining.'

He laughed, handed me a mug of coffee, and then sank into one of the two chairs in front of the large windows, from where we could observe the comings and goings of the hotel. I sat in the other and felt surprised how relaxed I was in the circumstances. Maybe because we shared the responsibility now.

'The hotel food here isn't wonderful, but good enough, so I think we're better staying here for dinner, if that's ok with you?'

'Of course.'

'You'll hand the stick over to your father tomorrow, when you meet him.'

'That wasn't the original plan, but I presumed that was what he was thinking. It makes little sense to go onto Florence now the route is known.' I said, wondering if father had contacted Julia to get the plan changed.

'That's right. After you rang your father, and in the light of all that's happened, we thought it better for him to take it from here.'

'Why can't I just give it to you?' I asked. It seemed reasonable to me in the circumstances that Giuseppe should take it, and cut me out as the middleman, as it were.

'That isn't the plan,' he said, but didn't elaborate.

There was much more going on than just the transfer of the memory stick, but I didn't know what and wasn't sure I wanted to know. Giuseppe was more than just a courier like me. He seemed to have knowledge of the wider situation. I felt exhausted. I just wanted to give the damned thing to my father and go home.

'Roll on tomorrow.'

Chapter Twenty-One

Later, alone, after Giuseppe had excused himself while he went to 'sort something out', I curled up on the less than comfortable bed and, for want of anything else to do, turned on the television. The programme, a game show of some sort, was mind-numbingly dull and my thoughts soon wandered and drifted over the events of the day so far. As Raisa was here in Rome, maybe it was too good an opportunity to just let her disappear again, when it could be the perfect time to find out a bit more about who she was, and more importantly, who she was working with. I sat thinking for a few minutes, and the more I thought, the more I convinced myself that we couldn't just let her drift back into the shadows, and that I should be the one to seek her out. It was the least I could do in the circumstances. I had promised Giuseppe I wouldn't leave the hotel, and I knew if he, or my father were here, they would advise me in no uncertain terms against doing anything and to just lie low and keep out of trouble.

I mulled everything over. After all, I had the memory stick in my possession and that was my only task in this operation, to collect it and then deliver it, but as I reasoned with myself, things had already changed. I knew it was through my own actions that the transfer was not going as smoothly as it should. So, if I could make sure something productive came from my detour, then my actions would not be wasted. These thoughts whirled around in my head. One moment I was all set to do something, the next I convinced myself it would be suicidal to go after her and risk making things worse. I tried again to concentrate on the television, flicking through the channels, looking for something vaguely interesting to watch, but failing.

A few minutes later, I stood up. My mind was made up. I was going out. Telling myself I would be careful, of course, but it was better than just sitting here doing nothing. Giuseppe would not be back for hours, so I could see what I could find out and be back before he returned. I wouldn't take any risks.

My bag was on the top shelf in the voluminous, antique looking wardrobe and I needed to stand on a chair to reach it. The items given to me by my father in case I needed a disguise, were turning out to be more useful than I had ever imagined. I pulled out the wig, a pair of glasses, and a loose navy jacket. When I felt ready, I looked in the mirror. I hardly recognised myself, so I was certain Raisa, if I was to come across her, would not give me a second glance. I took off my rings; they might be something she would recognise, as she commented on how pretty she thought they were when we first met. I locked them in the safe. My fingers felt odd, naked, without them. The only other time it was necessary for me to remove them was before a caesarean section when I gave birth to Jilly. I hesitated for a few moments, then removed my belt containing the memory stick and stashed that in the safe as well. It did cross my mind that if anything happened to me, Giuseppe wouldn't know the stick was in the safe, or how to open it. I shrugged. It was a risk, but a very small one, and I felt sure he could somehow open the safe if necessary.

Just in case things did not go to plan, and he returned before me, I wrote a note saying I would be back soon, and everything was safe. I kept it vague but underlined the word safe and hoped he would understand the note and that alarm bells would ring with him if I was very late. I was certain that would not happen, but felt reassured that if things went wrong, he would be looking for me. Another look in the mirror to make sure the wig was in place and looked natural. It did and looked quite good; a style I could maybe adopt for real in the future. Looking around, I found the tourist map of Rome inside the visitors' information pack left in the room and tucked it inside my bag, then made my way downstairs into the reception. Not wanting to be noticed, I loitered for a couple of seconds in the shadows until the receptionist was busy with another guest, and then slipped out of the front door.

The evening was still very warm, and I strolled passed the tables in the courtyard, which were filling up with people, most were tourists, enjoying pre-dinner drinks, how I wished I was one of them, with nothing to worry about except which cocktail to have next. I stepped through the arch onto the street and joined the bustle of people making their way along to the next historic site, or at this time of day back to their hotels to change before going out for the evening. When I reached a junction, I stopped, not being sure which way I should be heading. I opened the map, and after studying it, found the name of the street I wanted to head towards. It looked quite central, and as luck would have it, I was going in the right direction.

Raisa's mistake earlier in the café was to pull a packet of cigarettes and a book of matches out of her bag as soon as we sat at the table. She put them away again almost straight away after lighting her cigarette, but not before I read upside down - *Hotel Piazza*, on the matchbook. It looked new and as far as I could see, all the matches were still intact, which made me assume she must have picked it up very recently. If she hadn't already checked in, it was likely to be a hotel she'd stayed in before and would choose again. So, it was worth making it my first stop. I had only managed to see part of the address, as the writing on the matchbook was quite small, but I hoped it would be enough for me to find the hotel. I doubted there would be more than one Hotel Piazza in the vicinity, although it wasn't an uncommon name.

After plotting the route, I walked along memorising the names of streets on the way, and soon reached what I hoped was the correct vicinity. The Hotel Piazza was big, taking up one side of a small piazza. The other sides contained bars and shops. Traffic beeped and jostled its way noisily around all four sides without seeming to bother the numerous people sitting, eating, and drinking at the tables lining the pavements. Rather than head straight in, I walked past the hotel and along one side of the piazza. Keeping the front entrance in sight, I observed the people entering and leaving, some on foot, others getting in and out of taxis and juggling luggage. I sauntered back and waited until there were several people going in through the main entrance before following them up the steps and entering the reception hall.

It was a large and airy reception, with beautiful marble floors and several small tables with red velvet armchairs arranged around them. Large pot plants stood in each corner. The reception desk was on one side and opposite was a wide marble staircase. I could see a bar or lounge area through an archway to one side of the reception, and on the other side a dining room. It was a very smart hotel; Raisa obviously didn't believe in taking the cheap option. There were plenty of people milling around, so I didn't feel conspicuous or out of place. I sat down in one of the red chairs in a position where I could see all the comings and goings in and out of the hotel, as well as the various areas inside. Now what? I wondered if I should go into the bar and have a drink and just wait to see if Raisa appeared, but that felt too passive. I needed to be active.

It was, for once, my time to be lucky, because before I had a chance to move, a woman swept in through the main doors. It was Raisa. I picked a newspaper up off the table and pretended to read, watching over the top as she made her way to the desk to collect her key. It was only when she drew level with me, I realised it wasn't her. In fact, I felt quite foolish. This woman, apart from being roughly the same height as Raisa, bore no resemblance to her in any other way. I put the paper down and was about to get up and go into the bar when the lift doors opened in the far corner of the reception. Raisa emerged. This time there was no doubt. It was her. I picked up the paper again and watched her every move. She walked briskly to the reception desk. I put the paper down again and moved a little closer so that I could overhear what was said, and kept my fingers crossed she wasn't checking out. If she was, I would lose her, but I reasoned that was unlikely as she didn't have any luggage or even a handbag with her.

She asked for another pillow to be sent to her room, and when asked, she told the receptionist her room number, two hundred and fourteen, in a clear loud voice. I felt like punching the air. Instead of returning to the lift to go back to her room, Raisa walked through the arch into the lounge area. I followed at a distance and saw her greet a man, who summoned a waiter after kissing her on both cheeks. As discreetly as possible I took a photograph of them on my phone. I was torn between going into the lounge and finding a seat near to them, to see if I could overhear their conversation, or going to find Raisa's room.

In the end I took the lift to the second floor and walked along until I found room two hundred and fourteen. The door was, of course, locked. At the end of the corridor was a seating area, and I waited for a few minutes to see if the housekeeping staff arrived with Raisa's extra pillow. I knew it was a long shot that they would come straight away. I glanced at my watch and decided to give myself five minutes, and then if nothing happened, I would return to the lounge to eavesdrop. My patience was rewarded. After a long couple of minutes, a young girl, wearing a grey and white striped dress and white apron, appeared carrying a pillow. When she reached Raisa's room, she used her master key to open the door. I made my move, reaching the door as she opened it. I held my arms out for the pillow, thanked her for her prompt attention, slipped a couple of coins into her hand, and entered the room. I leant back on the closed door, hugging the pillow to my chest. I stood there for a few seconds, allowing my nerves to settle, and then went into the room and placed the pillow on the bed.

It was a very pleasant room, large and tastefully furnished. I knew I needed to be focused, do what I needed to do, and get out of the room before Raisa returned. Now inside the room, I wasn't sure what to look for, or where to look. Before doing anything, I took a pair of blue disposable gloves out of my pocket and pulled them on. I started with the wardrobe. It wasn't locked and swung open as soon as I touched the door. To my surprise, the standard hotel safe on the shelf was open and empty. Either Raisa had nothing of value to lock away, which I found hard to believe, or she was careless of security, which was equally surprising. I remembered she wasn't carrying a handbag when I saw her downstairs, so I assumed it must be in the room somewhere. It didn't take me long to find it on a chair, tucked under a small table in the corner of the room. I lifted it onto the table and opened the many pockets systematically; I carefully checked the contents and made sure to return everything to the same place.

In a central pocket I pulled out a dark red Turkish passport, in the name of Raisa Binici, so she was Turkish and neither Italian nor Russian. Being Turkish made a probable link to the man on the boat in Procida. I took my phone from my pocket and photographed all the relevant pages. There were also two small pieces of paper, folded inside the passport, covered in what I presumed was Turkish writing, so I photographed them as well, before putting them back into the central pocket. There didn't appear to be anything else significant in the bag, but I photographed other ordinary items as well, just in case. I put the bag back in place on the chair and pushed it under the table.

A soft-sided blue suitcase was on the luggage stand. It was closed, and I expected it to be locked, but to my surprise it wasn't, and it opened easily with a flick of a catch. I lifted out neatly folded clothes, being careful not to disturb them too much, and patted them to check for anything unusual. At the bottom of the case there was a small, brown leather, zipped folder. Without removing it from the suitcase, I unzipped it and found two more passports, along with a large amount of money tucked inside. I opened the green Saudi Arabian passport, believing it must have been stolen, and to my surprise, I saw a photograph of a woman. It was clearly Raisa, even though a scarf covered her hair.

The name inside the passport was Rana Anbar. I took several photographs of the different pages, including the front cover. The other passport was from the Republic of Ireland, and I was again confused, even more so, to find a picture of Raisa inside. The name on this passport was Roisin O'Sullivan. I was standing holding the passport, feeling rather bemused, when I heard voices outside in the corridor. I froze, then as fast as I could, put everything back in the suitcase and grabbed the pillow. I would pretend to be the chambermaid delivering the requested pillow, and just hoped that Raisa wouldn't notice that my clothes bore no resemblance to those of a chambermaid.

I stood still, my pulse thudding in my ears, and then the voices stopped. Nothing happened. The door remained closed, and I could faintly hear movement in the adjoining room. I heaved a sigh of relief and returned to the suitcase. I removed everything again and then photographed the Irish passport before putting everything back in its proper place and closing the catch.

As I scanned the rest of the room, I noticed a pen lying on top of a notepad on the writing desk. On closer inspection, I could see faint indentations on the blank top sheet of paper. It was impossible to make out any words, but I tore the page out of the notebook and tucked it into my pocket, so I could examine it in more detail later. Next, I moved into the en-suite and had a careful rummage through both Raisa's wash and make-up bag, which revealed nothing apart from her expensive taste in cosmetics and perfume. I twisted up a lipstick and opened a couple of bottles, but everything looked normal. Resisting the temptation to have a quick spray of her perfume, I returned to the bedroom. I looked around for other likely clues, but I was beginning to feel I was chancing my luck if I stayed any longer, so I opened the door and peeped out.

The corridor was silent and empty and in a déjà vu moment from Naples. I peeled off my gloves and made my way to the stairwell and walked up two flights of stairs, before walking to the far end of the corridor to catch the lift. The lift seemed to take an exceptionally long time to arrive and when it did, there were already at least half a dozen other people in the cabin. I squeezed in beside them and watched as the lights indicated the descent of the lift. It stopped twice, once on Raisa's floor and I held my breath, hoping that when the doors opened, she would not be standing there. Although I was sure she wouldn't recognise me in my wig, I didn't relish being in such close proximity with her. I relaxed again as a woman and young girl wriggled their way into the now over full lift.

At last, the lift reached the ground floor, and we all piled out and scattered in various directions across the large reception area. I followed a man and a rather large lady into the comfortable lounge, where I hoped I would still find Raisa ensconced with her companion. I veered away to the opposite side of the room to where I'd seen her meet the man earlier, before turning to see if they were still there. They were, and they were deep in conversation. Neither looked up to see the new arrivals entering the lounge. They were concentrating on each other, not expecting to see anyone they knew. Despite smoking being banned inside buildings for many years, Raisa held an unlit cigarette between her fingers, and the tell-tale book of matches was on the table in front of her. She fiddled with the cigarette, lifting it to her mouth and then putting it down. A sign that she was less than relaxed, and the body language of both her and her male companion showed they were both tense, although both were trying hard to appear calm.

I hesitated, wondering whether I should buy a drink and sit down to keep watch on what they did, or better, whether I could find a seat close enough to them to hear their conversation. It was impossible from where I was to even ascertain what language they were speaking. I looked around, weighing up my options, when I started in surprise. I recognised the man sitting reading the paper in a chair just to the left of Raisa and her companion. It was Giuseppe. My mouth must have dropped open. What on earth was Giuseppe doing here? How did he know where Raisa was staying? I was tempted to go and sit with him, to find out what was going on, but I knew my questions would have to wait until later. I imagined he could easily hear the conversation taking place only a few feet away. At least I hoped he could. I walked around to the far side of the bar and perched on a stool and ordered a soda water. I could still see Raisa and her companion and now Giuseppe, but I doubted they would notice me, as there were several other people sitting at the bar and milling around between me and them. Knowing Giuseppe was there, I relaxed and began to enjoy my surveillance.

I sipped my drink, but decided I would leave if the situation was the same after I'd finished it. After all, Giuseppe appeared to be in prime position and I was not really serving any useful purpose by staying, apart from satisfying my own curiosity. After a few minutes, Raisa and her male companion stood up. He was tall with an air of supreme confidence, which made Raisa appear less poised. I studied him as closely as I could, to see if he was anyone I recognised. He wasn't. From his appearance, I thought he looked about forty. His hair was dark and thinning and he wore small silver framed glasses. From his clothes, a navy jacket over a green shirt with a blue tie and beige trousers, although not totally unstylish, made me think he wasn't Italian. The man put his hand on

Raisa's elbow and steered her towards the reception. He was still speaking, but even though they were closer, I could not hear what he was saying. They turned right under the arch, which was away from the reception desk, stairs and lifts, so I presumed they were going out of the hotel to find a restaurant, or for Raisa to smoke the cigarette that she still held.

Chapter Twenty-Two

Giuseppe got to his feet, folded the newspaper and strolled out into the reception, without a second glance in my direction. He also turned to the right. I finished my drink in one mouthful and slid off the bar stool and followed. By the time I reached the reception, I could see no sign of Raisa and her male companion. Giuseppe was just heading out through the main door onto the street. Keeping a discreet distance, I went out after them, but decided I wouldn't follow if they were all heading off in a direction that wasn't towards my hotel. It was time to return and not chance my luck any further. The pavement outside the hotel was busy and from the top of the steps I scanned both directions. There was no sign of Raisa, but I could see Giuseppe appearing to look casually into a small menswear shop, although his eyes were darting in both directions.

I waited for a moment until he stepped away; he glanced at his watch and started to walk more briskly along the road in the direction of our hotel. Making sure there was no one in the street watching either him or me, I hurried after him, catching up just as he turned the corner into a smaller street leading on to the road where the hotel was. I slipped my arm through his just as he was about to cross the road. He jumped.

'What the…?' he looked at me confused, pulling his arm away, not having any idea who I was.

I took off my glasses and grinned at him. Again, he looked doubtful.

'It's a wig,' I touched my head.

'Katharine? What the…? What on earth are you up to?'

'I was at the Piazza as well. We can tell each other what we found out when we get back to the room.'

'OK,' he said, but was still looking at me doubtfully. Then he smiled, took my arm, as if to make sure I didn't run off and do anything else he wasn't aware of, and we walked back towards our hotel. 'Good disguise, by the way,' he said, after a pause.

'Thanks, it's come in handy a couple of times on this trip so far.' Just before we entered the hotel, I slipped into a small alleyway and removed the wig, stuffing it into my bag.

'That feels better,' I said, shaking my hair.

'Why take it off now? Why not wait?'

'We don't want the hotel receptionist to think you're taking a stranger up to your room. We need to create the minimum amount of attention and suspicion.'

He nodded and looked up and down the road before nodding again, and we crossed over and entered the courtyard in front of the hotel. It was still busy with customers, and despite being tempted to sit outside in the pleasant evening temperature, we made our way across reception, which looked dowdy compared to the smart interior of Raisa's hotel. We reached our room without anyone speaking to us or taking the slightest notice of us, which was a relief.

'I need a drink; how about you?' I opened the minibar, which wasn't particularly well stocked.

'Wait, they're stupid prices. I'll go down to the bar. Don't go anywhere,' he said, and was only half joking, but I flopped into a chair and waited, too tired to even think about anything else.

He was back in no time and placed two large glasses of wine on the small table.

'So how did you know where Raisa was staying?' he said and looked at me as he took a long drink of wine.

'She had a matchbook from the hotel, so it was a hopeful guess. How did you know?'

'Same, I recognised the Piazza Hotel logo on the matches when I dropped the tracker in her bag.'

We exchanged in detail everything that we had both found out during our separate forays into the Hotel Piazza. Raisa and her companion were speaking in a language Giuseppe didn't recognise, but he'd recorded most of their conversation on his phone. He played the recording to me; it was quite difficult to hear their voices amongst the background hustle and bustle of the bar, but no doubt there was enough for a specialist to work on. Giuseppe was impressed with the photographs of the passports, but like me, could not explain why she had them. He studied in detail the imprint on the piece of writing paper.

'It's not English or Italian, it might be Turkish. I'll get all these off for analysis as well when this is over.' He placed them in a plastic folder and locked it in his bag. 'Now then, are you hungry or have you already eaten?'

'Yes, I am, and no, I haven't eaten,' I said, realising that I was starving. This sort of work was much more fun when you weren't alone.

We made our way downstairs and, rather than sitting in the pretty courtyard, sat in a rather dark and uninspiring room inside, but probably sensible in the circumstances.

Our evening turned out to be quite pleasant, and the food was well prepared and tasty. We chatted about all sorts of things, but I was aware that every time I asked a question of any meaning, Giuseppe steered me back onto the superficial, or at least general, topics of conversation. He was very skilled at sidestepping questions that might reveal the real him. I knew no more about him, as a person, at the end of the evening than I did at the beginning. He was clearly well trained, or perhaps he was just less curious than me, but he was good company and very charming.

We returned to our room and Giuseppe was asleep on the small child's bed, or so it seemed, before I was out of the bathroom. I lay awake for a long time, mulling over the events of the day. Was it only a day it felt like a lifetime? So much had happened in the last twenty-four hours. After what felt like too little sleep I awoke, and the sun was nudging in through a chink in the curtains. I knew it must be late and I sat bolt upright in bed. I could see Giuseppe's bed neatly made across the room, and he was nowhere to be seen. My stomach contracted; something was wrong. I leapt out of bed, dragged the curtains back, flooding the room with sunlight. It had gone ten, and I was alone. I looked around and spotted a note on the table. It was from Giuseppe. He explained he had to go, and I should go ahead with my meeting with my father as planned. He wished me good luck.

I sank back onto the bed, feeling deflated. I thought Giuseppe would stay with me; at least until he knew I'd carried out my task. I tried to pull myself together; this was work not a social liaison. I could manage this on my own and rationalized that he would not have gone if he thought there was any risk I would mess up–again. I showered and dressed and felt better. I was annoyed at myself for feeling weak and needing Giuseppe's protection but could not help feeling a little let down he didn't stay to say goodbye in person. No doubt he wanted to get the recording and photographs to whoever could examine them as soon as possible. After all, if I had stuck to the original plan, I wouldn't be in this position now and wouldn't feel in need of a nursemaid. I had messed up big time, and I wasn't looking forward to the afternoon and meeting my father. In some ways, I hoped he would be angry with me. It was what I deserved and would be easier to deal with than his quiet disappointment, which was often his reaction to my childhood misdemeanours. I paced around the room berating myself and wondering whether I was still up to this sort, or any sort, of mission come to that.

I considered whether to book a flight and make arrangements for returning to the family but thought it more sensible to wait until after meeting my father, just in case he wanted me to do something else. In my head I felt certain he wouldn't but didn't want to second-guess what might happen. My bags were all ready to go, but I decided to leave them in the room and come back for them later. The belt with the memory stick was once again around my waist. In just a few hours, my part in this would be over. I ate a light lunch in the hotel, read a magazine, or at least attempted to read it, until it was time to go and meet my father.

Chapter Twenty-Three

The café, which father and I had been to a couple of times before, wasn't far from the hotel, but I left in plenty of time just to make sure I could find it. The last time we had been there was a year or so ago, when I met him with the children on one of our educational trips during the school holidays. It was an ordinary little place, but my father always liked to visit it when in Rome. I thought I knew where it was, but things change quickly and one side street in Rome looks very like another. A small knot formed in my stomach, and I wiped perspiration from my brow when it wasn't on the corner where I expected it to be. I found myself by the river and knew that I'd come too far, but at least now I could get my bearings and work back to where I should be.

My nerves were fraying and every few steps I stopped to look around and make sure no one was following me, which was difficult to ascertain as there were people everywhere, stopping and starting just as I was, looking at maps, or locals rushing about their business. Every eye that so much as strayed in my direction made me suspicious. I looked at my watch every couple of minutes, eager not to be late, and calmed down a bit when I realised there was still plenty of time. I turned a corner, feeling sure the café would be in front of me. Once again, it wasn't. There was just a street full of bins with scooters parked erratically between them. This was ridiculous. It must be here. I stopped, took a deep breath and made myself concentrate. I felt sure it was nearby. I knew I was in the right vicinity, a couple of streets in from the river, on the Vatican side. I walked down the street with the bins and out into a small piazza that I thought I recognised. There was a street leading off it with various shops and cafes, and as I made my way along, I relaxed. This was looking more familiar. As I reached a junction, I looked to my right and could see the place I was looking for. I even recognised the logo on the parasols. Thank goodness I'd made it; only a short time more and I would be rid of the damned memory stick.

I walked along the street to the corner to double check. It reassured me to walk past and glance in to see the bustle of people sipping coffee, chatting with friends, reading the paper and involved in all the other normal café activities. It wasn't full, so finding a table should not be a problem. The aroma of coffee and sweet cakes almost tempted me in to wait, but I carried on walking. I made my way round the corner on to another busy shopping street. For a reason I couldn't explain, I preferred my father to arrive first. The shops here were expensive, with glamorous clothes displayed on arrogant looking mannequins in the carefully styled windows. Most of the customers oozed wealth and indifference, and paid scant notice of me, although I kept a wary eye on all of them. I glanced at my watch and turned back towards the café. I was still a few minutes early, so I went into a shop and on impulse bought a pair of earrings for Jilly. As I put them in my bag, I knew it would mean having to look for presents for the boys, but that was the sort of stress I could cope with.

I stood aside at the door to let another customer enter the shop. Her perfume wafting from her clothes as she passed by took me straight back home and to Aunt Clare. It was *Beautiful* by Estee Lauder, her favourite. Although I knew it could not be her, I couldn't stop myself from looking back just to check it wasn't. I couldn't remember ever smelling that perfume on anyone else. Clare was clear-minded and sensible and somehow just the reminder of her perfume boosted my self-confidence. I could hear her saying: 'Of course you can do it Katharine, never doubt yourself.'

As I turned to go out onto the street, I could see my father striding out as he crossed the road, heading towards the corner and the café. I wondered whether to rush out and meet him, but knowing he was less than demonstrative, I hung back a little. Let him get settled at a table first. In the middle of the road, a group of tourists, who were intent on following a red-triangle-wielding-tour-leader, engulfed him. I smiled to myself. I could almost hear him tutting and could imagine his irritation, as he had very little patience with large groups when they were in his way. He emerged only to be caught up in another group of people trying to get across the road, dodging the inevitable scooters. Then he was gone. I could no longer see him; being tall, he was head and shoulders above everyone else, particularly Japanese tourists.

Mayhem suddenly erupted, and it felt like my world was moving in slow motion. People were shouting and screaming and for a few seconds they parted like the waves on the Red Sea. As they did so, I saw my father lying on the ground. Then the crowd closed around him once more, some on their knees, others gesticulating, but not before I saw a bright red patch forming on his shirt, and then oozing from his chest and forming a pool underneath his left side. I don't know whether I screamed. My mouth was wide open, and I was about to run to his side when someone grabbed my arm and dragged me along the street. I fought with my assailant. I must go to my father. Nothing else mattered, but he held my arm in a grip as strong as a vice. I twisted and yanked my arm to get him to release me – but failed. I turned just enough to see who was holding me and was about to shout out, but as soon as I realised who it was, my anger deflated into confusion.

'Giuseppe, what the…?'

'Just keep quiet and keep walking.'

He loosened his grip, but not enough for me to free myself.

'Keep calm Katharine, trust me.'

'Let go of me, my father he needs me, I must, …'

Giuseppe stopped but still held on to me with both hands. He shook me a little and stared into my face.

'There is nothing you can do; your safety is more important now. I saw him, a man wearing a baseball cap holding a knife, he stabbed your father. We need to get away from here. Now.'

'But he got away, the man in the baseball cap?'

'We're on to him.'

I knew he was right. There was nothing I could do. It was obvious, even from the glimpse I had, that my father was dead. Stabbed through the heart. It didn't appear to be just an average tourist mugging. The memory stick, and me, needed to be out of the way. This was turning into my worst nightmare.

'I'm sorry Katharine, really I am,' he said, and at last he let go of my arms, and this time, I didn't move.

'Why? Who was it? How did they know? Who's gone after him?' I started shaking and Giuseppe put his arm through mine to help steady me. He steered me further away from the scene along the street, past more shops and then turning round the next corner into a small square, where life was going on as though nothing had happened. The pavement cafés around the square were busy and Giuseppe guided me into one of the smaller ones and into a seat at a corner table, out of sight of the road. He ordered two strong espressos and two Grappas.

Our drinks arrived at the same time as sirens screamed along the road that ran parallel to the square. Too late, I thought. I tried not to imagine the scene and wondered for the first time if my father was carrying anything incriminating or papers showing his real identity. I took a gulp of coffee and a bigger gulp of Grappa. Both helped to ease my shakes. I sat, staring unseeing, into my cup; at last, I remembered Giuseppe was sitting next to me and looked up at him. He smiled, a mixture of sympathy and reassurance.

'What happened? Where were you? I thought you'd gone.'

'We were nearby, just out of sight. In case something might happen, but they caught us off guard by such a public attack.'

'Why? I don't understand and who are 'we'? Who else is involved?'

He didn't reply, just beckoned the waiter over and paid for our drinks.

'Come on, let's go.' He helped me to my feet and tucked my arm firmly through his, this time to stop me from falling rather than escaping. We made our way back to the hotel in silence. My brain was no longer functioning enough for me to think.

I stood in the middle of the room, watching as Giuseppe filled the kettle. How could he be so calm? Anger boiled up in me. My father was dead and all he could do was make tea.

'Coffee, tea?' he asked.

'No, I don't want another fucking drink.' I surprised myself with my language. 'I've had it. I can't go on.' I pulled the belt containing the memory stick off and flung it on the bed. 'That's it. I don't care what happens to this stupid thing anymore. You can take it or flush it down the toilet. I'm done. I'm going home.'

He walked over to the bed and picked it up, then guided me into a chair, where I burst into tears.

'You can't let your father's death be in vain. He would want you to carry on, you know he would,' he spoke gently but firmly, and I felt like a child being soothed out of a tantrum, but I wasn't ready just yet to be calm.

'Would he? Would he want to risk me getting killed as well? You take it if it's that important. I've had enough.'

Even as I spoke, I knew he was right, and I think we both knew that I would complete the task, but I was now certain that I would never get involved in anything again.

'You are a strong woman, Katharine; you'll do the right thing.'

He returned to the kettle and took a long time to make

some tea. I sat, not moving. My body felt numb, as did part of my brain, but the other part was now starting to work out what to do next. Giuseppe handed me a cup of steaming tea. Is there anything better in a crisis? He didn't have one himself and didn't sit down.

'I need to go out to get things sorted,' he said. 'Do not open the door to anyone. For any reason. Ok? I'll put the do not disturb sign on the handle. Promise me you won't leave.'

I nodded.

'Finish your tea and try to get some rest.'

'What's in it?' I took a sip. There was a faint taste I knew wasn't tea but was almost beyond caring.

'It'll help. I won't be long. Lock the door after me.'

I locked the door, then tipped the tea down the sink and made myself another one. This time with no additives. I needed my wits about me. I paced around the room, trying to put all the pieces of the jigsaw together, but the more I thought about everything, the less sense it made. How, and who, knew where my father was going to be? This entire mission made little sense. The memory stick seemed such a convoluted way of passing on information in this day and age. There was so much I didn't know, and I didn't like the feel of being kept in the dark.

I don't know how long Giuseppe was out, but I was still pacing when he returned.

'You look exhausted. Did you sleep?'

I shook my head.

'Well, sit down at least.'

I sank into a chair, relieved that Giuseppe seemed in control. I looked up expectantly as he pulled another chair over and sat beside me.

'OK, if you're feeling all right, let me talk you through what happens next.'

'I'm fine. Where have you been?'

He didn't answer my question but handed me a passport and an airline ticket. I glanced at them. Rosalind Amos was the name next to my photo in the passport. I looked at Giuseppe.

'Just as a precaution,' he said.

I shrugged and pushed them into my bag. He continued to explain that he had contacted Julia and booked me on a flight early the next day from Rome to Bristol. Then I was to make my way to Padstow, in Cornwall, where they had reserved a room for me in a hotel. Then I was to wait to be contacted by someone who would collect the memory stick.

'Padstow, why?'

'You know it?'

'Of course, but why there? I just wish I knew what was going on.'

'Don't worry. That's the plan. Now, I'll order some food. We'll stay out of sight tonight.'

The food arrived soon after. It might have been delicious, but I never noticed, just forced it down because I knew it was the right thing to do. I must keep my strength up to help me concentrate. After we finished eating, I fell into a deep, but troubled, sleep and was far from refreshed when Giuseppe shook me awake in the early hours of the morning. We took a taxi together to the station, where I boarded the Leonardo Express airport train alone. Again, I was surprised that Giuseppe wasn't coming with me, but he'd kissed me on both cheeks as he had when I boarded the ferry in Procida.

'Take care Katharine. Go straight through to departures after checking in, don't wait. You've got your belt with the stick?' he asked even though he already knew the answer, having watched me put it on in the hotel.

'Thank you, Giuseppe. I couldn't have managed without you. You take care as well.'

We parted rather awkwardly, I thought, after all we had been through together, but with a final smile and nod, he turned away.

Chapter Twenty-Four

The train was on time and busy for that time of day, but I found a seat and settled back to watch Rome awaken, as we sped through the city towards the airport. Half an hour later, I was inside the terminal building. I followed instructions and went straight to the departure lounge, after I had checked in. I looked back just as I went through and saw Giuseppe leaning against a pillar. He only gave a nod of acknowledgment, possibly feeling embarrassed that I'd spotted him, and turned away. His job was done. Lucky him! He must have boarded the train, instead of leaving, as I had thought. He was continuing to keep a lookout for me, or at least making sure I, and the memory stick, made it to the airport without further mishap. I assumed, as he was now leaving, that all was well, but then he couldn't follow further into the airport. I watched him leave and wondered if I would ever see him again. His presence these last couple of days had been a lifeline, and I shuddered to think what would have happened if he hadn't been there, more than once, in the right place at the right time.

I had disposed of everything except essential items. So, my luggage was just one small carry-on bag. The memory stick zipped inside my belt seemed to burn against my skin like a detonator and hard as I tried to look casual, I felt as though a sign was above my head saying 'Search her', 'Search her'.

Whatever was on the memory stick it caused my father's death, so it must be vital information. Despite that, I still felt like throwing it away, to be rid of it, but I knew that for his sake I must carry on and deliver it to whoever was going to meet me in Cornwall. I hoped that this time everything would be straightforward. Knowing I couldn't cope with anymore dramas. I left my belt on as I passed through security; I was feeling hot and agitated and wasn't surprised when a security man stopped me.

'Belt,' an official nodded without making eye contact, first at me and then the tray on which I'd placed my bag. I was unsure how he could see the belt under my top and so hesitated before doing anything.

'Belt, off.' He pointed to the tray this time, so I removed it and placed the belt under my jacket and bag on the tray.

I stared at the image of my belongings as they appeared on the screen when the tray slid through the x-ray device. They rarely scrutinised everything, did they? How many airports had I passed through before and never taken much notice, always eager to get through and get going? At last, it rumbled down towards my greedy hands. My sigh of relief must have been audible and suspicious, but no one moved towards me. I grabbed the belt, my coat and bag, and after securing it back in place, rushed into the departure lounge before anyone could change their minds. Could the scanner corrupt the information on the stick? I wondered. I presumed not, but it would have been the final insult in this debacle.

The wait for the flight seemed interminable, although it was on time, and as soon as they announced the gate, I was ready and waiting. However, I felt shocked when the officer in the booth examined my false passport, scanned it, and then stood up to discuss with a colleague. My legs felt like jelly, and I thought I was going to faint. I could see the plane through the window. So near, yet so far. Please don't stop me now. I waited, trying to look nonchalant, probably not very successfully. At last, he came back, sat down and slid my passport under the glass screen towards me.

'Everything all right?' The words were out before I thought about it and at once I wished that I'd kept my mouth shut.

He looked at me and for one moment, I thought he was going to ask for my passport back or ask me to step aside. It felt as though time stood still while we stayed, eyes locked, me trembling.

'Go through,' he said, as he looked over my shoulder and was already beckoning the next passenger forward.

At last, I was on the plane, and we were airborne. I felt safe for the first time in days and leant my head back, closed my eyes and tried once again to piece together the events since I left Naples. No longer did this feel like an elaborate game, exciting, with only a hint of danger. Now I felt as though I had been sucked into the middle of a maelstrom. I had no control over anything. All I knew was that whatever was on this memory stick was worth killing for. My hand reached to touch the stick in my belt. Why kill my father when they must have known he didn't have the stick? I was certain they knew, they seemed to know everything else, but maybe they didn't. Maybe my father acted as some sort of decoy to enable me to get away. That was the only explanation I could come up with, and I felt grateful, sad, and angry all at the same time. I doubted I would ever know the full facts.

Thoughts and memories of my father filled my mind. He was always an enigma, and I supposed he would remain so, even more now, after his death. As a child, he came and went from my life. I was always told he was busy working, and I just accepted the situation as normal. I never questioned what or why. Just enjoyed his company and made the most of the times when he appeared. He always arrived laden with presents, although his actual presence was often aloof. It struck me for the first time that in my own children's eyes, my father was an intermittent, benevolent being, who appeared from time to time to spoil them. Like many men, he was a more attentive grandfather than father. My children didn't even know where he lived, but they just accepted it as normal, as I had done as a child. I suppose they assumed he lived with Clare.

As I grew up, I knew father was involved in work for the government, something to do with security, but I wasn't that interested. His work was far less interesting to me than the latest pop band or fashion trend. The first time I 'helped' was a simple, or so I thought then, case of taking a small package to a man in rural France. I trundled off in my small car, caught the ferry and followed my father's detailed instructions to find a small hamlet and cottage. My job entailed passing the package to a man who could answer a simple riddle. It felt ludicrous, but my father's praise and rewards for a job well done made me suspect there was more to it. He swore me to secrecy about my trip to France, and I never mentioned it to anyone else.

Afterwards, I accompanied my father to an office in London, where he introduced me to a man and woman who complimented me on my good work and hoped I would continue to assist my father and work with them. Looking back, I realised I was being tested and vetted. I signed a contract, and that was when I started to work for the service. After a rigorous training period, I travelled to all parts of the world, often carrying out surveillance and reporting back to contacts, either in the country I was in or back to people in London. On very rare occasions I went to the headquarters, but more often I gave my reports to people in obscure locations and sometimes to my father. I loved my role and do not remember feeling in danger, and always felt a buzz knowing I was doing something secret.

As far as spying or surveillance went, I became a sleeper after we married and even more so after having the children. I knew having a family made me more of a security risk. Even the mundane jobs became fewer. Even father seemed less active. He was around a lot more and I presumed he was working towards retirement. We never discussed our roles. Then one day he said there might be another task he would like me to carry out. He wasn't sure when, but he would come and collect me, if the time came. He said it would be a simple collection and delivery task. Was he tense and more secretive? Did he hint at the possibility of it being risky, but at the same time assuring me that if I followed his instructions, there should be no problem? Was that the case? I closed my eyes and tried to remember everything he'd said. Did I think it was different or was I using the benefit of hindsight? Whatever, by the time the holiday came round, and nothing had happened, I'd put it out of my mind. I thought it must have been called off. Then on the second, or was it third, day of our holiday, he rang.

Sitting on the plane, I again tortured myself with the fact that if I hadn't gone off on a wild goose chase, lured by information about my mother, my father would still be alive, and I would already be back with the family. I gave a spontaneous sob, pushing my fingers in my mouth to stop others following, but I couldn't stop the tears from cascading down my cheeks.

'Don't worry, it's just a bit of turbulence. It shouldn't last long. Is it your first time?'

I looked at the rather frail elderly lady sitting next to me and gave a strained smile.

'I've never been a good flyer.'

She patted my hand and offered me a boiled sweet.

'Never mind dear, we'll be there soon. I always find sucking one of these helps when it gets bumpy.'

I gave in to floods of tears and the lady took my hand in hers and kept it there until we landed. She was wise enough not to question me but must have known that my reaction was over the top, even for someone terrified of flying; which I wasn't.

Chapter Twenty-Five

It was raining, one of those grey, dull days that suck the colour and warmth from the air. All I wanted was to go home, forget about everything that had happened; after all, it was nothing to do with me. As I tried to convince myself, my thoughts once again became negative and maudlin. I was just doing my father a favour, acting as the courier. I realised it was the same excuse used by women who were drug mules, and who often ended up in prison, sometimes in unsavoury jails in some godforsaken country for years on end. The thought made me shiver. I put my hand to my waist and felt the stick through the thin fabric of my jacket. I just needed to hand it over, and then I could go back to normal life.

Padstow was my destination. A pleasant place, but a strange choice for a rendezvous. Why not Bristol or Manchester, or at least somewhere nearer to an airport, so I didn't have to drive for miles? But Padstow it was. That was, I suspected, the precise reason why it had been chosen. I had never been to Bristol airport before and was surprised to find that it seemed to be in the middle of nowhere. There wasn't a railway station, and I felt certain that there would be no public transport heading to Cornwall. After I studied a map on the wall, I decided there was no point going into Bristol, I would have to hire a car from the airport and drive myself.

The journey down the M5 was terrible, slow traffic and blinding spray being kicked up from every passing vehicle. Feeling tired and weak, I persevered, and tempting as it was, I didn't stop. My focus was on getting there and getting the job done. In a day or two, at the most, I would be back in the villa in Italy. How often had I told myself that recently? At last, I arrived at the hotel, stiff, tired and fed up. As a tiny consolation, the sun broke through the grey clouds just as I turned into the car park, to shimmer on the incoming tide in the estuary. It looked beautiful and moody, but the stiff sea breeze made it chilly, and I realised that my clothes, ideal in Italy, were unsuitable for the unpredictable Cornish weather.

The hotel reception was empty, but I could see through large open doors, people enjoying cream teas in a pleasant sitting room overlooking the town and harbour. A young girl appeared when I reached the desk and confirmed my reservation. I wondered who had made it, and doubted it was Giuseppe, maybe Julia, but didn't really care. I was just relieved there were no complications.

'Is there anywhere locally where I can buy a coat? I stupidly forgot to put mine in the car.'

The girl behind the reception desk looked incredulous that anyone could go anywhere without a coat, but she composed herself and her face broke into a kind friendly smile.

'Oh yes, there are loads of good shops down in the town. Most will be open for at least another hour,' she said, and glanced at her watch as she handed me my key.

'You're on the first floor, with a nice sea view. Shall I have your bags brought up?'

'No, I can manage, thanks. I'm travelling light,' I lifted my one small bag, and she lifted her eyebrows, giving me a look that I chose not to interpret.

Once in the room I looked at the big bed and felt tempted to throw myself onto it and stay there for several hours. However, the dimming of the light outside, as the sun again disappeared behind clouds and threatened more rain, made up my mind. I needed suitable clothes and needed to hurry before the shops closed.

I spent a very enjoyable hour dipping in and out of the many shops, buying jeans, flat shoes, a jumper and the essential waterproof coat. Necessity and the proximity of closing time made me more focused than on a normal shopping trip. Usually, I liked to linger and try on all the options before making a purchase, but being decisive made a pleasant change. Feeling pleased with myself, I hurried back to the hotel and the welcoming bed. The receptionist nodded and smiled when I walked in loaded with bags.

'Successful shop by the look of it. Did you find all you need?'

I nodded and smiled but didn't linger to chat. Once back in my room, I dropped the bags on the floor and flopped onto the bed. I mulled over how and when I would be contacted, but before I could feel anxious, I fell into a deep, dreamless sleep.

When I awoke, it was dark outside, and I felt hungry. I freshened up and went downstairs. I peeped into the restaurant; it was busy with couples and chattering small groups of middle-aged people. The food looked and smelt delicious, but I felt that, as a lone female diner, I would draw too much attention to myself in this traditional dining room. Instead, I walked down to the harbour and chose to have fish and chips sitting on the quayside. They were divine; maybe the best fish and chips I had ever eaten, and my spirits rose as I devoured them with an appetite I hadn't felt for many days. I whiled away some time people-watching, again pondering about who might be my contact and how they might approach me. None of the people strolling around the harbour looked likely candidates. They were mostly older couples or young families. No one paid me the slightest attention, for which I was grateful.

I wondered as I walked back into the hotel reception whether there would be a message for me.

There wasn't.

Maybe someone would have slipped a note under my door while I was out.

They hadn't.

I sighed and hoped something would happen soon. The last thing I wanted was to be hanging around for days. I didn't even know how long the hotel was booked for and didn't want to ask the receptionist. Undressed and ready for bed with my mouth full of toothpaste, the phone in the room rang. I spat it out, dribbling toothpaste down my nightdress and rushed for the phone.

'Telephone call for you,' the receptionist said, rather stating the obvious, I thought. 'I'll put the caller through.'

I wondered if this was a secure way of contacting me as I heard the click. What if the receptionist was listening? What if she was a stooge? I knew it wasn't likely and I was overthinking the risk.

'Walk out to Stepper Point tomorrow. I'll see you by the Daymark tower at midday.'

'How will I know you?'

'Don't worry, I'll know you.'

The phone went dead. I sat on the bed, going over the instructions. Stepper Point and the Daymark tower. I had no idea where they were, but presumed they must be local landmarks. A folder on the small coffee table caught my eye; I picked it up and was relieved to see it was full of useful tourist information, including a map of the town and coastal paths. Stepper Point was marked as the promontory at the end of the estuary. The Daymark Tower wasn't shown, but I assumed it would be obvious once I reached the headland. It was almost over; midday tomorrow couldn't come soon enough.

I woke up late the following morning and just made it down to the dining room before breakfast service ended.

'How long does it take to walk out to the headland, to Stepper Point?' I asked a young waiter, as he poured me yet another cup of coffee.

'Depends how fast you walk,' he looked me up and down. 'About an hour, I would guess.'

'Thanks. Is the Daymark tower obvious when you get there?'

He nodded. 'You can't miss it,' he said, and started clearing away my empty plate the moment I put my knife and fork down, eager to be rid of the last breakfast customer and not interested in why I needed to know. I looked at my watch: ten thirty. Now I needed to get going. I didn't want to be late and didn't want to rush.

It was a beautiful sunny, if windy, day, and I was glad of my new jumper and coat. I felt the sea breeze sweep down the estuary as soon as I left the shelter of the harbour behind me and strode out onto the coastal path. It was an invigorating walk. The well-trodden path skirted the top of the beach for a while before heading up past some cottages onto the cliff top. I thought it would be a good place to come back to, in more relaxing times.

The number of people on the path thinned the further I went. Most stopped at the long sandy beach, where dogs and children ran around letting off steam. I would have liked a dog to be trotting along beside me. Somehow a dog gives legitimacy to a single person on a walk, but it was more because it would be company. I was feeling lonely and longed for uncomplicated company and mused for a while on the type of dog that would appeal to me. Perhaps a small spaniel like the one chasing after a ball on the beach, running back with it in his mouth and dropping at his owner's feet then jumping up and down waiting for it to be thrown again, or maybe a Labrador, walking contentedly by my side. I smiled at the thought; maybe it would be an option when I returned home.

I carried on along the path and turned at the headland, pausing to admire the rugged beauty of the coast. Once I passed the coastguard lookout station I could see the Daymark tower ahead of me. The waiter was right, you couldn't miss it. The white horses on the open sea were rushing towards the cliffs and crashing with a roar at the base. I took in deep breaths of the clear air and allowed myself to be entranced by the view, before turning towards the Daymark and my final rendezvous. There were several people looking around, taking photographs and admiring the scenery. None of them looked like my man, but it was still not quite midday. I found a position close, but not too close to the Daymark, where I could sit and lean against the low stone wall to wait. I would see anyone approaching from any direction before they saw me.

Several people came and went, walking in both directions, most were couples either out for a bracing stroll, or more serious booted walkers with rucksacks and sticks intent on taming the coastal path. One such couple sat down near to my vantage point, and I envied them their picnic of Cornish pasties and crunchy apples, and even more envied them their bottles of water. My stomach gave an involuntary gurgle. I was ridiculously unprepared. The couple got to their feet and, with a nod and smile in my direction, strode off in the opposite direction. For a few moments I was alone, with only the crying gulls swooping around the Daymark Tower on the fresh sea breeze. I got to my feet and walked slowly around the tower, checking in the small, empty interior to make sure 'he' wasn't waiting there. He wasn't.

I looked at my watch, and was surprised when it showed ten past one, over an hour late for our rendezvous. I touched the zipped pocket on my belt that contained the memory stick. Not for the first time, an overwhelming temptation to get rid of it took hold. I was so tempted to throw it as hard as I could over the edge of the cliff onto the rocks and crashing waves below, but I didn't. I dithered for a few more minutes, looking around to make certain no one was looking for me. Satisfied I was alone, I walked back along the path towards the harbour. I studied everyone who passed me. There were no single men walking along the path, and no one in the couples or small groups looked likely candidates. One of the coastguard cottages above a small cove was serving tea and cakes in the back garden. A thriving small enterprise meeting the needs of weary walkers like me. I demolished a slice of homemade lemon drizzle cake and drank three cups of tea before setting off again. I felt a little better after my rest and nourishment, although my nerves were close to jangling whenever I considered my position. There was only so much I could take, and I was very close to that point.

The thought struck me that if this man didn't show up, it must mean someone had intercepted him. Once again, I could be in danger. Beads of sweat formed on my brow, despite the chill wind. Since the killing of my father, everything had changed, taken a sinister turn, or maybe it was always sinister, and I was just unaware. What if this other man was dead? That must mean it was my turn next. Something was wrong, very wrong. Trembling now from head to foot, I leant over and put my hands on my knees and tried to control my breathing. Someone touched my back. I jumped out of my skin and only just stopped myself from screaming. I turned, my heart beating so hard it almost hurt. It was a young man. A wave of relief swept over me. He must be my contact, but before I could say anything he spoke.

'Sorry, are you ok? I didn't mean to startle you. I was just trying to get past.'

He wasn't much more than a boy, dressed in singlet and shorts and as I stepped aside, he muttered 'thank you' and edged past me on the narrow path to continue his run. Sweat was now trickling down the back of my neck. I took some deep breaths to calm myself and continued walking, keeping a wary eye over my shoulder. I would have to contact Julia, or Geoffrey, somehow. Although I didn't have a number for them, as my father was always my emergency contact, I was certain that I must have an alternative number somewhere. I just couldn't think where.

Frustration and anger welled as I realised that the only person involved in this escapade who didn't have a clear idea about what was going on, was me. Even Giuseppe, who told me that he only knew his part of the mission, seemed better informed. The knowledge that I wasn't on my own, even though that was how it felt at that precise moment, calmed me a little. Perhaps Giuseppe would make another of his miraculous appearances. The idea didn't seem too far-fetched. Or did it? Was it wishful thinking? I made it back to the hotel with no mishaps and had a brainwave as I walked into reception.

'Hi, I received a call in my room last night and like an idiot I forgot to write down the number. I don't suppose there's any way you can find it for me?'

It was the same girl on reception. She smiled at my request, but I could tell from the vague look on her face I was asking too much.

'Just a minute, I'll ask the manager.' She disappeared into the small office behind the reception desk, and I could hear the murmur of voices. She came out, still smiling but shaking her head.

'I'm very sorry. The manager says our system isn't sophisticated enough to recall anything but the last incoming number.'

'OK, never mind, thanks for trying.'

'My pleasure.' She gave me an odd look and then turned her smile towards the next person, a single man, who was waiting for her attention.

I slowed down, just in case he was my man. After only a couple of seconds, I reached the conclusion that he wasn't. He was fussing about where he had parked his car and whether it would be safe in the middle of the car park rather than next to the wall. The receptionist noticed me loitering and threw an almost imperceptible look of disbelief in my direction when she realised I was eavesdropping on the man's chuntering. I grinned at her and made my way to the stairs.

My momentary feeling of calm dissolved on the way upstairs and as soon as I was in my room, I sat on the bed and sobbed, once again feeling alone and anxious. I wasn't prone to feeling sorry for myself, or feeling out of control, but now I felt both. It was a sensation I hated. All I wanted was to return to my family and try to resume normal life.

Chapter Twenty-Six

'I think this may be your caller,' the receptionist's voice was music to my ears as she put the call through.

'So sorry I didn't make it. There was a pileup on the motorway; I was stuck for hours; I've only just got through now.'

Relief flooded through me. Nothing as simple as a delay on the road had even crossed my mind. I tried to sound cool and calm.

'Right, I see. No problem. What's the plan now?'

'Do you know the Camel trail?'

'I think so. I'm sure I can find it.'

'It's the old railway track, now a cycle path. There's an iron railway bridge across an inlet not far along. I'll see you there in half an hour.'

'Can I have your number, just in case there's another problem?'

'There won't be.'

The call ended, and I was left staring at the receiver. I was tired and the last thing I felt like was another walk, particularly as it was now drizzling; a low sea mist had once again swept in with the tide.

The girl at reception looked a little surprised that I was going out for another walk so soon. I double checked with her the direction of the trail and felt reassured by her directions and assurance that the bridge was not far. Part of me wanted her to know where I was going, just in case. I wondered whether she had listened in to the call, but why would she? There must be hundreds of calls coming into the hotel all the time and she did not look like she had time to sit and eavesdrop. Anyway, if she listened, she most likely would have assumed it was some sort of illicit romantic liaison. I pulled the hood up on my coat and pushed my hands deep into the pockets, put my head down and strode out past a couple of cycle hire places and the sailing club, towards the bridge. The memory stick stowed safely in my belt; this time it must be for the last time. If anything went wrong now, I would, without a doubt, throw the blasted thing away. There were very few other people around. Most were sensibly using the change in the weather as an excuse to retreat to a café or pub or spend their money in the numerous small shops.

The walk was shorter than I expected, which meant I was early, but as I approached, I could see a man standing in the middle of the bridge staring out towards the mouth of the estuary. I slowed as I reached him; he turned, smiled and held out his hand.

'Nice to meet you, Katharine.'

'Nice to meet you,' I said, which was an enormous understatement.

I nodded and smiled; his handshake was warm and firm. He wasn't quite what I expected. Not that I really knew what to expect. He was young, late twenties or early thirties maybe, with blonde shoulder length scruffy hair, under a beanie hat. Dressed in jeans and a parka type jacket, he could have passed for one of dozens of young men who made up the surfing set along this coast. That, I supposed, was the point. He blended in like a chameleon, and I wondered whether his hair was a wig. The wind, which was whistling in from the sea, made an eerie howling sound in the struts of the bridge. I found it quite unnerving and was glad when he suggested we move along to somewhere more sheltered. Once off the bridge, the path was protected in places by trees. We walked along in silence.

On impulse, I unzipped the small pocket on my belt and pulled out the memory stick. I didn't care if this wasn't protocol, I just wanted rid of it. He stopped, looked both ways along the path, then took the stick and without saying a word, put it in his inside pocket. I breathed a sigh of relief. It was done. It was no longer my responsibility.

'We were all saddened to hear of your father's death,' he said, turning to look at me.

I nodded my thanks.

'What in truth was my father doing? I mean, why was he killed? I know it must be something to do with the stick, but why? What went so wrong?' Sorry, lots of questions.'

He smiled. The sort of smile you give to a child when you are about to deny them something.

'Let's sit here for a moment.' He pointed to a bench overlooking the water, but away from the main path.

At last, the rain had stopped, and I pulled my coat down to protect myself from the wet seat.

'Your father was a very successful senior agent, as you know. I suspect he was killed because someone thought he was carrying more than the memory stick, but we can't be sure.'

I digested what he said. My suspicion was he was concealing something. I turned so that I could look straight into his eyes; he held my gaze and smiled that smile again.

'What else would he have been carrying? Couldn't they have just pickpocket him, or followed him and snatched the stick or whatever else, but to kill him? They didn't even stop to look in his pockets. I don't believe they were trying to take something from him. They set out with the intention of murdering him,' I said. My voice caught in my throat, and I swallowed hard to stop myself from crying.

He looked away and for a moment stared out across the water. He looked back at me; this time he didn't smile, just nodded his head a couple of times.

'You're right, of course. He was involved in something far more dangerous and important as well. The memory stick, although vitally important, is just the icing on the cake for us; he thought it would be a simple courier job that was why you were involved. I guess they killed him to take him out of the loop. It would have been an enormous bonus to them if they retrieved the memory stick as well.'

'What? What was he involved in?' I looked at him. His face wore a serious, undecipherable expression. 'You're not going to tell me, are you?'

'I'm sorry Katharine, I can't go into detail, but what I can tell you is your father has made the world a much safer place. His death is an enormous blow to us all, but the information he transferred on this trip, and previous trips, will make a big difference.'

'Safer, for now maybe, but new dangers seem to spring up all over the place,' I said. Still not feeling convinced by his explanation.

'That's true; we must keep going, keep one step ahead. You've done your bit as well.' He tapped an inner pocket where the memory stick was now secure in his custody.

'So has my life been at risk while I've been carrying that around, for days on end?'

He shifted his position as though reluctant to answer.

'No, I don't believe you were at risk. I don't believe anyone outside the team knew your real identity.'

'But what about the woman, Raisa, who claimed to know my mother? She knew about the stick, and she knew who I was and who my father was.'

'Yes, your father alerted us about her after you contacted him.'

'And? Who was she? How did she know who I was if my identity was secret?'

My suppressed anger started to bubble up inside me again. I needed to know more. I needed to know everything, but I knew I was only going to get very filtered information.

'We're working on it; on who she is and how she tracked you down.'

'Julia mentioned a leak in the department, so could that be it?'

He said nothing, just looked back out to sea. I wanted to

shake him. Who was he to withhold information from me? How dare he! He looked back at me. His expression was kind, friendly almost, but I knew I would never penetrate more than the surface. I looked into his eyes. I wanted to know everything, but I knew my wants would be frustrated.

'What's your name, by the way?'

'Sam.'

'Really?'

He smiled but didn't reply.

'Come on, Sam, can't you tell me what all this is about? At least tell me what was on that stick to make it so important?'

'No, I can't. It's better this way. Well, all I can tell you is that it contains very important, vital information, formulae, complicated scientific stuff.' He patted his pocket again. 'But it will take an expert to decipher it all.'

'My father told me there was only a minor risk, that it was straightforward.' My anger was melting away, and I was resorting to self-pity.

'We thought that was the case. It should have been.'

'Of course it should have been! Except I messed everything up by going to meet that Raisa woman. If I hadn't, my father wouldn't have needed to meet me, to sort out my mess. I caused my father's death,' I said, realising I must sound like a hysterical female. I felt sick with guilt.

'No, Katharine,' he put his hand on my arm and glanced in both directions. Even though there was no one in sight, he couldn't afford for me to make a scene.

'No one could anticipate what happened. That woman was under our radar, otherwise we would have warned you about her. So were the people on the boat. You uncovered a link we weren't aware of, and the details you provided about the boat are crucial in identifying them. So, that was good work. That's why we need people like you, who can think on their feet, not just follow instructions. What we don't know is how she knew about you, or more importantly, who told her where you would be.'

'Could they still be looking for me?'

'Very unlikely. Once your father was out of the picture, they would think you were no longer of interest to them, and as I said, I suspect they don't know your true identity. Your father was the big fish they were after.'

I said nothing for a moment. If they could find me in the first place, it couldn't be difficult to find out who I was. They knew a lot about me. They knew I was my father's daughter. I guessed Sam was trying to reassure me, but he must also know I wasn't stupid.

'Why kill him, that way they would never know what he knew?'

'Good question, but there's no answer to that at the moment.'

We sat in silence for many minutes. I expect it was less, but it felt longer.

'Do you think Raisa really knew my mother?'

'No, I doubt it. I think it was a ploy to draw you in.' He paused and turned towards me. 'How much *do* you know about your mother?'

His question surprised me, but when I considered it, I was even more surprised by how few facts I knew about my mother. My memories were now confused by Raisa's stories.

'Not much, when I think about it. I know she was Italian and died a couple of days after I was born, or so I thought before… Do you know more?'

He took a while to answer, just nodded his head slightly and looked as though he was weighing up what, if anything, he should tell me.

'I looked at her file before I came to meet you,' he said at last.

'Her file? What do you mean her file? Was she…?'

A slight flick of his hand made me stop. Instead of continuing our conversation we exchanged pleasantries about the weather with a couple I hadn't noticed, walking past with their small dog. Once they were well out of earshot, he continued.

'Your mother and father met when they were both working

on the same…' he hesitated. 'Working on something together. Your mother was half Italian and half Russian.'

'So, Raisa was right about that. I mean, I thought my mother was just Italian.'

'Her mother was Italian, and her father was Russian. I think she identified as Italian and was brought up in Italy. I don't know whether she had links with the Russian side of her family or not, although there is little evidence that she had any close living family connections, either there or in Italy. She was ideal, no baggage.' He paused for a moment before continuing. 'Your mother was going to stop working after your birth; it seems your father was as well. It happens, people hanker for a normal life after a while. I think they just wanted to be a family, but then, well…'

A lump formed in my throat, and I wanted to cry at the loss of the picture Sam was painting of an ideal family life. I needed to change the subject.

'Do you hanker after a normal life?'

He gave me that half smile again and shook his head.

'Not yet.'

'What else did my mother's file say? What was she involved in?' Curiosity got the better of me.

'Much as you've been doing recently, only she was full time and more, well more involved on every level, I suppose.'

I looked at Sam again; he was fiddling with something in his pocket.

'I'm no longer one of your people, by the way,' I said referring to his earlier comment. 'I only did this for my father. I told him it was the last time.'

'Your father held you in high esteem. He was confident in your abilities.'

The lump grew in my throat again. The realisation that I would never see him again felt like a stab in my chest. There was so much to ask him. So much to tell him. It wasn't fair.

'What's happened to his body? Where is it? What do I need to do?'

Another wave of guilt swept over me as I realised, I had given no thought to how I would retrieve his body or arrange his funeral.

'The Service will arrange to have his body repatriated. I'm not sure how long that will take. It shouldn't take too long. Then you can arrange his funeral.'

'My children, they'll want a funeral. I need to tell them. I need to go home.'

Tears started to sting my eyes as reality hit home. This, if it ever had been, wasn't a game anymore.

He laid his hand on my arm again.

'Perhaps you'd prefer a family service for the funeral, but I know there are a great many people who will want to pay their respects. We could arrange a memorial service for everyone to attend?'

I looked at him; he looked so young, yet he sounded as though he dealt with situations like this all the time.

'I don't know, yes, that sounds about right, a family funeral. I just don't know. Let me have time to think.'

'Of course, it must have been a horrible shock. Someone will be in touch when his body is back in the UK.'

Silence folded round us again for a few minutes while we both stared out across the estuary, which looked as grey and miserable in the sea mist as I felt.

'What now?' I asked.

'It's over, for now. Time to go back to your normal life.'

'It's over for good, as far as I'm concerned.'

He nodded, smiled that enigmatic smile again, and stood up.

'Thank you for everything Katharine,' he took my hand and pressed something into it. Before I could gather my thoughts, he was striding back along the path. He stopped and turned back, checking no one else was around, and hurried back towards me.

'Julia will be in touch for a debrief but carry on and make your plans.'

After he left, I flopped back onto the bench, forgetting to pull my coat underneath as I did so, and the damp soaked through my jeans. I shivered, not sure if it was due to the damp, or the thought of going back to my normal life, as Sam said. Fingers crossed he was right, and life would return to normal. I looked at the small disc he had given me, not much bigger than a coat button. I turned it over, wondering why he'd given me such a strange object. A talisman perhaps, or a strange souvenir of my time in espionage. As I glanced at it again the warmth of my hand was slowly changing the disc's colour; a series of numbers, barely visible, appeared. I turned the disc over and could just make out the words "in case of emergency". The numbers must be a phone number and I wondered what sort of emergency Sam had in mind. I pushed it deep into my pocket and sighed; I had no intention of being involved in any further emergencies. The sea mist was beginning to swirl ever thicker along the estuary, and droplets were dripping from my hair and run down my neck. It was time to go.

Even before I reached the hotel, my phone rang. At first, I ignored it, not realising what it was. It was the first time I'd heard it ring. It was Julia. She wanted to meet before I left. She assumed I would be flying out of Bristol tomorrow and had booked a secure room at the airport for us to discuss the recent events, as she put it. It wasn't a meeting I looked forward to, but at least it would draw a line under the whole debacle.

The debrief meeting with Julia was straightforward, professional and quite brief, almost perfunctory. I talked while she took notes and only interrupted to clarify the occasional detail. I wanted to ask more questions, but when I started, she just raised her hand and suggested I keep them for another time. She shook my hand and left, saying she would be in touch again when I returned home and felt more settled. I felt irritated and unfulfilled, but there were more important things I needed to deal with first. A couple of hours later, I was on the plane and on my way back to Italy to, with any luck, resume my family holiday. I was feeling sick with mixed emotions of anticipation and trepidation.

Chapter Twenty-Seven

At last, Katharine stopped talking and looked towards Jake. True to his word, he hadn't interrupted once, and Katharine had almost forgotten she was talking to him, as she became lost in her story. The relief at being able to offload was immense. It felt cathartic. The silence between them weighed heavily and uncomfortably and she realised Jake, not surprisingly, was not feeling the same sense of relief. Katharine didn't know what else to say or do. She had told Jake everything, as he had demanded. Information that should have stayed secret had spilled out, but what else was she to do if she wanted to win back his trust? Everything she had told him was the truth. Nothing left out. She could do no more. Now all she could do was hope that he believed her and did not reject either her story or worse still, reject her.

His silence when she stopped speaking was deafening, and she forced herself not to start up again. Not to apologise. He looked out to sea, then back at her, opened his mouth and then closed it again. He looked as drained as Katharine felt. Confusion, disbelief, and concern crossed his face. Katharine could not read his expression. At last, he spoke, but not the words that would satisfy her longing for forgiveness.

'You look tired. Why don't you go to bed?'

She looked at him, surprised, wondering why he wasn't bombarding her with questions?

'Don't you want to ask me anything?' she said.

'It's a lot to take in. I just need time to absorb everything first.' He stood up and moved to the rail, where he leant and looked out to sea, just as she had done on that evening that might now become the undoing of their marriage.

'Of course, I understand. Shall I sleep in the spare room?' A knot of anxiety tied itself into her stomach as she waited for his reply. She desperately needed to be held. Even more, she wanted him to tell her everything was all right.

'The bed's made up. Just one thing,' he said.

'Yes?'

'That disc, or button, or whatever it was, that Sam gave you. What have you done with it?'

She looked across. He was still facing away from her. She wanted to hold him, to reassure him, to promise him anything he wanted to hear, but she didn't. She knew now was not the time to plead for understanding. He didn't move.

'It's safe,' she replied, wondering why he wanted to know, and knowing her answer would not satisfy him. Katharine turned, and with a last glance at his slightly hunched back, made her way through the villa to the small guest room. At no time had Jake looked at her in any meaningful way. His eyes swept over her but did not meet hers.

The bed was not usually made up in this room and Katharine wondered if Jake had made it up himself in anticipation of this moment. The sight of the bed made her realise just how tired she was, exhausted in fact, but she was sure she would not sleep. How could she with such a big question mark hanging over her, over both their futures? She undressed, draping her clothes on a small chair and slid between the sheets. As soon as her head sank into the soft pillow, even before she could analyse the effect of her story on her husband, she fell asleep. It was a deep dreamless sleep, prompted by the subconscious knowledge that she could do no more, along with the relief of finally unburdening her mind, and knowing she was safe.

The following morning Katharine awoke late. She lay still for a few minutes listening for sounds, but apart from the distant hiss of the waves on the sand all was silent. She glanced at her watch and sat up; startled to see it was eleven o'clock. Not since she was a student, as far as she could remember, had she slept so late. Did she feel refreshed? She wasn't sure; she supposed it would depend on what lay ahead as the day unfolded. As full wakefulness returned, so did the knot of anxiety in her stomach.

She put her feet onto the cool tiled floor, and pulling on a dressing gown, padded barefoot into the main room of the villa. The balcony ran the length of this room and one quick glance around confirmed that she was alone. Where was Jake? There was no note. Nothing to indicate where he was or what was happening. Standing in the middle of the room, Katharine took a deep breath, trying hard to quell the rising feeling of panic, and then let out a sigh of relief as she heard a car door slam. Her legs refused to move, and she was standing in the same place, trembling inside, when Jake strode into the room carrying several bags of shopping.

'You're up.'

He hoisted the bags onto the kitchen counter, then turned to look at her.

Was it her imagination or was his look softer, more concerned than angry? She knew him so well, every contour of his face and body, but at that precise moment she felt as though she didn't know him at all.

'I looked in on you before I popped out, but you were out for the count. I left a note,' he nodded to the overlooked, unread scribbled words on a piece of paper on the table. 'You must have needed it, sleep, I mean. Coffee?' he held up the pot.

Katharine nodded. Feeling unable to move or speak. She just stood and watched Jake as he bustled about, making coffee, and putting the groceries away, resisting the urge to correct him when he put things in the wrong cupboard. She still wasn't certain where they were in their relationship, but she wouldn't allow herself to contemplate the worst-case scenario, that their marriage was over. Somewhere inside her a flame of optimism ignited. He wouldn't appear so relaxed or have been shopping if that was the case. Would he? His behaviour seemed normal.

'I spoke to the children earlier. They're on their way over. Should be here about five.'

'Are they all right?'

'They were delighted that you're back and are very eager to see you. They stayed with my sister last night, did I say? She's renting an apartment along the coast?'

Katharine nodded but didn't ask why.

'Am I? Back, I mean?' she ran her fingers through her hair and didn't quite catch his eye.

'Let's take this outside.' Jake handed her a mug of coffee.

As always, the smell of coffee made her feel better and she took a sip before she followed him onto the balcony. He looked tired and she wondered whether he'd slept, or even if he'd gone to bed after she'd left him the previous evening. She was about to ask, but he sat down at the small table, and without waiting for her to sit down, began to speak.

'I still have lots of unanswered questions.' He held up his hand, as Katharine was about to interrupt. So, she sat and listened rather than spoke. This was his turn to have his say.

'But I suppose those can be answered in time. I love you, Katharine, and I don't want this to come between us, but I must say it's shaken me. Made me realise there's a lot I don't understand about your life.' He turned and looked into her eyes. Her stomach flipped with relief and joy, but she felt sorrow and guilt at seeing the sad expression on his face. All she could think was everything was going to be all right. Whatever he asked or needed to know she could cope with, but at least there was a basis to build on and she knew deep down they were strong.

'I just need one thing for now and that's for you to promise that it's over. To assure me you won't disappear again in a few weeks, months or years. I don't want us to be forever looking over our shoulders, worried about being in danger from some unknown assassin.'

She reached for his hand and looked him in the eye.

'I promise,' she said, as solemnly as if taking an oath. There was only a tiny flicker of doubt concerning safety, but it was buried deep in her subconscious and that was where she planned for it to stay. All she wanted now was to step back into her rightful place with her husband and family.

Chapter Twenty-Eight

'Mum!'

The shout rang out from the taxi that had stopped close to the bottom of the steps, and with a flurry of activity the children tumbled out, grabbing bags and other teenage paraphernalia, almost falling over each other as they raced up the stairs to the balcony where their parents stood waiting.

'Mum, I've missed you. I've been so worried. Where have you been? Why didn't you call us?' Her daughter, face devoid of any make-up, threw herself into her mother's arms and she continued her torrent of questions into Katharine's shoulder.

'Good to have you back mum, not like you to do a moonlight flit.' Her eldest son just grinned at her. 'Any coffee left?' He looked at the now empty jug. Katharine reached out her hand and patted Dan's shoulder. She knew his flip remark covered his concern. Her younger son stood at the top of the steps. She looked at him over her daughter's head, and the dark circles under his eyes told her all she needed to know. She disentangled an arm and held it out; he dropped his bag and joined his sister in an embrace with their mother. Sobs racked his small body and nearly broke Katharine's heart.

'Let me look at you both.' She stood back and smiled, hopefully looking confident and reassuring. Come here, she pulled Oliver towards her and wiped his tears away with her thumbs. 'You look well,' she lied, but Oliver and Jilly's smiles told her they would soon be back to normal. 'You look so naturally beautiful without make-up.' She reached out and stroked her daughter's hair.

'Oh mum, don't start that straight away.' Jilly tossed her head and looked at her mother, who threw her head back and laughed. Yes, everything was going to be all right. Although Oliver, she realised, would need some careful handling. She needed to sit down with him and persuade him to talk. He, out of the three of them, was the one who took things to heart and often bottled up his feelings.

'Right, here we are.'

Jake put a tray on the table. Without Katharine noticing, he had refilled the coffeepot and filled a jug with juice. They all filled their mugs and glasses and started bombarding their mother with questions. Where had she been? What was she doing? Why didn't she tell them she was going to be away so long? Why didn't she ring them?

'Hey, give your mother some space, all in good time,' Jake said, as he rested an arm around Katharine's shoulders. 'All in good time. Let's put some lunch on the table first.'

Over lunch, Katharine tried to answer their questions truthfully enough for them to understand why, in their minds, she left in such a hurry, but leaving out many of the details she felt it was better for them not to know. It was difficult, and they weren't prepared to be fobbed off with what they thought was half a story.

'Wow! Was grandad a spy?'

She ruffled her younger son's hair and laughed, aware of all eyes on her.

'No, he wasn't, not really, not in the way you think of spies.' That was a bit of a white lie. 'He worked for an organisation, part of the government, who managed information.'

'Intellectual property?'

'Yes, that's right.'

She looked at her older son and was once again surprised by his knowledge. He was no longer a child, and she wondered if one day, far off in the future, she could tell him, well, all of them, the truth. She smiled at him, and he returned a knowing look. His instinct and quick mind would make him an excellent candidate for the Service, but Katharine would do everything possible to discourage him following in both hers and his grandfather's footsteps.

They were all, naturally, upset about their grandfather's death, which Katharine explained as an accident while crossing the road. They were also upset to hear that they would have to wait for his body to be returned to the UK before they could have a funeral. The questions they asked were deep and pertinent and were like those that Katharine had asked herself.

'We'll organise the ceremony together once all the legalities have been sorted out, but dying abroad can be more complicated,' Jake said, sensing that Katharine was finding this part of her story difficult to tell the children.

'Thank you,' Katharine mouthed to Jake, grateful for him stepping in at that point. She allowed herself a moment to bask in the relief that everything seemed to be all right. Despite having cupboards full of food they walked to the restaurant that evening rather than cook. Their meal was quieter than when they had last been there, the evening Katharine had left. All remembering that their grandfather was the centre of attention on that occasion. After their meal they walked back to the villa around the little bay, unaware that hidden in the trees high above them, on the hillside overlooking the bay, crouched a person with binoculars trained on their every move.

The family spent the last couple of days of their holiday relaxing and trying to get back to normal. The children swam and sailed, but they were quieter than before. Jilly and Oliver didn't like to be far from their mother for too long; 'Where's mum?' being a frequent question.

On the surface, Katharine felt that everything with Jake was as it should be, although she was aware that he was treating her with caution; he was being just too polite, which made her feel nervous, or was she being oversensitive? Her emotions appeared to be highly charged and at times a little erratic, causing her to over analyse every look and word. On their last day, she sensed a subtle change and Jake suggested that he and the two boys should spend the day taking the dinghy around the headland. They would not be back in time for lunch, but he suggested another family meal out that evening. They busied themselves with the rigging and pulling on life jackets and were about to push the boat out into the calm blue sea, when Jake ran back up the beach and gave Katharine a quick hug and peck on the cheek. For the first time since her return, she felt as though the old Jake might be breaking through. She watched as the dinghy bobbed across the sea towards a slight ripple on the water that indicated a light breeze, which once they reached it, filled the sails.

'Take care, have fun,' she waved them off, and then turned to Jilly.

'Anything particular you would like to do?'

'Not really. It's nice to just be the two of us for once.'

Katharine nodded. She had spent time alone with Oliver and felt he was more or less back to normal. Now Jilly was the one that concerned her most. She wasn't her usual chatty self, and since Katharine's return hadn't bothered with make-up or her appearance, not that she found that a problem. It was just out of character. They swam, then lay under the parasol on the beach, Katharine reading her book and Jilly flicking distractedly through a magazine.

'Mum?' she looked up from the magazine.

'Yes darling,' Katharine waited, and hoped that whatever Jilly asked she could answer honestly.

'Why did you live with Aunt Clare?'

Katharine was taken aback; it wasn't a question she was expecting. Clare didn't figure in any of Katharine's explanations to the children.

'Well, because my mother died when I was born, I must have told you that before, haven't I?'

'Yes, but why didn't you live with your grandparents, or why didn't granddad look after you?'

Katharine wasn't certain where this line of questioning was taking them but carried on. Something was worrying Jilly.

'I didn't have any grandparents still alive, and my father was working, so it was sensible for me to live with Aunt Clare. Your Grandfather used to visit as often as he could. We had some lovely times together, and I loved living with Aunt Clare.'

'I would hate that. I mean, not seeing you and dad all the time. It was horrible last week without you. I thought you might not come back. I thought you'd left. Then dad sent us to Aunt Lucy's for a few days. She's nice, but I hated it.' And with that, Jilly burst into tears.

'Oh darling, come here,' Katharine sprang to her feet and scooped Jilly into her arms. They both fell backwards onto a lounger, but Katharine held on to her daughter, rocking her in her arms. Jilly snuffled on her mother's shoulder.

'You silly thing, I was always going to come back. I just couldn't tell you where I was going and because of a few hitches, everything took longer than planned.'

'Why couldn't you tell us? We wouldn't have told anyone,' Jilly spluttered out between sobs.

'I know you wouldn't, but it was just the way it was. I wasn't allowed to tell anyone, not even daddy, but I was always going to come back.'

'Granddad didn't come back, did he?' Jilly pushed back from her mother's embrace and looked into her eyes.

'No, he didn't, and that is very sad, but he died in an unfortunate accident. It could have happened anywhere, and I was never in any danger.' Once again, Katharine felt another little white lie at this stage was justified.

'Was Granddad being chased or something, when he ran across the road and got killed? He was always so careful, he always made us look both ways.'

Katharine's explanation of her father's death, for the children, was just a vague story of him being killed crossing the road. Jilly's imagination had constructed a scene where he was running for his life. Katharine thought for a moment before replying.

'No, he wasn't being chased. He was just distracted for a minute. You know how careful you must be crossing the roads in Italy.'

Jilly nodded,

'I'll miss him,' she said, as she wiped her eyes and gave her mother a watery smile.

'Yes, I know. We'll all miss him. We'll do something special to remember him when we get home.'

After a few minutes sitting in silence together, Jilly turned to her mother.

'Would you like a peach?'

'That would be nice.'

Katharine watched as Jilly jumped to her feet and ran up the beach to the villa to collect some peaches from the bowl. She sensed her daughter was beginning to put her vivid imaginings to the back of her mind and move on, but it was yet another stark reminder of how much damage she had caused. She shuddered to think how they would have coped if something dreadful had happened to her as well as to her father.

For the first time, Katharine wondered about her own mother's death. She grew up believing her mother died due to a complication in childbirth, because of inadequate treatment. Thinking about it now, she realised that no one ever said that was what happened; all she was told was that her mother died when she was born, and Katharine had filled in the blanks and never questioned anyone further. When she was born did not have to mean during childbirth. She must have been a child who lacked curiosity, not like her own children. Yet now she wondered if her assumptions were correct. Had she not just told her own children a half-truth about their grandfather's death? What if she only knew half the story about her mother? She decided, as she watched Jilly skip back down the beach, that she would ask Clare for more information when they next met.

Later in the afternoon, Katharine spotted the white sails of the dinghy, rounding the small headland and sailing across the bay towards the beach.

'I'm going to swim out to meet them,' Jilly said, and was already running towards the water, waving madly at the boys on the boat. 'Why don't you come, mum?' she called.

'I don't want to get my hair wet,' Katharine said, using an excuse she knew Jilly would understand. She watched Jilly, now a strong swimmer, cut through the calm sea towards them, and within minutes she was bobbing beside the boat. Jake reached into the water and heaved her on board. Katharine smiled to herself, watching as her family crossed the water towards her. For the first time in many days, she felt at peace. The boat soon reached the beach and they all started talking at once telling her how fantastic their day had been. The wind was stronger once they left the shelter of the bay and both boys felt their sailing skills, although tested, were a match for the conditions. Jake beamed proudly at his boys, confirming that they were becoming excellent sailors.

'Right, let's get the boat up the beach, then showers and dinner.' He planted a kiss on Katharine's head before going to help the boys get the boat onto the launching trolley.

'Don't forget to pack. We're going home tomorrow.' For once, this comment wasn't met with the usual end of holiday groans. Katharine felt they would all be happy to be back home, to feel grounded.

Katharine was ready first and poured herself a drink to enjoy on the balcony, while she waited for the others. Dan was ready next and sat himself next to his mother. He checked that his brother and sister were nowhere to be seen and turned to his mother.

'Mum, what really happened to Granddad? He wasn't run over, was he?'

Yet again, Katharine was surprised by her eldest son's perception.

'I know it's easier for the other two to think that, but I'm not a child any longer and I could tell you were holding something back.'

'Am I that transparent?'

'Afraid so,' he leant forward with his hands on his knees, looking at Katharine and waiting.

'No, he wasn't run over. It's true he was killed crossing the road, but someone coming towards him stabbed him in the chest. It was instant.' Katharine looked at her son, trying to gauge his reaction.

'I'm presuming it wasn't just a mugging?'

'No, it wasn't. I don't know who it was, but he must have thought your grandfather was carrying something significant.'

'Was he?'

'No, he wasn't, but I guess there was no way they would have known that.'

'Wow, it's a lot to take in, all this subterfuge. What about…'

Katharine held up her hand to stop him.

'I can't tell you anymore, so please don't ask, and please say nothing about this to Jilly and Oliver. Let them believe it was a car accident.'

'No, of course I won't. Is it over now mum? I mean, are you safe?'

'Yes, I was never in any danger,' she repeated her white lie, but wasn't sure whether Dan accepted it as easily as Jilly. 'We'll soon be home, and life will be back to normal, so there's nothing to worry about.'

'Except exams,' Dan screwed up his nose, and Katharine was relieved that the conversation about her father seemed to be over.

'Let's make the most of our last evening. There'll plenty of time to think about exams when you get back to school.'

Dan groaned, stood up and went to search out the others, only pausing to toss the words, I love you mum, over his shoulder as he left the balcony.

Tears pricked Katharine's eyes as she watched him.

Chapter Twenty-Nine

'I think I'll go over to my father's apartment today,' Katharine said, fiddling with her butter knife. They had been home from holiday for just a day, but there were things she needed to do. Things that could not wait.

'Really? I didn't think he ever used it. Didn't he always stay with your aunt when he was in this country?' The realisation that he didn't know any detail about his father-in-law's life had been slowly dawning on Jake since Katharine's return with the news of his death. If he was honest, the whole affair had left him rather stunned and wondering what else he was in the dark about.

'He did, most of the time, but I think I need to go to the apartment. Just to check if there's anything personal or that type of thing, which I need to remove.'

Jake looked at her but said nothing.

Katharine continued, 'It was more of an office for him, but it all needs sorting. Anyway, I suppose I'll have to decide what to do with it in time.' She laid her knife down on the plate and gathered the breakfast paraphernalia together, ready to load in the dishwasher.

'Would you like me to come with you?' Jake folded the sheet of paper he'd been studying and pushed it back into an envelope. 'You might need a hand.'

Katharine looked at him, and her heart gave a very tiny leap. she would welcome his company; it wasn't a long drive, but the car would be a good place to talk. They had not talked in detail since the night she returned and although, outwardly, everything was normal between them, she still felt there was an underlying narrow thread of tension. It was easy in the hustle and bustle of daily life to ignore it, to pretend, but she felt they were just being a bit too careful around each other in a way they weren't before. Maybe she was imagining it; maybe he was just treating her more gently, assuming she was grieving. He was right, of course. She was grieving, but it felt more than that. Her emotions seemed bottled up for now, and she didn't feel able to open the floodgates. Not until she was certain everything between them was back to the easy trust, they had had before. Would they ever reach that stage again she wondered? She glanced at Jake and understood why he must feel wary but wasn't sure what else she could do.

'Yes, that would be great, if you can spare the time.'

'Of course I can, besides it's not something I like to think of you doing alone. I want to help.'

'Thanks, hopefully it won't take too long,' she said, smiling and reached out her hand. He took it in his.

'We're in this together, you know. You've been through a hell of a time and I'm here for you.'

'Thank you,' Katharine said, and squeezed his hand. As she did, tears cascaded down her cheeks and she gave in to big rasping sobs. Jake stood up and pulled her into his arms, making soothing noises and stroking her hair. They stood wrapped in each other's arms for what felt like a long time, until Katharine's breathing settled back down to normal.

'OK?' Jake pushed Katharine gently back and reached into his pocket for a tissue to dry her eyes.

'Yes, I'm fine. Thank you. I think I needed that!' she smiled and blew her nose. They'd taken a huge step forward and the relief almost started her crying again. Instead, she took a deep breath,

'Right, let me get organised.'

Jake smiled,

'Ever practical, but it's good to let go sometimes. Now then, do we need to take anything, boxes that sort of thing?'

'No, I'm not going to clear everything out today. Just look around and pick up a few personal items. We'll need a van later and then think about selling it at some time, but not today.' Katharine's main reason for going was to check that her father had left nothing important lying around. She didn't know what that might be, papers, his computer, that sort of thing. He was too careful to leave anything significant accessible, she felt certain, but she needed to satisfy herself, and remove it to safety.

'There's quite a good pub nearby. Perhaps we can have lunch there.'

'Sounds good to me. You ready? I'll get the car.'

Katharine nodded and picking up her coat and bag, set off feeling more positive than she had for many days. They listened to the radio in the car, discussing and debating aspects of the news, just as always. They held the same views on most topics, but there was a healthy margin of difference. A comedy programme had them both laughing out loud, and for the last ten minutes, they listened to music in companionable silence. They decided to go to the apartment first and then have a late lunch after they'd sorted everything, or at least decided what to do with everything.

They pulled into the parking space outside the building designated for her father's apartment. The apartment was in an old, converted mansion building.

'Nice place,' Jake said. He couldn't remember visiting his father-in-law here before. He knew he had a place in London but that was all. It was never really discussed as anywhere significant.

'Shouldn't his car be here or is it at an airport somewhere?' he asked as they climbed out. Katharine looked around as if almost expecting to see her father's car parked somewhere else in the car park.

'I don't know, the airport possibly. I never gave it a thought, but he always took a taxi to the airport. I'll have to try to find out.'

'There might be something inside to indicate where it is.'

Katharine nodded; she said nothing but thought it was doubtful. She entered the code and opened the door into the lobby area of the apartment block. The concierge, whose name she could not remember, got to his feet as they entered.

'Good morning.' Jake nodded and moved towards the lift.

'Good morning,' the concierge replied, looking at Katharine. 'I'm so sorry for your loss. Your father was a lovely man, a real gentleman.'

'Thank you.' Katharine answered automatically and was about to follow Jake to the lift but stopped dead in her tracks. The lift arrived, the doors opened and closed before she moved. Then she turned back to the concierge.

'How did you know about his death?' she stared at him, then took a step towards him.

'I'm very sorry. I didn't mean to speak out of turn. It was, well…'

'No, I'm sorry, I didn't mean to be rude, it's just that I'm surprised you knew.' Jake was back by her side, wondering what was keeping her.

'Danny,' Katharine said, looking at the concierge's name badge. 'Was offering his condolences.'

'How on earth…?'

'Mr Michelson's sister was here yesterday,' Danny interrupted. 'Very upset she was. Loaded down with boxes, I helped her up to the apartment and let her in, when she couldn't get her key out of her bag. She said you would probably be here in a day or two. I didn't realise he had two sisters, but she said she lived abroad.' Danny looked from Katharine to Jake and back again, taking in their look of confusion, as they looked at him, and each other.

'Oh, my God! Quick, let's get up there,' Katharine almost ran to the lift, followed by Jake, leaving a gawping Danny behind.

'I hope that was ok?' Danny called as the lift door shut. He'd been told never to let people in unless instructed by the owner, but Mr Michelson's sister was so distraught, and he was shocked and taken off his guard when he heard about Mr Michelson's death. He'd said goodbye to him only about two weeks ago and he seemed in fine health. Danny remembered meeting a lady who was Mr Michelson's sister a while ago, but to be honest, the gentleman was away more than he was here and was rarely visited by anyone. He knew Katharine, his daughter, of course, and there was another man who often came in with him, but he didn't seem to socialise much. This lady, who said she was his sister, was a lovely lady, so why would she say she was his sister if she wasn't? He sat back at his desk and mused that maybe there were valuables in the flat and the sister wanted to get in first to claim them. He knew from experience that death could cause family fights. Not that his family had anything worth fighting over, but even so he and his sister nearly fell out when their mother died.

'When did you tell Clare?' Jake asked as soon as they were in the lift. 'I'm surprised she didn't tell you she was coming up.'

'I haven't told her, at least, not told her in so many words. I rang her, and she sensed it was bad news, so she asked me not to say anything on the phone, but to go and see her as soon as I could.'

The lift seemed to be interminably slow, and Katharine felt a growing sense of agitation. As soon as the doors slid open, she pushed past Jake and ran along the corridor to her father's apartment.

'That's what's worrying me,' she said. 'I've got an inkling who it was, and it wasn't Clare.'

As she feared, the door was unlocked; she pushed it open and stopped.

'Jesus Christ! What the...' Jake looked over her shoulder. 'I'll call the police.'

'No, wait. Let's just look around first.' Katharine walked into the large airy apartment and surveyed the scene; every cupboard and drawer was open, furniture moved, and a rug pulled up. She walked from room to room, feeling lightheaded and sick. There was no doubt in her mind who was responsible.

'Don't touch anything,' she snapped at Jake, as he was about to pick up some papers on the floor.

'That idiot downstairs let a burglar in, without even checking who they were. Typical, a few tears and a sob story and in she comes.'

'This wasn't a normal burglary; how would a burglar know my father was dead? I wonder what I should do?'

The question was almost rhetorical and hung in the air for a moment. Then she remembered Sam's disc. She scrabbled around in her bag; she was certain it was in there.

'What are you doing? Don't we just need to call the police?' Jake watched as Katharine emptied the contents of her bag onto the table.

'Sam's disc, it's got to be here, somewhere.' She unzipped an inner pocket and let out a sigh of relief. Holding the disc in her hand, the warmth once again revealed the numbers. She picked up her phone and tapped in the numbers. Someone answered almost immediately, as though they were waiting for her to call.

'Hello, this is Katharine Carmichael, my father was…'

'Hello Katharine, it's ok I know who you are.' A woman's calming voice broke in. 'Sam's on his way up.'

Almost before she could register the woman's words, the entry phone rang and within minutes Sam and another man were in the apartment. Sam looked very different. His neatly cut hair and smart black jeans with a blue shirt and casual jacket were a long way from the surf bum look he had sported when they first met.

'How did you…? What's going on…?'

'We've been monitoring this place since your father's death. We thought something like this might happen. I came over yesterday after I saw the woman entering and leaving.

Made quite a mess, didn't she? This is Doug, by the way.'

'How did you know she was coming to this apartment?' Jake asked.

Sam pointed to an angle poise lamp high on a bookshelf. 'Surveillance camera,' he said.

'Why didn't you stop her or call the police? They could have caught her red- handed,' Jake said.

'It's not quite that straightforward, but don't worry, we're on to it.'

Jake took himself off and sat on a chair near the window. He felt out of his depth. This wasn't his world; he would sit there out of the way and just observe. He looked at Katharine, and she nodded and smiled as he sat down.

'Is this your woman from Italy?' Sam showed Katharine an image of a woman entering the apartment.

'No, I don't recognise her.'

'I didn't think it would be her, but we've got a tail on this woman, so hopefully we'll soon know who they all are.'

'It's all intact.' The other man, Doug, who had been carrying a black case, called from the second bedroom, and Sam and Katharine went to see what he'd found. Even Jake, his resolve to just watch forgotten, got up and followed to see what the excitement was about.

A cupboard had been pulled away and was standing at right angles to the wall. Behind was concealed an area not much bigger than a large wardrobe, in which there was a small desk with a computer and all sorts of other electrical equipment, the likes of which Jake had never seen before. Neither had Katharine for that matter.

'What on earth…?' Jake tried to push past Doug to take a better look. He knew a bit about computer equipment, but this was not like anything he had come across before. Doug looked at Sam, who nodded, and he stood aside. Jake stared hard at all the equipment, but when he reached out to touch something, Sam laid a hand on his arm to stop him.

'Sorry, just intrigued. That's quite a setup.'

'That's ok, you probably can't do any harm. All the data's encrypted, but just in case.'

Jake nodded. He wasn't interested in the data, but his fingers itched to check out the connections and find out how all this state-of-the-art equipment worked.

'Did you know all this was here?' He looked at Katharine, who shook her head.

'Fascinating,' was all she said.

'Download it all, then we can disconnect and remove everything,' Sam instructed Doug, who was already slipping into the small seat that pulled out from under the shelf and was logging into the computer.

He turned to Sam.

'Do we know if the laptop's still here?'

'Doesn't look like it. The rug's been disturbed, so I guess they found it.'

'I don't think my father had a laptop with him in Italy,' Katharine said. She couldn't remember seeing one, but then he would have had a less obvious, smaller device, with him.

'No, he wouldn't have.' Sam smiled at her and walked back into the sitting room to examine the area of disturbance and pulled the rug back.

Katharine and Jake leant over his shoulder as he pressed on a floorboard and flipped it back, exposing a small metal container.

'What the...? How many more secret hiding places are there in this apartment?' Jake stared into the empty container.

'That's good, it's gone.' Sam lifted the box out from under the floor and pushed the floorboard back into place. 'It's gone,' he called through to Doug.

'Good. I'll just be a few more minutes here.'

'Why is it good? If they've taken his laptop, that can't be good. Can it?' Jake said.

Katharine smiled; she was beginning to understand.

'It was a dummy, wasn't it?'

'That's right. Although, it will take them a long time to

realise that. It was full of encrypted data that will keep a decoder busy for quite some time. Some of it is just authentic enough to keep their interest, but most of it is just complete nonsense.'

'So why hide it, if you wanted them to take it?' Jake, even as he spoke, was figuring it out. 'If it's hidden and they find it, it seems even more real. Is that it?'

'Exactly. This sort of place.' He tapped the floor with his toe, 'is an old-fashioned sort of hiding place, but once the woman found it, I doubt she even bothered to look anywhere else. Even if she thought there was something else, she would not have been able to move the cupboard on her own.'

'Clever. She thought she'd hit the jackpot, but in fact she'd got the booby prize.' Jake was beginning to enjoy the intrigue.

'What are your plans for the place?' Sam turned to Katharine, who had picked up a photograph of her mother from a side table.

'Remove all the personal bits and pieces today and then eventually sell it, I suppose.' She looked at Jake.

He shrugged. 'It's up to you. I can't imagine we would want to keep it.'

'Well, it's possible we'd be interested in buying it. Can I let you know in a day or two, before you put it on the market?'

'Of course, that makes sense. I won't be doing anything about it in a hurry. There's probate and all that to do first.'

'Isn't the place compromised now?' Jake asked, wondering but not liking to ask who the 'we' that might be interested were.

'No, not really. It could still be useful.' Sam looked around approvingly. 'It's a good size, but don't let me stop you doing what you came to do. We'll be out of your hair in a few minutes anyway.'

Katharine went into her father's bedroom and started looking through his clothes and books. A few small items and some of her father's private papers she picked out and put into a pile. She was surprised to find how little he kept that wasn't functional and wondered where he stored photographs and other mementos; she couldn't believe he didn't have any.

'Is that all you want for now?' Jake looked at the small stash Katharine had gathered.

'It's all that I can find. I expect there's more, but I guess he must have kept most of his personal items at Clare's. We need to go and tell her as soon as possible.' Katharine turned to Jake, who nodded his agreement.

'Whatever you think best.'

'I think we should go straight away. She needs to know. It shouldn't take us more than a couple of hours to get to Gloucestershire at this time of day. I'll ring her on the way.'

Sam and Doug left at the same time. Jake helping them to carry the equipment they had disconnected, a big haul compared to Katharine's small bag of mementos. She was in no hurry to clear out the other contents from her father's apartment. The remaining items and furniture would not interest anyone now.

Before they all got into their respective cars, Sam took Katharine to one side.

'Are you OK?'

'Yes, I think so, thanks.'

'I think Julia will be in touch soon about your father's body. A lot of people in the Service would like to pay their respects.'

Katharine nodded. 'Of course, but I need to speak to my aunt, my father's sister, before I make any arrangements.'

'I understand. Well, goodbye for now.' He shook both Katharine's and Jake's hands and climbed into a car next to Doug and was gone.

Chapter Thirty

At last, after a slow drive down the M4, Jake turned the car into a narrow, no through road and drove along to the end, grumbling as he avoided the many potholes. He pulled into the gravelled driveway at the side of Clare's house and looked nervously towards Katharine. He did not relish the task ahead of them.

The afternoon was warm, and the sun illuminated the trees on the other side of the valley, creating an idyllic, peaceful scene, which Jake feared would soon be shattered. Katharine appeared much calmer. As soon as they set foot out of the car, they were met by the bounding Billy, Clare's large and rather out-of-control dog. He was a gorgeous animal, with a lovely, soppy nature, which was just as well because he was too big to be anything else. No one knew what breed he was, or more accurately, what mix of breeds he was. Someone found the poor thing in a box on the side of the road, along with his four other brothers and sisters when they were just six weeks old. When Clare adopted him from the shelter she was told he would probably be a medium-sized dog, but Katharine, stroking Billy's head, remembered the small puppy that just didn't stop growing.

'Hi Billy, still as mad as ever, I see.'

'I'm here.' Clare was standing outside a small summerhouse at the top of her large and rather steep garden that ended at the edge of a small wood.

Katharine waved and rushed up to greet her aunt, followed more slowly by Jake. Billy beat them both to her and was jumping around, barking in delight, hoping that Katharine might take him for a walk or at least play ball with him.

'Billy, be quiet. Would you like tea, or something stronger? Billy just lie-down.'

'Tea, please.' Katharine answered for them both. 'Come on, Billy, let me make a fuss of you.' Katharine sank into a garden chair and Billy sat next to her and let her scruff his head and neck.

Clare filled a kettle from a jug and busied herself making tea in the summerhouse. Jake stood admiring the garden and the view. They exchanged a glance just before Clare returned. Katharine was grateful to have Jake with her, but he wished he were miles away.

'Here we are.' She placed a tray on the table and sat down beside Katharine. Billy, now calmer, flopped on the floor at her side.

'So, it's lovely to see you, but I gather from your call that there's something seriously wrong. It's Duncan, isn't it? Bad news I imagine? I have my suspicions, of course, but just tell me. Get it over with,' she said, as she tucked her hair behind her ears and bit her lower lip.

Katharine nodded. She had tried very hard to keep her voice and tone neutral when she telephoned the day before, but Clare knew her so well and could pick up the slightest nuance in her words. Jake sat down on the other side of Clare and looked at Katharine. He needed to take his lead from her.

'OK, tell me.' Clare grasped her mug.

'Someone stabbed him in the heart in Rome. It was instant; he didn't suffer.'

Jake flinched at his wife's rather blurted, blunt clichéd words and wondered if she could have softened the news. Clare sat motionless, staring ahead but seeing nothing. She seemed to age in front of their eyes and slowly her face crumpled. Katharine leant forward and touched her hand. Clare turned her confused eyes, now filling with tears, towards her. She swallowed hard and focused on Katharine.

'I knew something like this would happen one day. It felt like I was waiting for something to happen every time he went away. I kept telling him he was getting too old for all this cloak and dagger stuff. Thank you for not telling me over the phone. I suspected, well deep down I knew, but I hoped…'

'You knew what he was doing?' Jake interrupted.

'Yes, not the specific details, of course, but when he was here a few weeks ago, I just felt that this job was different, more dangerous. Not that he said anything much about it, it was just in here.' She tapped her chest. 'I didn't know you were involved Katharine; I expect he thought it best to keep that fact from me. Were you there when he died?'

Katharine looked at her aunt. She sensed Clare wanted to be reassured that her brother didn't die alone, and not for the first time a wave of guilt swept over her that she hadn't rushed to her father's side, instead of being led away by Giuseppe.

'Yes, I was there,' she said, not daring to look at Jake. It was true; after all, she was there in the vicinity, just not there by his side.

Clare stirred her tea, and again her eyes had a faraway look. Although the news was not unexpected, she couldn't quite comprehend that Duncan wouldn't again walk up the path to greet her. Her lips quivered almost uncontrollably and at last she gave into her emotions. A large tear rolled down her cheek and plopped into her cup. She pulled a tissue out of her pocket and blew her nose.

'Sorry,' she said.

'Good grief, Clare, don't be sorry. You've just been told your brother's dead. You cry as much as you want,' Jake said, as he reached out and squeezed her hand. The caring gesture was too much for Clare and she fell into Jake's arms, sobbing like a child. Katharine, looking on, felt her own throat tighten with unexpressed grief. She jumped up out of her seat and was soon hugging them both. Her own tears soaking into Clare's hair. They stayed in this rather uncomfortable tableau for many minutes until Clare struggled away from them.

'I'll make more tea, this is cold,' Katharine said, and busied herself with the kettle.

Clare stood up, stretched, and walked around the garden, lost in thought.

'Leave her.' Jake laid a hand on Katharine's arm after she set the tea on the table and appeared to make a move towards Clare. Instead, she sat down, and followed her aunt with her eyes and tried to imagine what she must be thinking and feeling. They drank their tea in silence, watching Clare as she aimlessly wandered, sometimes touching a flower or just standing staring across the valley. Katharine remembered many happy afternoons spent in this garden. Often, she was reading or playing with a friend while Clare was busy digging, weeding or planting. The steeply terraced garden was one of Clare's great pleasures and relaxations. Full of winding paths, and different areas where you could happily lose yourself away from adult eyes. Not that Clare interfered with anything Katharine did as a child; she was the next best thing to having her own mother.

'Shall we go in? It's getting a bit chilly?' Clare said, when she made her way back to the terrace where Katharine and Jake were still sitting in almost complete silence. 'You will stay, won't you? I can rustle up something to eat and the spare room is always ready.'

Katharine and Jake exchanged glances, and Jake gave an imperceptible shrug.

'Yes, of course. The children are all sorted, so we don't need to get back. Let me come and help you. Are you sure you've got enough food?'

'Plenty. I popped to the village after you rang. I thought we might have a lot to discuss and hoped you would stay.'

They made their way, preceded by Billy, down the garden towards the house. The comfortable, familiar house where Katharine had grown up. It appeared cluttered and unintentionally shabby chic. An effect that other people would spend a fortune trying to create. This was Katharine's home, and no matter how long ago she had lived here, it still was her place of refuge when times were tough. Once inside, she curled up on the window seat, her favourite perch when she was young. This was where she would sit, and watch Clare cook or iron, or they would sit together and read a book. As she grew up, she would spend hours reading in one of the other window seats, on days when it was too wet to be outside and she would watch the rain sweep across the valley.

The windows were one of the key features of the house. Almost every room had a deep bay that was fitted out as a seat. From them, you could see people approaching the house from far down the lane. Katharine felt sad as she remembered many hours sitting, waiting, with her eyes straining, to catch the first glimpse of her father's car driving up to the house, after one of his frequent journeys away. In many ways she remembered, the anticipation was often better than his arrival; he was always kind and pleased to see her, but unlike her friends' fathers, he wasn't around much and when he was, he didn't seem to know how to play or have fun. He left her day-to-day upbringing to Clare. She understood now, of course, the reasons why he dropped in and out of her life when his work permitted, but as a child she was often confused and always worried he would not return. Now he never would.

The three of them enjoyed a simple meal along with a bottle of wine, which in other circumstances would have been the start of a convivial evening. Clare was always a good entertainer, but the atmosphere this time was more muted.

'He was a good man, your father,' Clare smiled at Katharine. 'And a wonderful brother. I'll miss him so much. I think I always knew it would end like this, but I was hopeful, because he was so near to retiring, I thought he'd got away with it.'

Katharine nodded; it was cruelly ironic that after all these years he was killed on his last mission. Not just his last mission, but hers as well.

'We went to his apartment this morning. I picked up some of his papers, but nothing significant.'

'No, he didn't keep much there. It's all here, his will and other important documents. I'll fetch them in a while. Have you decided about a funeral?'

'I wanted to talk to you about that. I was thinking of a small family service. What do you think? Did he have any wishes?'

'That sounds right, a small service here. I think he wanted to be cremated and have his ashes put with your mother's. The local crematorium's very peaceful.'

Katharine nodded but couldn't speak. She picked up her glass and took a big slug of wine.

'I'll sort all that, don't worry. I expect The Service will want a memorial in London.' Again, Katharine nodded and not for the first time felt surprised how aware her aunt was of her father's role. They sat in silence for a few minutes, both lost in thought.

'Did Duncan ever meet anyone else?' Jake asked, out of the blue. 'Sorry, my mind was wandering. A bit irrelevant, I know.'

'A lady friend, you mean?' Clare said and smiled, seeming pleased to be talking about lighter matters.

Jake nodded, amused at the old-fashioned turn of phrase.

'No, not really. There were women he would have dinner with sometimes, but I was never aware of anyone special, at least, no one he introduced to me. He never seemed to get over losing Mariana. Never got over the guilt.'

'Guilt, why did he feel guilty?' Katharine asked.

'He and Mariana were always busy, always active. Even when she was pregnant, she never rested, and I don't think your father realised she should. We talked for hours after her death, and on and off since, about what he ought to have done. I think he felt he'd let her down somehow, illogical, I know, but guilt and grief weighed on his mind. He wanted the best for you, of course.' She looked at Katharine. 'But I think every time he saw you, his heart broke again. You reminded him that Mariana wasn't here.'

'Their love must have been incredibly strong, unusually so, for him not to be able to move on.'

Clare turned to Jake; she understood his doubt; it was something she herself often wondered about.

'Yes, their relationship was intense, I expect because of the risks they took for their work. It was the Cold War then and very dangerous. Their work often forced them to spend time apart. So, the times they spent together when they weren't working were even more precious.'

'Did they work together?' Jake asked.

Katharine realised how little she had spoken about her parents to Jake over the years and put it down to the demands of everyday life with three children, and more likely because she knew very little herself.

'That's how they met,' Clare continued. 'Mariana's father was Russian, although he lived in Italy, but she, I imagine, still had contacts. To be honest, I knew little about their work. It was top secret, as you know, and she could become quite feisty if she thought I was asking too many questions. I know when she became pregnant, she changed and became anxious.'

'About what?' Katharine was hearing for the first-time information about the real Mariana, not just the idealised image portrayed by her father.

'Well, she wasn't sure she could settle at home with a baby, wasn't sure about living in England and was even less happy about your father continuing to work. She understood too well the risks. She was delighted to be pregnant, don't get me wrong, but she wasn't cut out to be a housewife.'

Clare leant across the table and touched Katharine's hand.

'They agreed to both leave The Service and concentrate on being a family, and were looking forward to it, but that never happened.'

'Living with all that danger and she died giving birth. It doesn't seem fair somehow,' Jake said, and picked up the bottle to refill their glasses.

'Did she die giving birth? No one's ever told me for certain what happened.'

Clare looked flustered and once again leant to take Katharine's hand.

'Oh Katharine, I didn't do a very good job, did I? Have you been wondering all these years?'

'Well, no, not really, just since, well, you know …'

'I'm sorry, we should have told you more but their lives were such a muddle of secrets. It was easier to say nothing. Let me tell you what happened.'

Clare closed her eyes while she gathered her thoughts.

'The night before you were born, Mariana became unwell. We called an ambulance and when it came, they rushed her into the hospital. Her blood pressure was dangerously high, and the doctors couldn't control it. You were born within an hour by Caesarean section, but even after you were delivered, her blood pressure kept rising. That caused her to have fits and other complications and they couldn't save her. She held you, though, and she knew she had a beautiful baby girl. Your father was with her all the time.'

'Was her high blood pressure caused by her being too active?'

'No, I don't think so, but maybe she did too much, but then so do lots of women. I think in some ways that's what made it so hard for Duncan to come to terms with. The doctor said it was something to do with her placenta, but Duncan still blamed himself.'

Katharine sat feeling numb, picturing the scene and imagining the heartbreak her father must have felt. She felt the loss of her mother more acutely than she could ever remember. Billy sighed, bored by their lack of action. He stood up and shook, then rested his head on Katharine's knee, looking up into her eyes as he slowly wagged his tail.

Chapter Thirty-One

'OK, wait a minute. Keep Billy here while I go and get some boxes.' Clare stood up and hurried out of the room.

The sound of the loft ladder being pulled down reached Katharine and Jake's ears, and they exchanged questioning glances. Katharine began clearing the table, assuming that her aunt was fetching her father's papers from the loft.

'Here we are. Leave that Katharine come and see this,' Clare returned with her arms full.

Katharine sat back at the table and looked, intrigued, at the rather ornate box, about twice the size of a shoebox, and a large battered brown envelope, both of which Clare placed in the middle of the table.

'What is it?'

'It was your mother's; she called it her box of treasures. I tried several times over the years to persuade Duncan to give it to you. Once when you turned twenty-one, and again on your wedding day, but he wouldn't. He used to say to me, he would give it to you when it felt right. I don't think it ever felt right while he was alive, but now I'm certain it is right that you should have it. It's been in the safe in the loft for too many years and by rights it now belongs to you.'

'I didn't know there was a safe in the loft,' Katharine said, distracted for a moment from the box. 'Is father's Will kept there?'

Clare smiled, 'It's behind the water tank. Yes, your father's things are here, in this envelope, but first, shall we look at this?' She was already fitting the tiny key into the lock of the box. A mixture of emotions swept over Katharine, and for a second her instinct was to say no, and to ask Clare to lock it away again, but the lid was already open. Jake was leaning forward to get a better look. Inside were several other boxes and large envelopes.

'Do you know what it all is?'

Clare nodded and pushed the box towards Katharine and indicated that she should look at the contents. Katharine stared at the items inside for several minutes, reluctant to touch them, and then feeling the pressure and anticipation from Clare and Jake, reached inside and picked up a small box. She flipped the lid and gasped. Inside were two beautiful rings. The first one Katharine picked up was platinum, with a large rectangular diamond surrounded by sixteen smaller diamonds. She stared at it and instinctively slipped it onto her finger, turning her hand so that the stones sparkled in the light.

'It was your mother's engagement ring, and the other one was her wedding ring.'

Katharine picked up the delicately engraved platinum ring and held it in her hand. A lump formed in her throat, and she swallowed hard to keep her composure. She slid the diamond off her finger and laid both rings back in their box. Her mother's gold bracelet watch was in another box, and a beautiful solitaire diamond necklace on a white gold chain was in yet another.

'Your father gave her that one on their wedding day, beautiful, isn't it?'

'He was quite a romantic, your father. Who'd have thought it,' Jake chuckled.

'I wanted you to wear it on your wedding day, but I don't think even after all that time he could bear to see it. It needs wearing, and the rings. I'm sure your mother would want them to be worn, not hidden away.'

'What's in this one?' Katharine picked up a larger, more ornate box.

'Open it.' Clare's voice trembled with anticipation as Katharine lifted the lid.

All three of them stared at the exquisite, deep red, delicately jewelled egg.

'Wow! don't drop it, Katharine.' Jake raised his hand as Katharine carefully lifted the small egg from its silk nest. She ran her fingers over the delicate jewelled surface, trying to imagine her mother doing the same.

'There's a little stand,' Clare pulled it from the box and set it on the table in front of Katharine so she could place the egg on it.

'It's stunning! Is it Faberge?'

'That was my understanding, but I guess you would need to get it verified and valued.'

Katherine opened the egg to reveal a perfect, deep red, rose jewelled brooch. After a few minutes of open-mouthed admiration, she reached into the box again and eased a small card out of an envelope. There was neat handwriting on it. Russian Cyrillic symbols inscribed in fading blue ink. Another piece of paper with it was, she presumed, the English translation:

To our dearest granddaughter Mariana, something to treasure on your twenty-first birthday, our love forever, Dedushka and Babushka.

Katharine ran her fingers over the Russian words, written by family members she never knew and felt a lump form in her throat.

'Your father wrote the translation, so you would know what it said. There are photos in the box as well. He's labelled them where he could.'

'I can't believe this has been hidden in the loft for all those years. What if there'd been a fire or a burglary?'

'I think it was quite secure; it would have taken an atomic

bomb to get it out of the safe. I haven't seen it for a long time. Your father sometimes used to take himself off to the loft and I presume he took it out, but I never asked.'

Both Katharine and Jake looked sceptical, but neither felt the time was right to say more.

Billy, feeling bored and ignored, without warning, leapt to his feet and jumped up at the table. The Faberge egg wobbled on its stand, then toppled over. There was a collective gasp, and they all stared, frozen in horror as it began rolling towards the floor. Jake, the first to react, lunged across the table, reached out his hand and grasped the egg seconds before its undignified demise. There was a collective sigh of relief, and Jake handed the egg back to Katharine.

'Best put it away,' he said, grinning with relief. 'Actually, I don't think it's as fragile as it looks.'

'I wouldn't be so sure. I think it is quite fragile, but don't think we should put it to the test. Billy to your bed, now.' Clare pointed towards Billy's basket and he, crestfallen, slunk off to lie down.

Katharine put everything back into the bigger box, before taking out the envelopes that contained photographs. Clare talked her through the ones where she knew the people. There were several showing her parents before and after their wedding. There were others of her Russian grandparents and people who she assumed must be her mother's friends. Clare understood that Mariana's grandparent's families fled from Russia after the Revolution and as far as she knew, they never returned. To Katharine's frustration, Clare didn't know where in Russia they came from, but she hoped there might be more information amongst the papers in the box.

'This batch is Mariana's mother's Italian family. I think Mariana always felt more Italian than Russian, although she was bi-lingual, of course. Well, tri-lingual with English. Katharine studied each one, hungry to learn as much as she could about her unknown relatives. This person looks like you,' Clare pointed to a young woman sitting under a tree.'

Katharine turned the photo over. 'Sophia 1967' was printed on the back.

'I think Sophia was a cousin. With any luck, there's more information in some of the other documents.'

Katharine nodded and put the photo back on the pile.

'That one's here, isn't it?' Katharine pointed to a photograph of her parents standing outside Clare's house, their arms around each other and both beaming.

'Yes, that was just after they bought the house. I think I might have taken that one.'

'They bought this house?'

'Yes, I must have told you that before, haven't I?'

'No, I wouldn't forget something like that.'

'Well,' Clare looked surprised. 'I suppose it was one of those things that just got lost in time and wasn't relevant to a child, but yes, they bought it just before they got married. It was here they planned to live a normal family life. After your mother died, it seemed logical for me to move in.'

'Did you just give up your life to look after Katharine?' Jake asked Clare.

'Well, that makes it sound too dramatic, but there was nothing very exciting going on in my life at the time and Duncan needed me.'

'Even so quite a sacrifice.'

'It never felt like that to me. I've had a good life; I don't feel like I've missed out on anything. In fact, I think I've been very lucky. Here, look at this.'

'What is it?' Katharine touched the envelope that Clare pushed towards her.

'Your father's will. I'm an executor. It shouldn't take too long to sort out. He's left everything to you, apart from this house and a small legacy, which he left to me.'

'I'm so pleased he's left the house to you. It's been more yours than his.'

Clare nodded. 'Yes, it's been my home and yours, of course, when you were young. It will again be yours when I die.'

'Well, let's hope that won't be for many years yet,' Katharine said, as she scanned the will. 'It says here that the villa in Italy comes to me. I never knew he owned the villa. I thought he... well, I suppose I never thought about it, he just seemed to arrange for us to stay there whenever we wanted. It's crazy, I can't believe I've been so uninquisitive all my life!'

'It belonged to your mother's family. She inherited it and then it became your father's and now it's yours.'

'It's a lot to take in,' Katharine said, as she closed her mother's treasure box and leant back in her chair, feeling exhausted. The contents filled many of the gaps about her mother's life, but more and more questions were pushing themselves into her consciousness. She just felt too overwhelmed to articulate them. Katharine also felt the regret of not asking her father more, not only about her mother, but about him as well. He always seemed to shut her down when she asked, not unkindly, but in a way that prevented her from asking more, and now she wished she'd persevered. Clare told her all she knew, but Katharine felt there was so much more that would now be lost forever.

After coffee, supplemented with a glass of port, they talked long into the evening, turning to Katharine and Jake's life and the children, but also about Clare and her life. Katharine, to her shame, had never given any consideration to Clare having a life of her own; she was just Aunt Clare, who was always at home when Katharine needed her.

Clare spoke a little about her life. She'd worked for a cartographer before Katharine was born and said vaguely that she'd helped her brother with maps from time to time. Katharine wondered if she'd been part of The Service as well, but Clare soon moved away from that aspect of her life. She had loved and been loved, she told them, but nothing that resulted in a long-term relationship. She had no regrets about how her life turned out. Katharine looked at Clare with new eyes, as though she was seeing the real person for the first time, and vowed to herself, to spend more time with her and get to know Clare the woman, not just her aunt.

Chapter Thirty-Two

The next morning, after one of Clare's special cooked breakfasts and a walk in the woods with Billy, Katharine and Jake set off home.

'What will you do for the rest of the day?' Katharine asked Clare, through the open car window, as Jake started the engine.

'Oh, I've got my friend Raisa coming over later. So, I think I'll potter in the garden this afternoon until she arrives.'

Katharine felt as though someone had punched her in the stomach. She managed a smile and waved goodbye as they drove away. Once down the lane, out of sight of the house, she demanded Jake stop the car.

'Are you ok? You look awful. Are you ill?'

'Did you hear what she said?'

'Clare? Something about gardening and a friend coming round.'

'The friend, she said the friend was called Raisa. I've never heard her talk about a friend called Raisa before.'

'You don't think…? There must be loads of people called Raisa.'

'What in a tiny Cotswold village?'

'Well, maybe you misheard.'

'No, I'm sure she said Raisa. Did I mention Raisa's name last night?' Katharine paused,

'No, I'm certain I didn't, and Clare would have said she had a friend by the same name. Oh my God, think Katharine, think.'

They both sat in silence for a few seconds, and then Katharine grabbed her bag and delved inside.

'What are you doing?'

'I'm ringing Sam. I don't like it. Something just doesn't feel right.'

Jake said nothing, just sat feeling bewildered, while Katharine spoke rapidly on the phone.

'He's sending someone straight down,' Katharine sighed, with a combination of relief and anxiety. 'He said we should carry on home.'

'Won't Clare be annoyed when someone rushes over to cross-examine her friend?' Jake asked, as he started the car and drove off once more. He felt again as if he was being propelled into a parallel universe, what with Faberge eggs, villas, and secret equipment. The Faberge egg, along with other precious pieces, was now locked away in Clare's safe until Katharine decided what to do with it all, but he noticed she was now wearing her mother's rings.

'It'll be discreet surveillance, at first. While they assess the situation.'

Jake said nothing, but wondered how anyone could carry out surveillance of any sort on Clare's house, without being spotted by Billy.

Once back at home, Katharine could not settle, and was grateful when the children returned from their various activities and sleepovers. They helped to distract her with their chatter and demands to find lost books and articles of clothing in preparation for the new school term. She cooked dinner for them all but struggled to eat anything herself. No one except Jake seemed to notice. It was gone eight when everyone had scattered to their separate rooms, and he put his arm around her shoulders.

'Never mind, you'll be out of it soon, and then you can relax. No more, promise?'

'Promise.'

Almost as soon as she spoke, her phone bleeped. Katharine picked it up and studied it, before bursting into laughter.

'What is it?' Jake had been watching her since the message came through.

She handed him the phone. It showed a photograph of a rather elderly grey-haired lady, who faced towards the camera, but she was unaware of the photographer. Billy could be seen in full flight in the background heading towards her. No doubt, Clare would be somewhere in the vicinity calling him back before he knocked the visitor over. Underneath was the message:

This is your aunt's friend, Rosa. You can relax, all is well!

'Rosa, Raisa, close I suppose,' Jake smiled, surprised by the wave of relief that swept over him as well.

'God, I feel such a fool,' Katharine said, and held her hand out for the phone to ring Sam to apologise.

'Don't worry Katharine, and thanks to you, we are onto the real Raisa and have uncovered an entire network we didn't know about. So, no need to apologise. Your gut instinct at the time really worked,' Sam paused, 'Are you sure you want to finish? You're a great asset.'

Katharine paused for a second too long. She knew her actions weren't down to gut instinct, but to pure stupidity, and she thought Sam knew that as well.

'Maybe, next time…?'

Katharine looked up; Jake was deep in conversation with their eldest son, who had reappeared looking for some lost item, and was not listening to her. She turned away. Her conversation with Jake, and her father's face, flashed through her mind, urging her to say no, but hard behind followed the thrill of the adrenaline rush, and a heady mix of fear and excitement. She stepped out of the room and lowered her voice.

'I'll think about it when the time comes.' As soon as she had spoken she felt wracked with guilt and knew, however tempting, her days in The Service were over.

At last, all the formalities regarding her father's body were complete and arrangements were made to repatriate him. A single stab wound to the heart caused his death; it would have been instant. Katharine assumed that was meant to reassure her, but the image of that moment would haunt her forever.

Clare and Katharine together arranged the small family funeral and cremation, as they had discussed, followed by a larger memorial service in London a week later. Clare came to stay for a few days to attend the memorial. Katharine was impressed by her resilience, and surprised by how many of The Service people she knew. Her discretion over the years had been admirable.

Many of her father's colleagues, including Julia and Geoffrey of course, along with several other people from work who Katharine recognised attended the memorial, but there were more people that she didn't recognise. Katharine read a poem and just about kept the quiver from her voice. The head of The Service spoke of her father's many years of dedication and how everyone who knew him would miss him. He touched only in a passing on the dangers of his role. Dan gave a beautiful eulogy on behalf of himself, Jilly and Oliver, which caused Jilly to sob on Clare's shoulder and Katharine to clutch Jake's hand even harder. Once the formal proceedings were over, they headed to a nearby hotel for refreshments. Katharine was acutely aware that Jake knew few people, except for family members, and after being introduced to some of Katharine's supposed colleagues, he drifted off to the bar. He felt uncomfortable, a bit like the first day at a new club, where everyone except him knew the rules. They were polite and friendly, but he wasn't one of them.

Feeling relieved, Katharine watched Jake sit down to chat to Jilly. Most people, regardless of whether she knew them, gravitated towards her to offer their condolences and say how much they'd admired her father and valued his input into The Service, but Geoffrey, for some reason, was not amongst them. One or two also mentioned Katharine's own role, but she preferred not to dwell on that too much. Over the shoulder of one, rather boring colleague rambling on about her father's outstanding abilities, Katharine could see Dan deep in conversation with Richard, one of the senior officers. The last thing she wanted was for Dan to be drawn into The Service. She had tried hard to play down her father's role, and her own minor involvement, and to convince Dan it was nothing like James Bond. In fact, mostly, it was quite boring and tedious. She made her apologies to the rambler, who seemed reluctant to stop talking, and sauntered over to where Dan and Richard were standing.

'Ah Katharine, I've just been talking to this fine young man of yours.'

She felt her heart quicken and was about to comment when he continued,

'He's been telling me about his plans to become a vet. So, lost to us, I'm afraid.'

'Oh yes, he's very good with animals,' she said, feeling wrong-footed. It was the first she had heard about Dan wanting to be a vet but managed not to look surprised.

'Well, I'd better be making a move. Lovely service Katharine. Your father will be sorely missed. See you anon. Goodbye young Dan, good luck with the studies.'

Dan and Katharine both said goodbye and shook Richard's hand.

'I didn't know you wanted to be a vet. Aren't you taking the wrong subjects?'

'Oh mum, of course I don't want to be a vet. I just wanted to stop that guy trying to recruit me into some dodgy role. It might look exciting in films, but it's definitely not for me.'

Katharine laughed,

'I thought that might be his ulterior motive. Well, done for putting him off. So, is it still art college?'

'Of course. I've got some prospectuses I'll show you and dad when all this stuff is over.'

'Yes, sorry, we have been a bit distracted.' She and Jake had been concerned about Dan's choice of studying art rather than an academic subject, but now Katharine felt pleased and relieved that Dan was clearly developing his own mind. All she wanted for all her children was for them to be happy.

Chapter Thirty-Three

The following evening Katharine and Jake enjoyed a rare time of peace and relaxation together, because the children were either visiting a friend, at the cinema, or in Dan's case, just out. They sat in companionable silence, listening to music, reading and sipping wine. It was the first time in weeks that life felt normal.

'What do you think you'll do with your mother's possessions?' Jake asked during a lull in the music.

'I don't know. I've been thinking about them. It still feels unreal. Some of them are too valuable to keep here, don't you think? They'll be safer in the bank. And then there's the villa. How did I not know Father owned it? I must be so dim, I just assumed he booked it somehow whenever we needed it. I suppose I just thought he knew the owner. Did you ever think about it?'

'Well, no, not really, but it's amazing to know it's ours. We should …'

The doorbell rang before he finished his sentence. Jake looked at Katharine, who shrugged. 'I'm not expecting anyone.'

'I'll go.' Jake put his wine down, feeling irked by the intrusion.

Moments later, he was back.

'Someone for you.' He stepped aside and elderly, dishevelled looking man stepped into the room.

For a moment Katharine looked blankly at the man, then recognition hit her.

'Geoffrey, I didn't recognise you at first. Are you all right?

Come in, sit down. Would you like a drink?'

Geoffrey raised a hand to silence Katharine's questions and sank into a chair.

'Jake, this is Geoffrey, a friend and colleague of my father.'

Jake nodded. At a loss for what to say, he sat back down and looked at Geoffrey, who appeared to be not quite in control. Jake could not work out whether Geoffrey was drunk.

'Katharine, I'm so sorry, your father I mean, I am so, so, sorry,' he looked almost close to tears.

Katharine didn't reply at once. She knew Geoffrey and her father were acquaintances, but his reaction to his death seemed well out of proportion. After all, as her father said from time to time, it was a hazard of the job. Like Jake, she wondered if he might be drunk.

'Thank you, Geoffrey, we'll all miss him of course, but, well…'

Katharine didn't want to ask him why he was here, now, so late in the evening and looking, if she was honest, a total wreck, not at all like the sprightly Geoffrey she met a couple of months earlier.

'I'm so sorry,' he said again, then looked at Jake. 'Does he…?'

'It's OK. I've told Jake what happened.'

Geoffrey nodded.

'It wasn't supposed to happen. Your father, I mean, he shouldn't have been there, neither of you should have been there. I thought I'd…' he paused again, and once again Katharine thought he might cry. Silence descended on the room, and they were all lost in their own thoughts. Katharine's brain was working overtime, and she was surprised that the others couldn't hear the whizzing of gears changing and realisation dawning.

'Geoffrey, what are you trying to tell me, are you …'

'Yes, yes, I've been so stupid, a stupid old fool. I should have been put out to grass years ago.'

Jake looked confused, his eyes darting between the two of them, while wracking his brain, trying to remember all the relevant pieces of Katharine's story. He was sure he remembered her mentioning Geoffrey. Then he remembered the leak. But Geoffrey was one of the people she told him had briefed her that first night. He looked at Katharine, a question in his eyes, and she nodded, putting a finger to her lips. So, he sat, determined to remain silent, feeling like an observer in a strange game, or play.

'I think you better explain.' Katharine, now in total control of the situation, picked up her glass and took a deep slug of wine, before leaning forward and staring directly at the crumpling old man.

Jake couldn't help himself from having a twinge of sympathy for him. He'd seen that look in Katharine's eyes before and knew it was no use arguing with her. Geoffrey sat up; pulling himself together, he looked more like the Geoffrey Katharine remembered.

'I'm too old for this game,' he said, echoing her father's words. 'Things are changing so fast; I suppose I got out of my depth. I didn't know who to trust anymore, and…' he paused, looking at Katharine, perhaps trying to gauge her mood, 'And I trusted the wrong person. It can get lonely, this life, and she was so charming, so understanding.'

'Raisa?' the jigsaw pieces were falling into place for Katharine. 'Do you mean Raisa? Did you know her?'

Geoffrey nodded; a slight flush of shame tinged his wrinkled cheeks.

'The classic honey-trap. I was such a fool. I thought we meant something to each other.'

'She could be very convincing,' Katharine said with a note of understanding. 'Tell me what happened. I presume that is why you're here?'

Geoffrey nodded, 'Could I have a glass of water, please?'

Katharine looked at Jake, who got to his feet and rushed out of the room, wanting to get back before he missed anything. He could not quite shake off the feeling that this was all some strange sort of play-acting, not real life, that involved his wife. Once back, he handed the full glass to Geoffrey, who took a long drink, wiped his mouth with the back of his hand, then put the glass on a small side table, slopping water as he did. He looked sadly at Katharine.

'I've been such a fool,' he repeated. 'I never in a million years intended to let information get into the wrong hands, and Duncan, your father, he was such a good man, a friend, and a stickler for doing the right thing. So, I thought the least I could do, in the circumstances, was to come and explain to you,' he said, and looked up at Katharine with such a look of pain and self-disgust that she found difficult to see and not feel touched by.

'You haven't explained anything yet,' she said, gently.

'No, I haven't, have I.' He stroked his grey beard, which now looked very ragged, not well groomed, as it had been when they last met.

'It was many months before I realised, and by then I was in too deep. I met Raisa or Roisin as I knew her at a music club I belong to. She was new, but I noticed her the first time she came. We didn't speak for a couple of weeks, just nodded and exchanged smiles. Then one evening we left at the same time. It was raining, so I gave her a lift home. Then the following week we went for a drink afterwards and it just grew from there. I had no idea who she was. She told me she was a musician but that she had retired after damaging her ear drum.' Geoffrey paused and took another long drink of water before looking up to check Katharine was still listening. He needn't have worried. Both Katharine and Jake were listening intently, Jake on the edge of his seat.

'We became a couple. I thought we were in love and, like the old fool I am, I started telling her odd snippets of information. It was a relief, a comfort, in some ways to have someone outside of the organisation to confide in, to trust, wrong and stupid, I know.'

Katharine and Jake exchanged a look, both wondering about their recent conversation and the amount of information Katharine had passed on, but that was different.

'We chatted, of course, like people do, and I told her about my friend Duncan and the tragic story about how your mother died. I told her a few stories about your parents' early life, how they met, that sort of thing. I didn't tell her in detail about the work we did, but then I guess she already knew that. It must have been because I trusted her, more came out than it should have. It never occurred to me that the leaks were coming from me. I even talked to her about my concerns that there was a mole in the organisation, can you believe that? I feel such a fool. She was so supportive and caring. I trusted her I really did. I thought we …' Geoffrey looked up, tears forming in his reddened eyes. He took another drink of water.

Katharine nodded,

'Go on.'

'Well, a few things happened that made me suspect something wasn't right. She became more insistent on knowing details of the mission you were involved in. She said it was only because she cared about me, and wanted to reassure herself I would be safe, but I felt uneasy. I fed her a few false trails just to see if anything came up. When they did, I felt sick. How could I have been so stupid. I think she realised I was on to her because one day, a few weeks ago, I returned, and she'd gone. She left me a note about her mother being ill, but I knew the real reason.' He sat staring at the floor for several minutes.

'Why didn't you say something?'

He looked up, and the look of torture in his eyes touched Katharine.

'Oh Katharine, that is the question I have asked myself over and over again. I think, perhaps, I still didn't want to believe it. Maybe her mother was ill. Anyway, I tried to see you in Naples.'

'Was it you who came to the Hotel?'

'When you weren't there, at first, I thought I would wait, but then I saw Roisin entering the lobby and I knew, so I just left. I had to get out. She didn't see me I'm certain of that. I didn't know what to do, couldn't think straight.'

'Why didn't you come back, or ring my father, or Julia, or just do something?'

'I don't know why I didn't. I've asked myself that so many times. Pride, shame, fear, stupidity? All of them, I think. I still didn't want to believe it. Perhaps I was wrong, jumping to conclusions. When your father contacted me to tell me about the incident on the boat, and about your contact with your supposed aunt, I knew Roisin, or Raisa, or whatever she called herself, must have met you. It was me who suggested the change of plan to Julia, for you to give the stick to your father in Rome, rather than continue to Florence. I thought it would be safer for you. Raisa wouldn't know where you'd gone, and I thought you would be safe. I didn't bargain for the tracker.'

'But I don't understand why they killed my father,' Katharine interrupted.

'No, I don't understand that, but desperate people act irrationally, and they were desperate to retrieve the memory stick.'

'How did they know someone hadn't already copied it, or sent the data electronically as well?'

'I think at one time I told Raisa we were only using the one stick, so I guess she told them it was the only copy.'

'Jesus Christ, what have you done?' Jake could hold his thoughts no longer. 'Katharine could have been killed as well. Just because you felt too ashamed to tell someone you'd been shacked up with a foreign agent.'

Geoffrey recoiled, and Katharine laid a hand on Jake's arm. Jake felt like thumping this stupid old man but kept still and said no more.

'It's ok, he's right,' he looked straight at Jake. Nothing can make me feel worse than I do. I have failed the most fundamental principle of an agent.'

Katharine glanced at Jake. Hadn't she failed on the same principle? But telling Jake was different. Of course it was– wasn't it? She trusted Jake …

'I was going to tell you after your father died, when you were back in Italy.'

'At the villa?'

Geoffrey nodded. 'I saw you, but … I couldn't. You were with your family and …'

'You were at our villa? I never saw you,' Jake said, getting to his feet and pacing across the floor. This was getting too much for him.

'No, I was on the hill behind, watching through binoculars. I'm so sorry Katharine. You know what to do now.' Geoffrey looked at Katharine. 'I expect you need to make a phone call,' he said, when Katharine didn't react. He now seemed quite calm and in control.

'Yes, of course, but thank you, Geoffrey, for telling me yourself. It can't have been easy.'

Jake looked aghast that Katharine was thanking him; he wanted to shake the old man until his teeth rattled.

'Could I have a few moments alone first?'

Katharine nodded and stood up, holding out a hand for Jake to follow her.

'I'll make the call from the other room.'

'Thank you,' Geoffrey whispered in a strangled voice.

'Katharine, are you mad, leaving him alone?' Jake said as soon as they were out of the room. 'He'll be gone when we go back in.'

Katharine was already picking up her phone. 'No, he won't,' she said, and turned her attention to Sam on the other end of the phone.

Jake looked aghast at her seeming stupidity. All Geoffrey needed to do was open the French doors, and he'd be gone.

'He isn't physically going anywhere, just leave him. Let him have his last moments of dignity,' Katharine said, as she ended her call.

Jake opened his mouth and shut it again, then opened it again.

'You mean he's going to, no, you can't mean that, not in our sitting room. He needs to go on trial or whatever they do with bent spies. Katharine this is total madness. What if…?' Jake stopped talking, he couldn't think. He was about to return to the sitting room when Katharine caught hold of his arm.

'Just leave him, please. It's too late.' Katharine turned away to look out at the garden, but when she turned back, tears were pouring down her face. 'It's almost too much to take in.'

Jake gathered her in his arms. He wanted to speak but could think of nothing coherent to say. So, he just held Katharine not sure who was needing the comfort most. They stayed like that until the doorbell rang for the second time that evening.

'In there.' Katharine pointed to the sitting room, and Sam, followed by a man she didn't recognise, opened the door and stepped inside.

Chapter Thirty-Four

Not long after Sam's arrival, Geoffrey's body was carried out to the waiting van. Sam returned and took copious notes as Katharine related the events of the evening. Just as she was ending her statement, Julia arrived. She sat down, waiting for Sam to finish.

'Well, I wouldn't have guessed that in a million years.' Sam closed his notebook and stood up. 'Are you OK?'

'I'm fine, thanks, and Sam, when the time comes, don't contact me. I really am backing out.'

'Shame, but understandable. I'll see myself out, take care.' He shook Katharine's hand and nodded towards Julia.

'Let's go in here,' Katharine said, opening the dining room door and ushering Julia inside. Jake hesitated in the hallway, then retreated into the kitchen.

'I'm not going to interrogate you as well, don't worry. I know Sam has all the details. I just wanted to make sure you're all right,' Julia said, as she sat down at the table opposite Katharine.

'Thanks Julia. I'm feeling a bit drained by it all.'

Julia smiled and leant over and took Katharine's hand. 'I'm not surprised. It's been quite eventful.'

'Did you suspect Geoffrey?'

'Not at first. In fact, I didn't want to let myself consider him, even when a few things were pointing in his direction.'

'Were those pointers before or after our meeting that night in Italy?'

'That night, I thought he seemed unusually agitated. He

refused to stay. That's why we left so late. I was worried he might be unwell. Then he disappeared for a few days and when he returned, he tried to persuade me to abort the mission, but gave no proper reasons and became quite insistent that we should change your route. He said he'd received intelligence that Florence wouldn't be safe and suggested that the exchange should happen in Rome. I did nothing at the time. I'm not one to act on other people's hunches, but maybe I should have.' Julia looked down at her hands and appeared to be studying her nails. Katharine waited.

'That was before you contacted your father,' she continued. 'I then advised your father to meet you in Rome.' Her voice quivered at the memory, but quickly recovered. 'After we heard the dreadful news about your father, Geoffrey just vanished. No one knew where he was, or what he was doing, until he appeared at the memorial. That was when I knew. I asked him to come in for a meeting the next day, but he never turned up. So, when Sam called me this evening, I felt shocked but not surprised.'

'My father was concerned about him; he thought it was a problem with a woman. I suppose he was right, in a way.'

'Hmm, you can never be too careful. Maybe that's why I've stayed single for so long. You're lucky having someone you can really trust.'

'I know, but don't sell your soul to the service, Julia. There's more to life.'

'You're right, but for now, it is my life.' She stood up. 'I must go. I just wanted to make sure you were coping.'

'Before you go, the memory stick. Was there more to it?'

Julia hesitated, then sat down again. She'd hoped Katharine wouldn't ask too many questions, but decided almost immediately that she owed her at least a brief explanation.

'It's just that it seemed a strange way to transfer information, and the convoluted route …'

'You're right,' she looked into Katharine's eyes and half

smiled. 'There was vital information on the stick, of course, but there were also two small capsules in the lid which contained material ...'

'Material?'

'Blood and skin cells in one. They're being analysed for DNA so that identification can be in no doubt.' Julia hesitated for a second.

'And the other?' Katharine couldn't wait while Julia contemplated her reply.

'The other is also being analysed. We think it will prove the existence of a new form of bacterial weaponry. Something we've suspected for some time.'

Katharine opened and closed her mouth; thoughts were spinning around her mind. She wasn't sure she could take anymore.

'It was safe. I mean safe for you to carry it, if that's what you're thinking.'

'It was, but is it still valuable now they know we've got it?'

'I'm not sure they do. They know about the data on the stick, but I doubt they know about anything else. We won't know ourselves how useful it is until the lab's worked on it. When they killed your father, they probably assumed he was carrying the stick and needed to stop him from passing it on. I think they were panicking.'

'But they didn't stop to check if he had it. The man just ran off.'

'They would have contacts.'

Katharine shuddered at the thought of foreign agents searching her father's body.

'And you leaving under a different name would have ended any link to you, but just in case, that's why we sent you to Cornwall rather than London, where they might have expected the stick to end up.'

She nodded. She was feeling exhausted by it all.

'Did Geoffrey know?' she said.

'Not entirely. He knew about the data and DNA, but not

about you leaving under a false name or where you were going. Do you remember I told you a lot of technical information?'

Katharine nodded. 'I was going to ask about that.'

'Sorry, it was a bit of a red herring. I wanted to see if any of it leaked…'

'And did it?'

'No, nothing, and Geoffrey didn't ask me about it after we left. I think, sadly, poor Geoffrey was an inadvertent leak. There was nothing malicious about it, but he was a fool to be taken in. He'll be missed. He was a good agent and I'll try to make sure his reputation isn't ruined by all this.'

'He knew he'd been taken for a fool as well,' Katharine said, and they both sat lost in thought.

A tap on the door startled both women.

'Can I get you a drink?' Jake popped his head around the door.

'No, thank you. I really must be going.' Julia stood up and walked into the hallway. 'Goodnight Katharine. I'm glad you're OK.' She walked towards the door, then turned back and stepped towards Katharine, touching her on the arm. 'You're sure? About giving up, I mean.' A shiver ran down Katharine's spine and she hesitated for a second too long. Taking a deep breath, she pulled herself up and looked into Julia's eyes.

'Yes, I'm certain.'

'OK. I'll be in touch about the formalities.'

'Take care, Julia, and thank you.'

Just as Julia was about to leave, she turned around and hugged Katharine.

'I will. Thank you and you take care. We'll miss you.'

Katharine closed the door behind her and leant against the wall in the hall, all her energy and resolve seemed to drain away.

'Are you OK?' Jake moved towards her.

She shook her head, and for the second time that evening burst into tears.

'Hey, come on now,' Jake pulled her into his arms and Katharine sobbed into his shoulder, letting all the tensions of the last couple of weeks flood out.

He stroked her hair and as her sobs subsided put his hands on her shoulders and pushed her gently back, so he could look into her eyes.

'No more,' he said quietly.

'No more,' she whispered back.

'Promise? No more secrets?'

She nodded. 'I promise. No more, it's over.'

Jake pulled her back close and kissed her. Katharine's body relaxed, feeling the relief and comfort of the first proper physical contact between them since her return.

'Oh God, must you?' Dan burst through the front door, pushed past his parents and galloped two at a time up the stairs to the sanctuary of his room.

Katharine and Jake pulled apart, laughing.

'Normal service is resumed,' Katharine said. 'Come on, let's have a drink and toast to ordinary life.' As she said these words, a niggle in her brain wondered how she would now fill her time.

Printed in Great Britain
by Amazon